HIS MOUTH CAME BACK TO HERS WITH AN URGENT DEMAND.

"Indy, if you had any idea how long it's been . . . and what you're doing to me."

"No. My God, no," she protested, afraid of him now that she understood what he wanted of her. Afraid of herself because she didn't want him to stop. Her complaint died under the onslaught of his kiss spreading the fire of passion through her body. Off in the distance, a lone coyote called out to its mate, and she felt his muscles tense as he lifted his head to listen. It came a second time, and he whispered close to her ear. "Don't make a move or say a word. We've got uninvited guests."

Alarmed and frightened, she saw his hand remove the wicked-looking blade from the sheath attached to his belt, then slowly bring it up between them. "As soon as I make my move, I want you to run. Don't stop for anything or anybody." He placed a quick kiss upon her trembling mouth and pushed her away. "Now!"

Indy ran like she had never run before. Behind her she heard a frightful cry. Shatto's cry. . . .

FIRES OF HEAVEN

FIRES OF HEAVEN

by

Chelley Kitzmiller

A TOPAZ BOOK

TOPAZ
Published by the Penguin Group
Penguin Books USA Inc., 375 Hudson Street,
New York, New York 10014, U.S.A.
Penguin Books Ltd, 27 Wrights Lane,
London W8 5TZ, England
Penguin Books Australia Ltd, Ringwood,
Victoria, Australia
Penguin Books Canada Ltd, 10 Alcorn Avenue,
Toronto, Ontario, Canada M4V 3B2
Penguin Books (N.Z.) Ltd, 182–190 Wairau Road,
Auckland 10, New Zealand

Penguin Books Ltd, Registered Offices:
Harmondsworth, Middlesex, England

First published by Topaz, an imprint of Dutton Signet,
a division of Penguin Books USA Inc.

First Printing, April, 1994
10 9 8 7 6 5 4 3 2 1

 Topaz is a trademark of New American Library,
a division of Penguin Books USA Inc.

Printed in the United States of America

I'd like to dedicate this book to my daughter, Gina Luree Kitzmiller, my best friend. For the joy and the utter chaos you bring into my life that keeps my blood flowing through my veins.

And to David Faust, curator of the Arizona Historical Society, operating at the Fort Lowell Museum, who brought me some of the best laughs I've ever had and whose first lesson in military detail was teaching me that cavalry rides and infantry walks!

And finally to Paul Thompson and Larry Ludwig, rangers at Fort Bowie Visitors Center, for little bits of information here and there.

Chapter 1

Arizona Territory
September 1, 1869

Independence Taylor stood behind the door listening to the troopers' descriptions of the four dead miners they had come across on their way to the San Simon stage station. Bodies riddled with bullets and arrows. Stripped naked and tied to the wagon wheels. Burned beyond recognition.

Despite the summer heat Indy felt chilled to the bone. She closed her eyes and bowed her head, then whispered a short but fervent prayer. "Dear Lord, I know I've been a trial to you over the years and to my father, but I ask you to please watch over the troopers and me when we leave here. Watch over us and keep us safe. I have so much to make up for, Lord. I can't die knowing Father hasn't forgiven me."

Captain Aubrey Nolan had been about to put his hand on the door latch when he heard the beginning of Indy's prayer. He turned away, not wanting to intrude, and went back to his men. "Keep your voice down, Sergeant," he said in an authoritative voice. "She's praying for our safety."

"Yes, sir, Captain sir, but I was thinkin'. Mebbe it ain't such a good idea t'take her back with us, what with Chie on another of his killin' rampages. Mebbe if we was t'tell her how things was here, she'd catch the next stage home and get the hell outta here."

"There won't be another stage for two days, Sergeant, and I don't think the colonel would look too kindly on me, or you, if I left her here with no womenfolk to look out after her. It wouldn't be seemly. Besides, with the station keeper being shorthanded, it would be more dangerous to leave her here than take her with us."

The burly sergeant removed his forage cap and rubbed his fingers through his graying hair. "I sure would hate t'see anything happen t'her. She's such a li'l thing, not much bigger than a child, but I can see she's all growed up and right purty if I do say so, with them big hazel eyes all bright and shiny. Reminds me of a girl I knowed back in Georgia, afore the war," Moseley said with a touch of melancholy. "Fragile, like one of my mama's roses, she was. Would have wilted out here in this damnable desert heat in no time. I'm thinkin' Miss Taylor's jes' about as delicate as that li'l girl. Why'd the colonel let her come, anyway? Smart as he is—or thinks he is—seems he'd have better sense. Damn fool thing lettin' her come, if you ask me. Yep, a damn fool thing."

"Nobody's asking you, Sergeant, and I might add, it's none of our business. Now, order the men to mount up. We'll be leaving momentarily."

Moseley wheeled around and walked away, barking orders to the men.

Not once since leaving her St. Louis home had Indy doubted the wisdom of her decision to follow her father to his new post and make a proper home for him. Not until a few moments ago, anyway. What the troopers had described seeing on their way to the stage station was the reality of the "Indian problems" in the territories—the reality she'd read about in shocking detail in the Army reports sent to her father to study in preparation for his new command at Camp Bowie. The reports told a completely different story from the innocuous newspaper articles that were occasionally printed. Yet she had minimized the seriousness of the reports because she didn't want them to deter her from making the journey. She had convinced herself that her coming such a long distance to make a home for her father and be his companion would somehow break the awful barrier that had existed between them these last seven years.

She realized now, too late, that she'd been a fool. The dangers were real and every bit as horrible as the reports had indicated. She could very well die within the next few hours and all the years' efforts to gain his forgiveness and win back his love would have been for naught.

Indy took a deep breath to marshal her composure and forced a smile to her lips. It simply wouldn't do for her to let the nice captain or the troopers know she'd overheard them talk. No, indeed. It wouldn't do at all, she thought, opening the door and stepping outside into the bright sunlight.

"We're ready to go if you are," the captain intoned flatly.

"Yes, I'm ready," she replied, making certain that nothing in her voice betrayed her burgeoning anxiety. She lowered her head, lifted her skirt, and walked down the pebble-strewn path toward the open-sided military ambulance. Averting her gaze, she stepped up to the back of the vehicle and accepted the captain's gloved hand to help her inside.

"With your permission, Miss Taylor, I thought I'd ride with you until we reach Camp Bowie."

"Why, of course, Captain. I'd be pleased to have you." Crouching to avoid smashing her hat beneath the canvas roof, she contemplated the best place to sit. There was none. Rough wooden benches, which served as beds for the wounded in the field when they were needed, stretched along each side of the wagon bed. She moved to the right and sat down.

The captain took his Spencer carbine out of the leather boot hanging from his saddle and tied his horse's reins to the back of the ambulance, then climbed in and sat on the opposite bench. "I can lower the canvas curtains if you like. It might help cut down on some of the dust and dirt."

"No thank you. I'm sure it will be fine as it is. Besides, I'm beyond the point of worrying about my appearance," she said, making her point by pulling a long stray lock of hair over her shoulder. She held it between her two fingers and frowned. More than two weeks of round-the-clock travel, with only brief basin baths at the more civilized stage stations, had turned her light brown hair, which had been glossy with good health, to a sickly gray-brown.

The real reason, however, that she wanted the

canvas curtains left up was so she could see everything going on around her. She'd grown up in a military household on military strategies and knew that one should always be aware of one's surroundings, especially when going into the unknown.

"If you don't mind my saying, Miss Taylor, you look just fine. It'll be a real treat for the men to have someone as pretty as you in their midst." He smiled appreciatively.

Tilting her head down, Indy demurred. "You flatter me, Captain, but I thank you for it." The last two weeks had opened her eyes to many things, one of them being that men found her attractive—even pretty, where she had always considered herself plain. Having been something of a recluse these last seven years, socializing only with her father's stuffy officer friends, who talked of nothing but the art of war, there had been few opportunities to experience the company of a young man, let alone hear a word of flattery or admiration.

Blushing beneath his admiring scrutiny, she tugged downward on the braided hem of her jacket to smooth out the wrinkles. She had selected her travel clothing carefully, making it clear to the dressmaker that comfort, durability, and practicality should take precedence over current fashion. The skirt was of a dark blue serge, not nearly as full or long as the skirts and dresses she'd left at home in her wardrobe. The matching jacket had black lapels and was trimmed with black braid. It was nipped in at the waist and flared flatteringly over her hips. Beneath the jacket she wore a simple white muslin blouse with a tiny, rounded collar. Her hat was her only concession to frivolity, a black velvet sailor hat, low-crowned with a moderate brim, turned down over her forehead.

The driver took up the double set of lines, released the brake, and called out to the mules. "H'yaw! Hee-yaw! Gee up, thar, you longears." Leather snapped smartly over the team's backs and the ambulance lurched forward. To keep from being thrown off her seat, Indy held on to the wooden framework that supported the canvas top. Once the four-mule team moved onto the road, the ride smoothed out and conversation again became possible.

"How far is it to Camp Bowie, Captain?" Indy asked. The captain had hardly looked at her since they'd left San Simon. He was watching out for Apaches, she supposed, forgiving him his negligence. So far he hadn't said a word to her about the dangers they could be facing.

"Twenty-two miles," he replied. "Three and a half to four hours . . . depending," he added a moment later.

Indy waited for an explanation but soon realized he hadn't intended one. "Depending on what, Captain?" she prodded, wishing he would talk to her and tell her exactly what problems, if any, he was anticipating.

His gaze came slowly back to hers. "Depending upon the mules, the road, the weather. All those things," he said, then quickly changed the subject. "I'm sure you must be anxious to end your travels and get some rest. I know what it's like to try to sleep sitting up in a crowded stagecoach."

"It was an experience I will never forget, I assure you," she answered coolly. She was beginning to resent the way he tried to protect her with his silence. He should give her credit for knowing a little something about the dangers they faced—she was, after all, the post commander's daughter. He obviously thought she was one of those fragile females who would panic and become hysterical.

It was everything she could do to hold her tongue, but she knew if she didn't, she'd regret it. He seemed a nice enough man; he simply wasn't accustomed to a woman who knew her own mind and went about as she pleased.

She turned away and focused her gaze on the flat open terrain. Having studied botany in school, she recognized beargrass, agave, sotol, and several other species of desert chaparral.

Her interest quickly waned. It was hard to think about anything when at any point in time an Apache warrior could jump out from behind a rock and attack the detachment. She wished there had been more information available for her to read on the Apaches as a people; it would help to understand them, which, in turn, would help her to know what to expect. But very little information existed—only accounts of their attacks, raids, tortures. They seemed to be little more than savage beasts who preyed upon soldiers, white settlers, miners, and travelers.

She hoped the captain was more informed than she. She also hoped he was well trained in the

event there was an attack. Acting with speed, or
celerity as her father always phrased it, was the
key to a success in any battle—no matter who
the enemy. Being well informed ranked a close
second. After several minutes of entertaining her
own thoughts, which were succeeding only in
making her more nervous, she decided to broach
the subject of her father. Perhaps she could glean
some insight into how he would receive her,
though she was fairly certain she already knew
the answer.

"Tell me, Captain. My father—is he well?"

"Yes, ma'am. The colonel is fit as a fiddle."

Indy laughed lightly. "I don't think I've ever
heard anyone use that phrase to describe Father."

A flash of humor lit the captain's face. It
changed his entire countenance and made her
take a second, harder look. She liked what she
saw. He was younger than she had first thought
when he introduced himself at San Simon. In his
late thirties, she guessed. It was the tint of his
skin and the tiny sun lines radiating from his eyes
that had given her the impression of an older
man—the indelible marks of a cavalry officer.

The captain's clean-shaven face was pleasing,
though far from handsome—a sincere and kindly
face—a face that inspired trust. He had a high
wide forehead and his brows rode low over deep-
set eyes that were an unusual light blue. A
ghostly gray layer of dust covered his well-fitted
dark blue fatigue blouse and stole the shine from
his boots. Beneath his hat, his hair appeared to
be a rusty brown. Both his manner and dress
were militarily correct, and he exuded compe-

tence, but displayed none of the self-important airs she had seen among her father's friends.

"Will you be staying at Bowie long?" he asked, giving her his full attention.

"Until my father is reassigned, I expect. He's convinced, as I am, that someone in the War Department made a mistake sending him to the frontier, when his expertise is in civil engineering. He appealed to President Grant as soon as he got his orders, but there wasn't time to hear back before he had to report to his new post." Indy paused a moment to bolster her courage before broaching the question that would give her the answer she sought. "Captain, I hope you won't think me presumptuous, but I was wondering— would you happen to know—was Father *terribly* upset when he received word of my arrival?" No sense pretending that she thought her father would welcome her with open arms.

The captain raised one brow and looked away. Out of the side of his mouth he said, "He was . . . surprised."

Indy rolled her eyes. That wasn't the answer she had been looking for. "Please, Captain Nolan, it would help me considerably if I knew just how upset he is so I can prepare myself."

His expression turned grave. "Well, then, Miss Taylor, I suggest you prepare for the worst."

"Oh," she breathed and looked down at her gloved hands. "It's possible I may have underestimated his objections. He did, after all, give strict orders that I was to stay in St. Louis and maintain the house." She lifted her gaze. "Father doesn't like being disobeyed." The captain nodded as if he understood, but of course he didn't really, and she wasn't about to enlighten him. "I hope he doesn't send me back. It's not a trip I would relish making again so—" She broke off, her eyes widening in alarm when the captain took his Spencer carbine in hand. "What is it? What's wrong?" She swung her head left, then right, trying to see what had prompted the action. But there was nothing to see. A second later she realized he had merely been changing his position. Her face colored with embarrassment.

"Sorry, ma'am. I didn't mean to startle you."

She struggled to regain her composure. "I'm afraid I owe my anxiety to one of the stage passengers," she lied, drawing on the incident as she had seen it affect the whiskey drummer. For some reason she couldn't bring herself to admit *her* fear of an attack. "The poor fellow hadn't slept in three days and was convinced that we would be attacked by the Apaches," she continued. "Eventually he became so hysterical that he had to be restrained. He's staying on a day or two at San Simon to rest."

"Things like that happen more often than you'd think. It's a difficult journey, especially now with Cochise, Juh, and Chie leading their braves in all-out warfare, but I'm certain you knew that, what with the colonel being sent here specifically to deal with the Indian situation."

Finally, he was admitting that there was a *situation*! "Yes," she said pointedly. "I'm aware that there have been problems. I don't envy you having to go back for the man."

Nolan looked up. "Begging your pardon, Miss

Taylor, but we won't be going back. The colonel has called a halt to civilian escorts until we can get things under control. The gentleman will have to find his own transportation."

"Halted the escorts? But—you came for me."

"No, ma'am, not exactly." Clearly embarrassed, he adjusted the brim of his hat. "Officially we came to pick up the mail. The stage line has refused to deliver it as long as the attacks continue."

"Oh . . . I see . . ." There was a catch in her voice and she felt the threat of tears. But for the mail, she would have been forced to find her own transportation just like the poor whiskey drummer. Staring down at the thin canvas mail pouch near her feet, she tried not to reveal her dismay. After a moment, she queried, "Is it customary to send an ambulance after so little mail?"

"No, ma'am, but I told the colonel that I had reason to believe the stage might also be bringing the *Harper's Weekly*s and newspapers we ordered. They're a month overdue and the men are anxious over what's happening in the East with the President and his Indian policies." He inclined his head and grinned.

Indy perceived the small conspiracy and smiled gratefully.

The ambulance rattled along, rocking and swaying like a storm-tossed ship. Jagged-topped mountains ringed the valley floor, one range feeding to another, the crevices and folds purpling as the sun slowly sank into the western sky.

Looking for a more comfortable position, Indy moved to the front of the wagon where she could lean into a solid corner. The ill-smelling Concord stagecoach, with its lumpy leather seat cushions, had been luxurious compared to this.

It was nearing dusk by the time they reached Siphon Canyon, a broad, sandy wash, leading into the mouth of Apache Pass. For the past hour the captain had talked continuously about Camp Bowie and the men who garrisoned it. His description of Army life had been so entertaining that she had all but forgotten her fear until Sergeant Moseley rode up next to the ambulance.

"I've ordered the men to flank you through the pass, sir."

"Very well, Sergeant. Let me know if you see any signs of trouble."

"If we see any signs of them, Captain, it'll be too late to do anything about it." The sergeant touched the brim of his cap in salute, then fell back into position with the other troopers.

Indy *had* to ask, "Are you expecting an attack, Captain?"

If the captain was surprised by her question, he didn't show it. "I'm always expecting an attack, especially there." He pointed to where the mountains came close together. "Apache Pass."

"I'm afraid I don't understand, Captain. I read that the pass *used* to be dangerous for travelers and freighters, but I was under the impression that Bowie had been built to protect the route and that, indeed, it had done just that."

"You've got your facts right, Miss Taylor. Once Bowie was garrisoned back in '62, the trouble stopped . . . but recently—" He floundered before her questioning look. "There's been some incidents," he finished in a low voice.

His hesitancy was disturbing. She wondered what he was trying so hard *not* to say and cautioned herself to leave it alone; it was none of her business. Or was it? A disturbing suspicion crept into her thoughts and she threw caution aside. "How recently, Captain?"

He stiffened, obviously uncomfortable with the question.

"Right around the first of June."

Indy thought back. "That's about the time my father took command, isn't it?" She watched him struggle for a reply and knew that her father had something to do with the reason the pass was no longer safe.

"Yes, I—" He broke off, turning his attention to Sergeant Moseley who had suddenly reappeared alongside the ambulance.

"We've got company, sir." Moseley inclined his head toward a high ledge overlooking the pass.

Nolan grabbed his carbine and swung around, his gaze lifting and searching the mountainside.

Indy followed his gaze. A half-naked Apache warrior sat astride his horse, looking down upon them. A second later another appeared, then another, as if from out of nowhere, reining their war ponies side by side until there were more than a dozen of them.

"I've never seen them sit out in the open like that before," said Nolan, his tone was touched with surprise. "They usually don't show themselves like that." To Moseley, he said, "Keep the men close to the ambulance, Sergeant. Order

them not to shoot until we know the Indians'
intentions." As soon as the sergeant dropped back
to relay the message, Nolan untied his horse and
let him go.

Indy crossed her arms and hugged herself.
Dear, God. Please don't let them attack. Fearful
images of the savage atrocities described in the
reports came back to her now in vivid detail—
images she had chosen to disregard, thinking that
nothing like that could happen to her.

"Can you use a revolver?" asked Nolan, his
voice jolting her from her thoughts. He was
kneeling in front of her, a worried expression
deepening the lines around his eyes and mouth.
Indy nodded, even though her mind rejected the
question. "Here, take this." He took the revolver
from its holster and put it in her hand. "You've
got six shots. You need to make every one of them
count. Don't shoot until I do and don't shoot
unless you're sure you can't miss. And, Miss Taylor," he paused, pinning her with a hard look, "I
don't know how this is going to turn out, but save
the last shot for yourself, just in case. You don't
want to be taken captive. Understand?"

Oh, yes, she thought, she understood all too
well. This was one time when she wished she
didn't. "Y-yes," she stammered. "I understand."
His expression told her he was doubtful that she
would be able to defend herself. "Please, don't
concern yourself about me, Captain. I *know* how
to use a revolver." Her brother, Justice, had indeed taught her to shoot, and she had become
fairly competent, but she had never shot at a

human being before, only bottles and painted targets.

Seeming convinced, the captain moved up front to converse with the driver. The man acknowledged Nolan's orders with a nod, then shot a stream of tobacco juice out of the side of his mouth.

All at once, the warriors raised their rifles high over their heads. Shots exploded and they whooped and shouted like demons.

"Go!" Nolan shouted to the driver.

The whip popped and the driver called out a string of profanities sharp enough to slash through the mules' thick hides. Sand and pebbles, kicked up by the team's sudden burst of speed, flew back and stung Indy's face.

She turned her gaze back to the rear of the wagon and saw the Apaches' horses break from their orderly position and come scrambling down the side of the mountain. They had the agility of a mountain goat and the speed of a cougar. Paralyzing terror stole her breath. No one had to tell her what their intentions were, and neither did she have to be a mathematician to know that the detachment was badly outnumbered.

"Get down on the floor," Nolan ordered, shouting. "And take off that hat. It's too good a target."

Indy slid off the seat onto the floor, curling her legs beneath her, and unpinned her hat. The wagon's paneled sides rose up two feet from the floor, not much protection, but better than nothing.

An arrow whistled over the top of her head and embedded itself into one of her carpetbags. She stared dumbly at its quivering feathered tail, realizing that but for the captain's command, she might now be dead.

"Yo, you mules. Get on out there." Again and again the driver cracked his whip.

Peeking over the side panel, Indy saw that the Apaches had reached the road and were now bearing down upon the detachment. Their war whoops mingled with the staccato bursts of rifle fire, the shouts of the six troopers, the driver's curses, and the wagon's rattling.

Twisting half around in their saddles the troopers fired their carbines at their attackers. Beside her, Captain Nolan shot straight out the back of the ambulance, then ducked down behind the drop gate to reload.

Indy cried out when the trooper riding directly behind the wagon flew off his horse. Without thinking, she clenched the revolver in both hands, raised it over the edge of the drop gate, aimed, and fired. Her shot went wild, missing the crouching warrior by a cannon length. She tried again, this time taking care with her aim. *Squeeze the trigger gently. Don't pull it!* The long-ago lesson came back to her, detail by detail. She nudged the trigger back another fraction of an inch and the shot exploded. The spine-tingling recoil threw her back against the mail pouch.

"Good shootin'. You got him, ma'am," said Nolan, offering his arm to help her up.

Regaining her position, Indy searched for the warrior and saw that both he and his horse had fallen. She gasped at the enormity of what she had done. Somehow it didn't matter that the Indian would have killed her had he been given the opportunity. He was a human being, and in spite of being a career soldier's daughter, raised in a home where the subject of war accompanied every meal, it went against her grain to deliberately take a human life. Even an Apache's, who, according to her father and everybody else, was something less than a human being.

Mortified, she lowered the revolver and prayed that God would forgive her yet again, if indeed He had forgiven her the first time, seven years ago, when she had killed her mother and brother.

Chapter 2

Above the din of pounding hooves, rattling wheels, and savage war cries came the driver's bellow of pain. He stood up, frantically trying to reach his hands around his back to pull out the arrow that had lodged near the center of his spine.

"Captain—the driver!"

Nolan twisted around. "Marcus!" He scrambled across the wagon bed on hands and knees toward the driver's seat. The wagon hit a deep rut a second before he reached him. The driver flew forward over the dashboard, down in between the rear mules and then beneath the wagon. "Marcus!" Nolan gained the driver's seat and leaned over, looking down. "Christ, Marcus!"

"Oh, God," Indy breathed, seeing the driver fall. She swung her head to the left and through the cloud of dust she saw the driver lying face up, spread-eagled on the ground behind the ambulance.

"Keep me covered, I've got to get the lines or the team will bolt." Nolan climbed over the seat and leaned down for the lines that had caught on the corner of the dashboard.

Indy refused to panic. She accepted her task without question and raised her revolver. Squinting down the barrel, she rotated the sight until she found a suitable target, one close enough that she couldn't miss. Her thumb eased back the hammer.

Something hit her shoulder, making her lose her concentration. Turning sideways, she saw it was the captain's hat. "Captain?" When he didn't answer, she swiveled around. "Captain Nolan!"

He was holding on to the driver's seat, his face a frozen tableau of shock. An arrow had entered his right shoulder from his back and come all the way through to the front. "Stay down," he ordered in a strangled voice when he saw her starting toward him.

Indy paid him no attention. He needed help, and though she had no idea what she could do, she was the only one available. On hands and knees, as she had seen him do, she crawled up the center of the wagon. By the time she reached him he was beginning to fade.

"Captain!" She leaned over the driver's seat and grabbed his left arm and pulled him toward her. "Climb over the seat," she demanded firmly, brooking no resistance. If he fell into unconsciousness before she got him over the seat, she wouldn't be able to get him back into the wagon bed. She didn't have the muscle. The effort was almost his undoing, but he did it, evidently as determined not to be weak as Indy was determined to be strong. "All right, now, let's set you down." She was breathing hard; all one hundred ten pounds of her had gone into getting him into the wagon bed. The wagon pitched sideways, jerking him from her grasp. He fell against her, knocking the wind out of her. Momentarily, she caught her breath and tugged and pulled until she had him sitting down and propped against her carpetbag.

He was as breathless as she, and obviously in a great deal of pain. "Re-remember wh-what I said." He clutched her hand and squeezed so hard she winced. "Save the last shot for yourself. Do you hear me? You can't let them take you!"

His eyelids started to close. Indy called his name and brought him back. "Please, Captain. I don't know what to do. I need you— Please!"

"Can't h-help— Wanted to bring more men, but the colonel, he wouldn't—"

He slipped into unconsciousness.

Feeling helpless and alone, Indy worried her bottom lip and stared down at the mail pouch. What was she to do? The troopers had all they could do fighting off the Apaches. They probably hadn't even noticed the loss of the driver or that Captain Nolan had been wounded. She had only herself to rely on.

"The reins! I have to get those reins!" She made a dash for the front of the wagon and peered cautiously over the seat. The reins were nowhere to be found. Puzzled, she looked for where they came off the team's rigging and sighed when she saw them hanging down behind the mules' rumps, slapping the ground. Even if she climbed over the seat and laid down across the dashboard, she wouldn't be able to reach them.

Tears seemed to fall of their own accord and she didn't attempt to brush them away.

Another bone-jarring jolt sent the driverless team off the road. Now, it was only a matter of seconds before they would bolt.

The fusillade of rifle fire behind her sent her scurrying back into position against the drop gate. The Apaches seemed to be everywhere, on the right, the left, behind the ambulance. She picked up the captain's carbine and braced herself for the recoil, then squeezed off the last three shots.

Another volley of fire came from somewhere in front of the ambulance. Indy whirled in that direction and saw a second band of warriors approaching from the west. Their war whoops resembled a thousand coyotes yipping and howling at the moon.

"Oh, God!" Frantically she searched the wagon for the captain's revolver, looking beneath her skirt, then moving the carpetbags. Finally, she slid her hands beneath Captain Nolan's legs and gave a cry of relief when her fingers closed around the wooden grip. There were four shots left. Only four. Three to use and one to . . .

She refused to think about that last shot.

The team turned sharply, throwing the ambulance up onto its right wheels. Tossed to the side, Indy struck her right temple against the long wooden seat. Blinding pain exploded inside her head and everything went blurry. Groaning, she lifted her hand and touched the side of her head. Warm blood trickled down the side of her face.

"Please, God. Don't forsake me now. I need you!"

Blinking and squinting, she located the new band of attackers and raised the revolver. If she hit anything it would be a miracle, but she had to try. Her first shot went high. Lowering the sight and willing her eyes to focus, she squeezed off another, then a third, but had no idea if any of them found their mark.

They galloped toward the ambulance—a boiling mass of horses and hostile Apaches. In a blur of motion they rode on past. More than a little confused, Indy stared at the cloud of dust they left behind and thanked God that for whatever reason they hadn't attacked.

The troopers, she thought, a second later. That's where they were headed. They would help their friends kill off the remaining troopers, then they would come after her and Captain Nolan.

A screeching noise came from out of nowhere. "Hai—eee! Hai-eee!"

Indy swung around. She was wrong. Not all the Indians had ridden past her after the troopers. *One* had stayed behind, watching from a rise the ambulance had yet to reach.

Perched like a big golden hawk upon his great pinto war pony, the Apache was tall, lean, and proud—an invincible force of one. His piercing gaze touched upon her for a scant second, but it was long enough to let her know he had seen her. Again, came that dreadful sound, "Hai-eee. Hai—eee." He kicked the pinto into a gallop and raced down the hillside after the wagon, seemingly intent upon catching the runaway team.

He was naked but for a tan breechclout and knee-high buckskin moccasins; his body was a sweat-glistened golden brown. The sun glinted off the brass cartridges in his belt, sending flashes of white light radiating from him in all directions.

His horsemanship would have won him top honors at West Point, she thought absently. Inch by inch the pinto swallowed up the ground, gaining on the lead mule, and a moment later they were running side by side. Switching the reins to his right hand, the Apache leaned to the left and caught hold of the mule's collar.

Indy's eyes widened in disbelief when, incredibly, he hurtled himself over onto the mule's back. And almost immediately the team began to slow. Now, it would be only moments before the Apache brought the team to a stop, and then . . .

It was as difficult to focus her eyes as it was her thoughts. Then she remembered that as long as she had the revolver, she had freedom of choice and the power to decide her own fate. She tucked the six-shooter into her right skirt pocket. There wasn't going to be any *and then,* not if she could help it!

Captain Nolan groaned and Indy moved to help him as he struggled to sit up. "Come on, Captain, lift up a little and lean against me," she whispered. Using his left arm, he raised himself up and moved back. Careful of the protruding arrow, Indy assisted as best she could. She was beginning to feel a little dizzy and disoriented herself, and realized she probably had a concussion. Once the captain settled against her, he sagged, his strength having given out.

"Ma'am?"

"I'm here, Captain." Wrapping her left arm

around across his chest, she held and comforted him. Blood oozed from his back and penetrated the layers of her clothing.

The team had been brought to a stop. Indy listened carefully for sounds that would tell her the Apache was on his way to claim his prize. Aside from the jingle of harness, the mules' winded blowing and stamping feet, there was only the echo of distant rifle fire. The Apache made no sound at all and without moving the captain, she was limited in what she could see. But there was no help for it, so she watched . . . and she waited.

A flash of red caught her eye. She moved her hand slowly to her pocket.

The Apache stood at the back of the ambulance, taller than most men and straight as a pine. His shoulders were wide, his arms bulging with muscle even now, when he wasn't straining. His skin was tight against the broad expanse of his chest and stomach, not an ounce of spare flesh anywhere. Around his forehead a faded red headband kept the mane of long, dark hair back from his face—a face that intrigued even as it frightened. Hadn't one of the Army reports described the Apache people as being flat-featured, with small, compact bodies?

This Apache certainly didn't fit that description. In fact, he didn't fit any standard description she could think of. He was arrestingly handsome with dark slashing eyebrows, a straight nose with flaring nostrils, and a jaw and chin so unyieldingly set that they could have been carved from the mountains that surrounded them.

But it was his eyes that made her die inside. Darkly cold—killing eyes that didn't even blink as they stole quickly but thoroughly over her face and body.

With the captain's right shoulder providing cover, Indy slipped her hand into her pocket and curled her fingers around the revolver's smooth wooden grip. Until now, she had thought only of sparing herself from being taken captive, not a thought of what would happen to the captain! He was already in great pain, maybe even dying. She had no idea if his wound was fatal. But if it wasn't . . . She needed only to reflect on the conversation she had overheard at San Simon to know what the captain's fate would be.

It would be immoral to leave him to die so horrible a death. Strategically positioned, the one remaining shot *could* do the job of two.

Captain Nolan stirred and opened his eyes. Indy turned her attention away from the Apache and nuzzled her lips against his forehead, trying to soothe him. "Don't worry. I'm here. I'll take care of both of us."

"Shatto." The word was garbled.

"What?"

He groaned and raised his right hand toward the arrow.

Guessing his intention to purge himself of the arrow, Indy screamed, "No! You can't do that!" She wrestled his hand, but even in his weakened state he was the stronger.

With baffling swiftness, the Apache vaulted up into the wagon bed and threw his fist into the captain's face, knocking him out.

The revolver, Indy. Now. Don't wait. Do it now! She pressed her lips together to keep from crying out as she drew the Colt from her pocket. Before she could cock the hammer, the Apache pushed the captain aside and seized her wrist. A small scream tore from her throat. Desperate to hold on to the revolver, she clamped her other hand around the length of the barrel. "Let me go," she said between her teeth, bringing the barrel around. His savage look told her he had no intention of letting her go or letting her get off a shot. "Damn you!" She couldn't let him stop her—couldn't let him take her captive. Summoning all her strength, she twisted away from him. If she could roll over with the pistol beneath her . . .

Almost effortlessly, he flipped her back, climbed on top of her, and straddled her hips. In the midst of the fracas, Indy had managed to shove her index finger into the trigger guard, but had yet to cock the hammer.

The Apache beat her to it, then forced her finger against the trigger. The bullet shot straight up and blew a hole through the canvas top. Five more times he cocked the hammer and made her pull the trigger. The cylinder clicked hollowly at each empty chamber. After the last one, his hostile gaze met hers and she read the anger in his eyes.

"Yes." She hissed like an angry rattler. "I saved the last one for me. I'd rather be *dead* than have you or your friends touch me!" Sobs choked her and tears blinded her. She couldn't move, not even her legs, which had been bared when he'd straddled her and forced her dress up. They were beginning to go numb beneath his weight—her whole body was going numb, except for her head, which felt like it might explode.

He leaned over her, blocking out the daylight. His dark hair fell forward over wide, muscular shoulders the color of saddle leather. He was watching her like a hawk watches its prey. Would he kill her quickly, she wondered, or would he tease and torment her until she screamed for mercy?

His gaze inched downward, lingering on her heaving breasts, clearly making an appraisal of her assets, yet acknowledging nothing of his summation in his expression until his gaze moved lower.

He spoke suddenly, a guttural foreign-sounding word that she could barely make out the pronunciation, let alone understand what it meant. Then, before she could guess his next move, he tore open her jacket and pulled her blouse free from her skirt.

"No!" she cried, assuming his intent. "No, please!" Of all the things she'd imagined would happen to her, she hadn't ever considered rape. Somewhere she thought she'd read that Apaches didn't rape . . .

Fear and blinding pain transported Indy to another part of her mind where she no longer felt the Apache's hands intimately examining her body, where she couldn't see his measuring expression, and where there were no sounds to intrude upon her trancelike stupor.

Slowly, she became aware that there was someone hovering above her. It was Sergeant Moseley. He was kneeling beside her, his craggy features tight with worry. Indy fought to keep her eyelids from closing, but they felt heavy, as if they'd been weighted.

"Sergeant—" she breathed, unable to complete her question. Her tongue felt thick.

"Shh, don't talk. You're safe now. Everything's gonna be all right." He patted her hand reassuringly.

It seemed to Indy that she must be hallucinating. How was it possible that the sergeant had escaped the attack after the second band of Apaches had joined the first? Was he the only one who had survived, or had he and his men somehow managed to fight the Indians off? Questions rolled around inside her head like tumbleweeds, but she couldn't seem to grab hold of one long enough to ask it. She looked up, bewildered.

Moseley tipped his canteen and soaked his neckerchief. "You've got quite a knot on your head, big as a bird's egg," he said, carefully pressing the cloth to the side of her head just above her ear. She yanked back sharply. "Come on now. Easy. This'll take down some of the swelling. You'll probably have a headache for a few days, but all things considered, I'd say you was real lucky. Thought for sure this old wagon was gonna roll." When she started to move around, he slipped a hand beneath her back and raised her up, propping her against her carpetbag.

He offered her the round, canvas-covered canteen, and she drank greedily, swallowing down several large mouthfuls before she actually got a taste of it. It hit her all of a sudden. She made a face and shuddered simultaneously. The water was cool but had a distinctly metallic flavor.

In spite of its repulsive taste or maybe because of it, Indy was suddenly able to think more clearly. She knew she hadn't fainted—she *never* fainted. But obviously she had blacked out for a moment or two. Curious now about the sergeant's description of her injury, she reached up and touched the injured area. He was right. It was the size of a bird's egg, and the way it was throbbing, she thought it might even hatch.

"Hey, Sarge! You got any more water in that canteen?"

Surprised by the voice, Indy grabbed at the sergeant's forearm and pulled herself up onto her side. She saw a small group of soldiers gathered next to a large boulder several yards behind the ambulance. Their images were blurry, but the blue—the wonderful cavalry blue of their fatigue blouses—broke through the blur and she felt a soothing rush of relief.

It was a miracle. Odds had been against any of them surviving and yet here they were. Later, when she had her wits about her, she would have to ask Sergeant Moseley how they had managed to run the Apaches off.

The trooper who had asked about the water detached himself from the group and ran over to the ambulance. "Shatto says the arrow has to come out now, else Cap will bleed to death. What should we do?"

"Shadow." Indy repeated the word in a whisper. Or was it a name? She vaguely remembered the captain mumbling a word that sounded similar. On a sudden thought, she spoke the captain's name and bolted upright.

Moseley caught her by the shoulders, stopping her from going any farther. Over her head he answered the trooper's question. "If *he* says it's gotta come out, it's gotta come out. Shatto knows what he's doin'. Probably better than Doc when it comes to arrow wounds."

Inside Indy's head shades of black, gray, and white whirled, swirled, mixed, and separated like a kaleidoscope. She moaned at the shifting, dizzying patterns. "The captain," she said with an effort, "where is he?" She felt an urgent need to see for herself that he was still alive and if there was something she could do to help him.

Sergeant Moseley pointed to the group of troopers. "He's bein' well taken care of. Ain't nothin' you can do. Shatto's gonna take out the arrow—"

There was that word again. *"Shadow?"* she interrupted. "Did you say shadow?"

Moseley gave a wry smile, lifted his hand, and scratched his beard-stubbled cheek with a dirt-stained finger. "There's times I think he *is* a shadow, the way he shows up all of a sudden like, right there beside you. But no, ma'am. It ain't shadow, it's Shatto," he emphasized the two t's. "And he's a—" At a voice behind him, Moseley glanced over his shoulder, then leaned back on his heels. "Speakin' of shadows . . ."

It was just like before: the Apache appeared at the back of the ambulance. Only now her fear had a name: Shatto. She would have screamed had she been able to find her voice, but it had become lodged in her throat. She threw herself against the sergeant and held on tight.

Her gaze met with the Apache's and she went breathless with fear.

The dark moments Indy had lost came into her head like the awakening blast of a sunrise reveille. He'd been touching her, her breasts, her stomach, her abdomen, and she'd been too winded, too afraid, and too much in pain to fight him or even make a verbal protest. Then, he'd withdrawn his blood stained hand and raised himself off her. She'd closed her eyes, sucked in great gasps of air, and when she'd opened them again . . . Sergeant Moseley.

It *wasn't* just like before, she realized a second later. Moseley was holding her and telling her there was nothing to worry about. Then, pushing her gently away from him, he said, "The fightin's over, Miss Taylor. Shatto here, he's a friend. He don't mean you no harm. Weren't for him and his braves being out huntin' and comin' on us as they did . . . we'd a had us some serious trouble. As it was we lost three good men."

"Friend?" she echoed, but her mind wasn't able to accept the word.

The Apache looked away from Indy and he spoke to the sergeant in that same guttural language she'd heard before.

Moseley translated. "He says he needs somethin' for a bandage and figured maybe you'd have somethin' in that carpetbag of yours."

Unable to turn her gaze away from the Apache, Indy spoke out of the corner of her mouth. She was shaking so hard she could hardly form the words. "I don't understand what is going on here. Why would you want to help him? He's one of the Indians who attacked us."

"Yes, ma'am, he's one of them all right, but then again he ain't. Like I said, him and his braves are friends. They've helped us out a time or two the last couple of months. It's been real bad since the colonel come and changed the way—" He stopped abruptly, obviously realizing his error.

Indy didn't have the interest or energy to question him further. "But, Sergeant! You don't understand. He tried to—"

"I know what you was thinkin', ma'am, but he weren't tryin' t'hurt you. He said he saw the blood on your clothes and thought you'd been shot, then he realized it was Cap's blood."

The sergeant's words were finally sinking in and so was the realization that the Apache— Shatto—had saved her life—their lives, she and the captain's—by stopping the runaway team, then by preventing her from using the revolver.

Apparently at the end of his patience, Shatto reached into the ambulance and grabbed for one of the carpetbags.

Indy saw the movement out of the corner of her eye. Impulsively, she reached out and closed her fingers over his forearm before he could carry it off. It was a foolish move, prompted by her natural sense of decency and her guilt, but once the physical contact had been made it virtually paralyzed her. Beneath her fingertips she could feel him tense, feel the sinew and muscle expand and contract, feel the heat of his skin.

Again, their eyes met and locked, but this time it wasn't fear she felt, but something else—some nameless thing that made her body ache with yearnings. It was almost painful in its intensity. She blinked and looked up.

It took her a full minute to remember why she had grabbed on to him. Then she rushed to explain, the words tumbling out too politely, coldly. "It seems I misinterpreted your intentions. You deserve my thanks not my condemnation. I'm sorry."

For all the courage it took for her to apologize, it had been a wasted effort. His unflinching stare told her he didn't understand her words. She turned to the sergeant to ask him to interpret, which he did, but there was still no change in the Apache's expression.

She removed her hand from his arm and he took the bag and returned to the captain. It was then that Indy saw the other braves, standing beside their horses, silent and watchful.

All but one of the troopers surrounding the captain moved back, giving Indy a good view. Stripped to the waist, Captain Nolan was propped up against the trooper behind him. He was very much alive and alert. He drank from a small glass bottle and grimaced after each swallow. Finally, he pushed the flask away from him and roared like a lion.

"God Almighty! Which one of you men has the audacity to call this whiskey?" No one confessed. "Ah, never mind. It seems to be working. But if I die real sudden like, it won't be the damn arrow that killed me. Hear me?" he yelled, then groaned, obviously in great pain. After a moment he turned his gaze on Shatto who was kneeling down in front of him. "I'm ready. Do what you have to do, but do it quick, dammit."

Shatto drew a knife from the leather sheath attached to his cartridge belt and sliced through the arrow shaft, just behind the arrowhead. Nolan clenched his teeth and grunted.

Indy cringed. She had always had a hard time bearing up to other people's pain. Shatto, she noticed, seemed totally unaffected. He was fast and efficient, as if he'd removed a hundred arrows. Maybe he had, she thought. Maybe he was some sort of Apache medicine man.

"You sure you know what you're doing?" queried Nolan, looking up skeptically at the Apache.

If Shatto answered, Indy didn't hear him. He got up and moved around to Nolan's back and hunkered down.

"Don't move, Captain," cautioned one of the other troopers. "Don't even breathe."

"Will you hurry up?" Nolan grated out.

The words were hardly out of his mouth when Shatto grabbed hold of the feathered end of the shaft and pulled straight toward him.

The captain cursed at the top of his lungs, then fell forward, unconscious. The remainder of the whiskey was now used to pour over the front and back of the wound, then his shoulder and upper chest were bandaged with strips torn from one of Indy's petticoats.

Finished now, Shatto moved back and watched as the troopers mustered to pick up their captain and ease him into the ambulance and place him on the long bench.

Minutes later, everyone was in position: a new man in the driver's seat, Sergeant Moseley sitting next to Indy watching over her and the captain, and the remaining troopers mounted and ready to go. Moseley lowered the canvas curtains and gave the order for the ambulance to start forward.

Indy glanced back and saw the Apache hurtle himself onto his pinto. He sat his horse with an arrogant, loose-limbed casualness that said he was a man who knew he had complete control, over his mount and everything else. His proud, handsome face wore an expression of supreme confidence—a confidence that manifested itself in every gesture he made, every word he spoke.

Was he an Apache chieftain? she wondered. She had read a little of Cochise, and one or two others, but the name Shatto had never come up in any of the reports. Perhaps he was a newly appointed chieftain, having stepped into the position as the result of another's death.

Even as the ambulance moved forward, she stared at him. There was something about him . . . something that set him apart from the other braves.

It was that *something*—that difference—that had sparked her awareness of him. She wondered if their paths would ever cross again, and she wondered why she was curious about such a thing.

She stared after him even after the ambulance had rounded a curve and she could no longer see him. "How much longer will it take to get to Bowie?" she asked Moseley.

"We'll be there in no time, ma'am. No time at all."

Chapter 3

Camp Bowie sat on a plateau at the base of a domed mountain overlooking Apache Pass. A clear sky and a full rising moon held back the dark of night. From inside the curtained ambulance Indy looked uninterestedly between buildings at the raw, crudely constructed post that would be her home for the next few months. A dozen or more buildings built of wood and adobe made a broken square around the parade ground, which by day, when the regimental flag waved, would become the center of activity.

The events of the last hours had left her body numb, her spirit languishing, and her clothing and hair disheveled. In her present condition, even if Bowie's streets had been paved in gold, she would have thought them ugly. In fact, Bowie had no streets, no grass, no trees for shade, or any amenities as far as she could tell. It was by far the most primitive, uncivilized-looking post she had ever seen, and she had seen a good many of them, all east of the Mississippi, she reminded herself, which may have had something to do with it, but didn't give her any comfort.

The bugler blew the 8:30 P.M. tattoo as the

ambulance creaked and rattled between two adobe structures. In half an hour he would blow taps and the day would officially be over. Turning right, and entering the far northwest corner of the parade ground, the driver pulled up beside a large, flat-roofed, L-shaped adobe. Soft yellow light spilled from the windows onto the team, glancing off the metal rings on their rigging.

Soldiers who had been heading for their quarters started running toward the returning detachment. Of the eight men sent out, five had survived the attack. The dead—Private Marcus, the ambulance driver, and two green recruits—were being towed behind the troopers, tied face-down to the horses' saddles.

The tranquillity of the evening erupted into chaos as word of the detachment's return passed like wildfire from mouth to mouth. In less time than it took to brake the team, word had spread into the barracks and officers' quarters.

Inside the curtained ambulance, Indy sat quietly in the right front corner, behind the driver's seat, trying to keep her eyes open and her mind alert for what she knew was coming. She heard variations of excitement, concern, and fear—the latter from the women.

In a minute or two she would have to abandon the ambulance. She trembled at the thought of having to present herself to so many people at once, especially in her present condition. Besides her dishabille, and a bruising headache, she had yet to recover from the fear of the attack. She wondered if she ever would.

"Stand back, now. Out of the way," ordered

Sergeant Moseley in a tone that brooked no argument, not even from the commissioned officers. He waved his hand to move the people away from the back of the ambulance, then opened the drop gate. "Somebody get Doc and tell him he's got a couple of patients." On an afterthought he shouted, "And get Colonel Taylor."

Indy shivered at the mention of her father's name. She dreaded the confrontation, *had* dreaded it from the moment the idea of joining him had been conceived, though she'd convinced herself that once he saw what a help she was, he'd forgive her for disobeying him. But now, after what Captain Nolan had unintentionally revealed, she wasn't so sure.

Her eyes stung with welling tears, but she quickly squeezed them back, took a deep steadying breath, and straightened her shoulders. She would not let her father catch her with tears in her eyes; he loathed crying or weakness of any sort.

Sergeant Moseley asked the man closest to him to help with the captain. Together, they lifted Nolan down to two other soldiers who carried him into the hospital.

Captain Nolan had not regained consciousness, but the sergeant assured her that his chances were good, thanks to Shatto's field doctoring.

Shatto.

The formidable Apache warrior had not been out of her thoughts since they'd left Apache Pass. Stamped upon her memory were the hostile planes and angles of his face—lean and hard—his skin darkened by the sun and burnished by the wind. And his eyes ... God, his eyes ... She would always think of them as *killing eyes*. Looking into their cold, black depths had frightened her as nothing ever had, but later, when he'd come after something for a bandage ... his eyes had fascinated her—the *man* had fascinated her in a way that was completely beyond her understanding. Even now, just thinking of him produced an odd emotional reaction and an even more peculiar physical reaction that made her clamp her knees together.

"Ma'am?" Sergeant Moseley stood before her.

Indy looked up, interrupted from her thoughts. She rose slowly, holding on to his arm for support, and moved to the back of the ambulance. A collective gasp of surprise went up among the onlookers, followed by one woman's "Oh, the poor child."

Sergeant Moseley jumped down, then reached up for her. Just as he set her on the ground there came a sharp command.

"Attention!"

Officers and enlisted men alike came to attention at the commander's order. The few women present, officers' wives and several laundresses, moved back out of the way.

Colonel Charles Taylor, a flint-eyed career soldier, shouldered his way through the assemblage. "You may take your ease, gentlemen," he said in a carrying voice. "Report, Sergeant!"

"With all due respect, sir, your daughter has been injured. I was just about t'see her into the hospital, but now that you're here, you might want t'take over."

"I would not, Sergeant. Miss Taylor is here without my permission. I want no part of her."

"Well, then, sir. Could my report wait just a moment till I get her inside?"

"It could not."

Indy felt herself begin to sway and grabbed on to the sergeant's arm for support. "Father, please. I know you're angry with me, but I really don't feel well—"

"Quiet, daughter. You will speak only when spoken to. Now, you were about to report, Sergeant?"

Sergeant Moseley gave Indy an apologetic look, then turned to the colonel. "We were attacked by Chie's bunch on our way back from San Simon."

"Any wounded or casualties?"

"Yes, sir. Captain Nolan took an arrow in his left shoulder and we lost Private Marcus and the two new recruits you assigned me. Would've lost more, including your daughter here, if Shatto's band hadn't showed up and driven them off."

"Shatto. His name seems to keep coming up quite often around here. Do you have any idea why he would come to your aid? What his motive is?"

"Motive, sir?"

"Yes, Sergeant. Motive. Has he asked for anything? Food? Supplies? Guns or ammunition? Information?"

Sergeant Moseley shook his head. "No, sir. He said they was out huntin' when they saw us. I can't say why they lent us a hand, but hell, sir, them Indians is always fightin' each other. They don't need no reason." He shrugged expansively.

The colonel appeared to give the answer some consideration. "I suppose anything is possible, but I don't understand how a few breechclouted savages could accomplish what your detachment could not."

"If we'd had us a few more men and better horses, we might have been able t'stop 'em sir. But as it was, we didn't stand a chance."

"More men, Sergeant? Perhaps you think I should send the entire garrison after the mail? Have you considered the possibility that the ambulance and its unauthorized passenger slowed you down and made you less effective against the enemy? And speaking of the ambulance, Sergeant Moseley, where are the magazines and newspapers Captain Nolan was to pick up?"

"They wasn't there, sir. Just the regular mail."

"Then there was no need for the conveyance after all?"

"We couldn't have known that, sir."

"I'll expect a full report on my desk first thing in the morning, Sergeant. Dismissed." He turned on his booted heel and walked away.

Indy gave a gasp of disbelief. What kind of father was he that he could leave her after all she had been through? Certainly not the same man who had long ago held her and Justice on his knee and sang military songs to them. That man had loved her, cared about her, and called her his "little girl."

Stricken by her father's coldheartedness, Indy felt her spirits plummet. Had she been so absorbed for the last seven years in trying various ways to gain his forgiveness that she had failed to recognize the truth—that he would never forgive her—or that he no longer loved her? She couldn't bear thinking about it. Maybe when she felt better she would give it her consideration, but not now.

Taps blew but no one moved. Indy saw the women's expressions of confusion and pity and wished she'd used the good sense God gave her and had stayed in St. Louis.

From atop his pinto, Shatto watched the ambulance disappear around a bend and out of sight. Two questions nagged at him. Why had Chie attacked the mail detachment? What would have been the detachment's fate if he and Toriano hadn't spotted the dust cloud and brought the whole hunting party to investigate? He knew the answer to the second question but not the first. The troopers would have been tortured and killed in various ways and the woman . . . Chie was particularly fond of raping white women. Because of having a white father, Chie didn't hold with the Apache belief that raping a woman would take away his luck.

At Toriano's signal, Shatto reined Valiente around and followed the others back into the pass to begin the unpleasant task of gathering the dead Chie had left behind.

Much later, after the band had made camp for the night, Shatto hunkered down near the campfire and set the rabbit he'd caught to roasting. Beside him, Toriano sat cross-legged, poking a broken arrow shaft into the burning mesquite wood.

Toriano was the first to speak. "Chie is no more Apache," he said, staring morosely into the flames. "No Apache leave warriors behind for vultures to eat."

Shatto's dark eyes reflected the firelight. "You must accept what Chie has become. He no longer calls you his brother. He calls you enemy, and he will kill you if he can."

"I know what you say is true, but it is very bad here." Toriano placed his hand over his heart. "I cannot forget that we were children together."

Shatto leaned forward to sniff the roasting meat. The rabbit was young and fat; its meat would be tender and tasty. Roasted rabbit was one of his favorite meals and normally the smell made his mouth water, but tonight he was immune to it and to his hunger. "I have been thinking," he said in a low voice. "Chie is many things, but he is not a fool. He would not attack the bluecoats unless he had something to gain: guns, ammunition, supplies . . . something." His voice trailed off.

"But there was nothing," said Toriano.

Shatto stirred the fire. After a long moment he said, "There was the woman."

Toriano cocked a brow. "Chie has three wives already. Why would he want the white woman?"

"Because she is the bluecoat colonel's daughter," Shatto stated without inflection. "There was no reason for Chie to attack the mail detachment, *except* to capture the woman. Such a woman would be worth many rifles, ammunition, and horses." Fat drippings fell into the fire and sizzled, sending the flames higher.

Toriano cut Shatto a sideways glance. "Do you think the bluecoat colonel would pay so much for his daughter?"

"I don't know, but Chie must have thought so. His band grows larger each day. He calls himself their chief. It is for him to find ways to get his band the rifles and horses they need to fight the white eyes." Shatto rose to his feet and moved away from the firelight. Other thoughts snapped at his heels but he forced them back. The bluecoat's daughter was not his concern.

Speaking over his shoulder, Toriano said, "Your thoughts are quiet like thunder, my friend."

Shatto crossed his arms and assumed a spread-legged stance in defense of Toriano's mind reading. "If my thoughts are so noisy, then tell me what they say."

"They say Shatto would like such-a-woman for *his* woman."

Shatto drew a long breath. "And can you hear my thoughts now, shaman?"

Toriano cupped his hand around his left ear. "They say . . . Shatto is angry at Toriano for listening to thoughts."

Shatto nodded. "Then you only heard half of them." He returned to the fire and removed the rabbit from the long stick.

Toriano looked up. "Half? What other half?"

Shatto bit into the rabbit and started to walk away. "That you can go catch your own rabbit!"

At the bugler's call of reveille, Indy woke with a start from a deep sleep. In reaction to the ear-piercing blast, her eyes flew open and her body stiffened.

The morning light barely penetrated the dirt-encrusted windows, but it was enough to see the neat row of iron bedsteads that stretched down the wall beside her. They served to remind her that she had spent the night in Camp Bowie's hospital.

Her brow creased with memories from yesterday—the attack, her father's hostility, and Dr. Valentine's pronouncement that she had suffered a concussion and would need to be watched throughout the night.

She rolled over onto her back, moaning with the effort. There wasn't a muscle in her entire body that didn't protest at being disturbed. She could only guess at the number of black and blue marks that must cover her body.

Surprisingly, her head didn't hurt all that badly—just a sort of dull ache instead of yesterday's merciless pounding. And the blurriness and disorientation were gone. All in all, she felt better than she had expected.

"Miss Taylor?"

She jumped at the familiar voice that came from the other side of the curtained screen. "Is that you, Captain? Are you all right?"

"Yes, ma'am," he replied weakly. "Doc says I'll be laid up awhile, but the arrow didn't hit anything vital." There was a long pause. "What about you? When Shatto was working on me, he said you'd been hurt. I—I figured maybe you'd shot yourself . . . like I told you to do. God Almighty,

I wouldn't have told you to do it if I'd had any idea we'd be rescued."

Indy curled her fingers around the edge of the woolen blanket. The thought of what she had nearly done chilled her from head to toe. "I thought he—Shatto—was like the others," she began, her mind taking her back. "He was so—so fierce-looking . . . He didn't say or do anything to lead me to believe he was friendly. He just stared at me." She paused, remembering. "I was so frightened. Then, he grabbed me . . . and took the revolver away. I thought he was going to ra—" She broke off and lowered her gaze to her hands and unclenched her fingers. Her knuckles were white.

"Thank God," said Nolan, relief evident in his voice. "I know how he must have frightened you—what you must have been thinking. I'm sorry. I remember seeing him there at the back of the wagon. I tried to tell you, but I must have passed out."

Indy sat up in bed. Beneath the thin hospital mattress, the straw-filled bed sack rustled and crunched.

The door opened and Dr. Valentine came in, carrying their breakfast trays.

"Well, now. How are my two patients this morning?" Though the silver-haired doctor looked old and frail, he walked with a spring in his step. He smiled as he set one of the trays down on Indy's lap. "You look a mite pale, young lady," he observed. "Are you feeling all right?"

"I'm a little sore, but I guess that's to be expected."

"Yes, I should think so." He leaned forward and examined her eyes and the side of her head. "No more disorientation?"

"No."

"Nausea?"

She looked down at the tray on her lap. "Not yet."

The doctor winked and laughed, then left her to deliver the captain's breakfast. Minutes later he excused himself, saying he had some reports to write up.

Indy didn't touch her food. Her growling stomach stated in no uncertain terms that she was hungry, but she felt as jittery as a beehive, a fact that she had chosen not to tell the doctor for fear he would make her stay in the hospital longer. She looked down at the tin plate. Over the years, her father and his friends had had a lot to say about Army food, but she'd never seen it or tasted it before now. The salt boiled beef had fallen apart like wet straw and lay atop a disreputable-looking biscuit that was surrounded by lumpy brown gravy.

Nerving herself for the worst, she plunged her fork into the biscuit and broke off a bite-size piece. Much to her relief, it tasted better than it looked, but after a few mouthfuls, she put the fork down and set the tray on the bedside table, deciding the challenge was too great after all.

Sometime later Dr. Valentine came back and sat on the edge of the bed. In many ways he reminded Indy of her maternal grandfather, with his sky-blue eyes and drooping white mustache. He'd put on square spectacles and they rode close to the end of his bulbous red nose. He peered at her from over the top of the wire rims. "I see no reason to keep you here another night; there's really nothing I can do for you that a little time won't cure. You will, however, need to rest for a couple of days." When she opened her mouth to speak, he held up his hand and effectively cut her off. "I know that you've just arrived and you need to unpack and get yourself settled in . . . but I can't allow it. You've suffered a severe blow to your head, young woman, and you need time and rest to heal. You could do yourself some serious damage if you don't follow my orders." He paused.

"Now, I've taken it upon myself to get someone to help you. In fact, I spoke to the woman last night and told her the situation. She was more than willing to offer her services. She assured me that she would call on the colonel this morning right after reveille and request his permission to prepare a place for you within his quarters. Her name is Prudence Stallard. She'll be here late this afternoon. Until then, I want you to rest."

Indy knew the moment Prudence Stallard entered the hospital that she was one of the laundresses. Her hands gave her away. They were rough and red.

"Please, call me Pru," said Prudence when Dr. Valentine made the introductions. "Everyone does." Likewise, Indy requested Prudence use the shortened form of her name. Dr. Valentine excused himself and left.

"Word is around camp that Shatto and his

band came to your rescue," Prudence said. At Indy's nod, she went on. "I've only seen him a time or two. Once on my way to Tucson for supplies, and last spring when he sent word to Captain Nolan that he had a present for Peter Clarke, the former post commander's little boy. It was a puppy to replace the dog Peter had lost the night his father was killed."

"That was kind of him," Indy said.

"I thought so too. I've never heard of an Apache doing anything like that before. That's when I got the notion that there was something *different* about Shatto, something that set him apart from the other Apaches. He's still a dangerous savage, mind you. I've heard about how deadly he is with a knife—but it's like he has . . . a heart . . . if you get my meaning."

Indy recalled thinking exactly the same thing right after the attack—that there was *something* different about Shatto—*something* that set him apart from the other braves. She might have told Pru how much in agreement they were and she might have elaborated on the subject by saying how Shatto had prevented her from killing herself and Captain Nolan, but she found herself oddly reluctant to share her thoughts.

"Nobody seems to know much about him," Prudence went on. "In fact, nobody had even heard of him until five or six years ago, then all of a sudden there he was." She lifted her chin and looked straight into Indy's eyes. "You saw him up-close. What did you think of him? How did he impress you?"

"Impress me? He terrified me."

Prudence clucked her tongue. "No, that's not what I mean," she said, laughing and shaking her head. "Once you realized he wasn't going to hurt you—what did you think of him? You know, as a man?"

Indy looked confused. "As a man? Why, I don't think I know what you mean. Of course I think of him as a man. What are you saying?"

Prudence gave an exasperated sigh. "Where did Doc say you were from? St. Louis? Did you grow up in a convent, or did your papa keep you locked up in the attic?"

Indy was taken aback at the woman's bold affront, but Prudence didn't seem to notice. "Most Apaches I've seen are sort of broad in the face. Now, Cochise. I saw him once in '62. He's handsome as far as Apaches go, and very distinctive-looking, but Shatto—he's so—" The bridge between her eyes wrinkled, then she smiled and shrugged her shoulders. "There's just a look about him that takes my breath away." She gave a delicate shiver.

Indy took a moment to think of a reply. "He's a fine-looking Indian," she said at length, refusing to indulge in an evaluation of Shatto's physical attributes—attributes that were deeply etched into her memory.

Prudence laughed again. "Oh, for heaven's sake, Indy. You aren't going to be like those stuffy officers' wives are you? They're so worried about trying to impress your papa so he'll look upon their husbands with favor at promotion time, they can't say a word unless they've rehearsed it first! But you— Now, you don't have to impress anybody. So you can speak up and say whatever is on your mind. Especially in front of me."

Indy laughed in spite of herself. She had never met anyone quite like Prudence Stallard before, and she had a feeling it was going to be a very interesting relationship. "Thank you, Pru. That's good to know, but I really don't have anything to say, at least not at the moment. And as far as men go, I never had much time for that sort of thing. I was always so busy taking care of the house and Father." She shrugged.

"I see. Well, then, you'll just have to take my word about Shatto. He'd have every woman here dreaming about him if he were a white man . . ." She rolled her eyes and made a funny face.

Indy wasn't amused.

"Well now, let's get you up and dressed. I've prepared your quarters so that at least you have a place to sleep and bathe, but I have to tell you there's a lot yet to be done." She gave a heavy sigh. "Your father—I mean, the colonel—it's apparent he hasn't lifted a broom to the place since the day he moved in. I cleaned the bedrooms, but that's as far as I got, so consider yourself warned."

On the other side of the privacy screen, Captain Nolan snored loudly. The two women looked at each other and broke into laughter.

In spite of Prudence's warning about the condition of her father's quarters, Indy was shocked and appalled. She had been prepared for dirt and disorder, typical of any man who didn't have a woman to take care of him, but she had not been prepared for this—this went beyond dirt and disorder.

The main room—the sitting room or parlor—was a perfect square, with a front window facing the parade ground, and a southern window looking out to the detached kitchen and a domed mountain that backed the camp. The inside adobe walls looked much the same as the outside walls, except lighter in color.

The furniture, what little there was, consisted of a scarred pine table, two camp chairs, and an iron bedstead like the one she'd just vacated. Several half-eaten meat pies, no doubt provided by some of the officers' wives, were so old they'd grown fuzz. Tin plates, encrusted with food, had been pushed to one end of the table and haphazardly stacked. A saddle, in need of mending, had been tossed in the corner beside the window, along with a sword belt, an old pair of riding boots, and an obscene boot jack, the iron cast in the likeness of a naked woman sitting down, her legs spread wide open.

Army regulations allotted a colonel four rooms with an added detached kitchen. Yet, it was obvious that her father used only this one room to eat, sleep, and live in. It seemed a great waste when there were probably several officers with families who could have made good use of the extra rooms.

Slowly she walked across the room to the hearth. There, on the mantel, above the stone fireplace, was evidence that this was indeed her father's quarters: several well-worn books by Scott and Irving, and Dennis Mahan's textbook,

Course of Civil Engineering. Mahan was a renowned instructor at West Point where her father and U. S. Grant had learned the *art of war.*

Indy lifted the book off the mantel. The leather binding had recently been oiled. The book fell open at a page long held by a child's golden curl. She reverently touched the silky lock and recalled how she had teased her little brother for having such beautiful, golden, curly hair.

"Do you happen to know where my father might be now? I'd like to talk to him."

"I wouldn't expect to see him until tomorrow anyway. He took a patrol out right after I spoke to him this morning. They went hunting for Chie. It's a waste of time and energy as far as the men are concerned, but your father is the one in command."

Indy looked up from the book. "Why do you say that?" she queried in an even voice that belied her irritation. She resented people speaking badly of her father.

"The Apaches know every inch of this land— every mountain crevice, every arroyo, every canyon. If they don't want to be found, no soldier on earth can find them, *especially* the colonel."

Indy stared at the textbook in her hands. The author had taught his students warfare strategies based on those of Frederick the Great and Napoleon—civilized men—not desert nomads. What Pru had just said, combined with what Captain Nolan and Sergeant Moseley had said, made Indy realize just how serious the situation here at Bowie was. She took a deep breath. "Does *everyone* think my father incapable of dealing with the

Apaches?" she asked, almost afraid to know the answer.

"I'm afraid so, Indy," Prudence said in earnest. "The problem is he's convinced that his way—by that book—is the right way. The *only* way. He just doesn't seem to realize that things need to be done differently here. He refuses to listen to the men with experience."

Indy bowed her head. "You don't like him, do you?"

"The colonel's a hard man. But I don't have to tell you that, do I? I was there when you came in last night. I saw your expression when he rebuked you. I saw how much he hurt you." Prudence looked suddenly weary. "I know I've spoken out of turn, and you can hate me if you want. I wouldn't blame you a bit. But you're going to be living here and you'll soon be meeting the women of Bowie—the wife of the soldier who was killed yesterday and others."

Indy felt suddenly sick inside. "No doubt they blame my father for their losses."

"They won't openly admit it, but yes."

Indy nodded, resigned. "I know Father is a hard man, but he wasn't always that way. You have to believe that. He used to be . . . different. He was kind. Patient. Loving."

"Come on now," said Prudence. "I've prepared a bath for you. The water was practically boiling when I left to get you. It should be just about right now. After your bath you need to get into bed before Doc sounds a charge. And while you're resting, I'll get working on this . . . mess."

"Oh, no, Pru. It's too much. I can't ask you

to clean this up. I can't ask anyone to clean it up. I—"

"Oh, pshaw! There's nothing here I haven't seen before. No, I insist!"

Unlike the parlor, the diminutive sleeping room Prudence had prepared for her was neat and clean. There was a bed, a chip-sided washstand, and a chair with a rawhide seat. The fragrance of fresh straw from the bed sack beneath an invitingly thick goose-down mattress filled her nostrils and made her think of long-ago afternoons when she and Justice used to play in the stable behind their house.

"All right, if you insist." Indy gave in.

"I'll leave you now. Enjoy your bath, then get into bed!"

Indy swung around and took Prudence's hands into her own. "You've been awfully kind. Thank you."

Prudence smiled and squeezed Indy's hands. "We're all sisters out here. We need to help each other. And you're welcome." She turned and left, closing the front door gently behind her.

Indy stood staring at the door moments after Prudence had left. It had been so long since she'd had any female friends that she had almost forgotten what it was like. Friends laughed together, cried together, and shared secrets. It would be nice to have a friend again. "*Sisters,*" Prudence had said. She smiled and gave a little laugh. Sisters would be even nicer.

Indy was about to return to her room when she looked out the window and saw the patrol ride two by two into the parade ground, her father in the lead.

"Prepare to dismount," Colonel Charles Taylor called out. "Dismount." He dismissed his men, tossed his reins to a waiting orderly, and started across the parade ground to his quarters.

Indy opened the door and waited for him, her fingers tightly gripped around the door handle. With a cheeriness she was far from feeling, she smiled. "Hello, Father. I was told you probably wouldn't be back until tomorrow. What a nice surprise."

He continued toward her, his gray eyes appearing as hard and cold as gunmetal. "You're the only surprise around here, miss, and it isn't one that pleases me."

The bath Prudence had prepared would have to wait.

Chapter 4

Indy backed into the parlor to allow her father to pass, then closed the door, leaned against it, and watched him survey the room. By rights, he should be embarrassed knowing that one of the laundresses had come in and cleaned up part of his deplorable mess. He should also be ashamed. But she knew he was neither.

Standing in front of the table, facing the window, he removed his hat and tossed it on the table. A cloud of dust rose up off the brim and crown. Then he stripped off his gauntlets and threw them on top of the hat. "Well, daughter, what do you have to say for yourself? You were told to stay home and take care of things there."

Indy drew a steadying breath and spoke to his back. "Yes, Father, I know, and I fully intended to do just that, but the servants do everything that needs doing around the house and there really wasn't anything for me to take care of once you were gone."

"In other words, you were bored and thought coming here would be a great adventure?"

"No. The fact of the matter is that I was worried about how you would manage without someone to see to your needs. I thought I might be of help." She could tell he was furious by the way he rolled his shoulders back and straightened his posture.

He turned around quickly and stood on the balls of his feet. "Well, miss, you thought wrong! If I had wanted help, I would have hired a striker!"

His anger hit her like a hard slap making her suck in her breath. She felt herself weaken, then chided herself, telling herself that this was no more or no less than what she had been expecting. She likened his fury to that of a hurricane. At the moment he was all wind, but he'd eventually blow himself out. With that thought in mind, she resolved to weather the storm and not let him see how he upset her.

She forced a light laugh as she pushed away from the door and walked around him to the hearth. "I beg to differ with you, Father, but you are very much in need of help," she said with a calm that belied her jumpy nerves. "Why, I couldn't believe these were *your* quarters when I first saw them. I've never seen such filth. I'm surprised you weren't overrun with vermin!" She turned to face him. "And to think," she scolded, narrowing her eyes and lowering her voice, "of all those lectures you gave Justice and me about being neat and tidy."

"You blatantly disobeyed my orders, Independence. If a soldier disobeyed me the way you did, he'd be charged with insubordination and made to ride the cannon."

It was a fagged, used-up threat that she had

heard him use a thousand times before with his subordinates. Hearing it now, directed at her, made her bold. "Oh, for heaven's sake. As long as I can remember you've wanted to punish someone by making them *ride the cannon*, but you haven't done it yet, and it's unlikely you ever will. Besides, I'm not a soldier, Father. I'm your daughter, therefore, I'm not subject to military punishment." She paused to catch her breath. "Now, what's done is done," she told him in a dismissive tone. "I know you would like to send me back, but you can't. It's too dangerous. So why don't we just make the best of it until you get your new orders? Then we'll both go home." She struck a match to light the kerosene lamp sitting on the mantel.

He stood behind her, glaring. "It seems you leave me no choice," he said in a tight voice, barely moving his lips. "But from now on, you'll do exactly as I say without question, and you *will not* under any circumstances interfere in my business or Army business. *Do you understand?*"

She lifted her chin and met his gaze. "I understand completely."

The dreaded confrontation was over and she would stay. Through weary eyes, she studied him. The harsh contours of his face gave him a cold, intimidating demeanor. His mouth curved down in a perpetual frown as his lips were unused to smiling. And his eyes, gray as chimney smoke, were deep-set and hooded beneath a sharp, jutting brow.

"He's a hard man," Prudence had said. Even harder now than before he'd left St. Louis, Indy

decided, studying him covertly as he lit his cigar. She wondered if the change was the result of his assignment to Camp Bowie. He had put in for Washington. The President had hinted that there might be a position for him helping to create the new Indian policy. But when that time came, Grant called on a civilian friend instead. Her father had felt betrayed and considered his assignment to Camp Bowie a slap in the face.

The confrontation left her exhausted and brought back her headache. She was about to sit down when someone knocked at the door. "I'll get it," she offered before he could say anything. The diversion was just what she needed.

Three women greeted her with cheerful smiles. "We're the official welcoming committee," one said, taking a single step forward. The movement made Indy notice that she was pregnant—very pregnant. "I'm Ava Burroughs, Lieutenant Burroughs's wife, and this," she said, gesturing to her right, "is Aphra Sinnett and Opal Dillehay. We didn't think you'd be up to preparing meals yet, what with your injury and all, and we thought you might like some supper."

Indy had steepled her hands in front of her mouth. "Oh, yes, thank you." She could have cried she was so grateful. "Won't you please come in? You'll have to excuse the place. I'm afraid I haven't had time to do anything with my father's quarters yet." Stepping back into the parlor, the three women paraded past her with their fragrant offerings.

"Think nothing of it," Ava Burroughs said on her way to the table. "We've all been where you are now, some of us more times than we can count. Good evening, Colonel Taylor," Ava said, holding her ceramic stew pot in front of her enormous belly. "I know how much you like my beef stew, so I brought enough for you and your daughter." Turning to Indy she added, "The vegetables are from my garden behind our quarters and the beef is range beef, a little different tasting than the eastern beef I know you're used to, but I think you'll like it."

"I'm sure I will," Indy returned with a wide smile.

Aphra set her gingham-checked bundle down on the table and unwrapped it like a baby. It was a loaf of freshly baked bread with the most beautiful golden crust Indy had ever seen. She almost swooned at the aroma that wafted up from the table and filled her nostrils. The last, from Opal, was an apple pie, reminiscent of the apple pies her mother used to make.

"Everything looks absolutely wonderful. I can't tell you how grateful I am—and hungry. I haven't eaten a thing since breakfast. Thank you. All of you."

As if tied together by an invisible thread, Ava, Opal, and Aphra started for the door at the same time. Ava reached out and touched Indy's arm. "You're quite welcome. As soon as you're feeling yourself, you come by. All three of us live just up from you on Officers' Row."

Indy closed the door, then went in search of eating utensils. In a day or two, she promised herself, she would return the dishes and become acquainted with the women of Officers' Row.

*   *   *

The next morning, immediately after she heard her father leave, Indy set about moving his personal belongings from out of the parlor into the next largest bedroom. Among his things was the leather pouch in which he kept the letters Justice had written him from West Point. Her father prized those letters more than gold and reread them often, but had never shared them with her. Someday, when things improved between them, she would ask to read them.

Indy had just opened the front door to sweep the dust outside when the bugler blew the nine o'clock call. A moment later her father and a number of the troopers—all in full dress uniform—and a half-dozen women assembled on the parade ground in a semicircle around three wooden coffins. She leaned on her broom listening as the chaplain read the burial service. Then the coffins were lifted into the ambulance and the procession made its way down the hill to the cemetery while the trumpeter played the funeral march. They had been gone a quarter hour when Indy heard the honor guard fire off three volleys of shots.

The troopers were the first to return, marching at quick time back to their quarters. The women followed at a slow walk. Indy didn't have to be told which one was the new widow; she was the one walking between Opal and Ava. She was the one crying.

Indy's heart went out to her. She didn't envy the choices the young woman would have to make. If she didn't have family or money, none of them would be easy. And what with it being so dangerous to travel now . . . The choices, Indy realized were even more limited than she had thought.

The very thought of packing up and leaving sent Indy into a panic. She clung to the broom handle and stared at the flagpole in the center of the parade ground. If not for Shatto coming to the detachment's rescue, where would she be now? The army reports had not censored the horrors the Apaches inflicted on their captives. Slavery. Repeated beatings. Starvation.

Thank God Shatto had come along when he had.

Shatto.

His name was becoming a habit in her mind— just thinking his name triggered an image of him—an image that would take her away from the present and put her right back in the ambulance, watching him bring the team to a stop, feeling his weight on top of her and his hands on her body.

Closing her eyes she imagined she could *feel* them now. Warm and strong. Demanding but not hurting. They touched and explored, frightened her, and, she had to admit it, excited her.

Beginning in her shoulders, a tremor moved with excruciating slowness down her body, radiating into her breast, her stomach, then moving straight to her abdomen where it lingered and ignited a soft, sweet fire. A sensation like none she'd ever known took root deep inside her and blossomed like a summer rose. The feeling stayed with her only a moment, then disappeared leaving her breathless and wanting.

Wanting what?

Her eyes flew open at the unexpected question and she began sweeping with a vengeance, taking her frustration out on the broom, as if it were to blame. It was just a daydream, she told herself. A silly daydream. There was no harm in it, and it didn't mean anything. So why did her face feel so hot, and why did she feel as if she'd done something naughty?

Thundering hoofbeats put an end to her discomfiture. Picking up the broom she stepped outside. A horseman galloped through the center of the parade ground. Pulling a tight rein he slid his horse to a halt right in front of her.

"I need Colonel Taylor!" he shouted.

"He isn't here, Private. He's at the adjutant's office. What's the matter?"

The soldier wasted no time on polite chatter. "Apaches ridin' in," he shouted as he reined sharply to the left and spurred his horse into a gallop.

A cloud of dust engulfed her, filling her nose and mouth. She tried to wave it away but was forced to give it up and retreated, coughing and choking, back inside her quarters and closed the door. What did he mean that Apaches were riding in? Were they attacking the camp? Biting down on her thumbnail, she perched herself on a chair in front of the window, hoping to get a glimpse of something or someone. As the dust began to settle, she saw the riders. There were six of them—naked but for their breechclouts, cartridge belts, and moccasins. They were walking their horses through the camp, and though they looked frighteningly dangerous and menacing, with their stolid expressions, they were not brandishing any weapons.

Shatto rode in front of the small party, a head taller than the others. Slung facedown in front of him, over his horse's withers, was a body—an Apache. Even from where she sat she could see the blood covering the dead Indian's back. With an effort, she switched her gaze to the others and was horrified to see that each of the riders had an Apache prisoner that they were towing behind them.

What was going on here? Why would Shatto make prisoners of his own people? And why would he bring them to Bowie?

From every direction troopers ran from whatever task they had been doing to the parade ground. There was chaos and commotion the likes of which Indy had never seen at any fort. Her father emerged from his office, pulling on his gauntlets. He was wearing his revolver. Four soldiers followed close behind him, their rifles at the ready. She heard him shout at an orderly to find Captain Nolan and bring him to the parade ground on the double.

Curious, Indy went back outside and stood directly in front of her door where she had an unobstructed view of the parade ground and Shatto.

Shatto hadn't seen her, and even if he had, she doubted he would bother to take a second look. He probably thought of her as some namby-pamby, high-minded white woman who got frightened at the least little thing. Prudence would be more to his liking, she thought. Besides being tall and slender as a reed, Prudence exemplified the frontier spirit. She was so absorbed in her thoughts that she failed to notice Prudence come up beside her.

"What is it? What's going on?"

Indy gave a start. When she saw who it was she blanched even as she breathed a sigh of relief. "You caught me off guard," she accused. She took Pru's arm and pulled her back against the door. "I'm not sure what's going on, but Shatto and his band just rode in and it appears they have prisoners."

Captain Nolan came out of his quarters, moving slowly and cautiously. He kept his left arm close to his side as he made his way toward the colonel.

"Captain Nolan," said the colonel. His voice carried to where Pru and Indy stood. "You speak Apache. I want you to find out what they're doing here."

"This is Shatto, Colonel," the captain offered as if it would made a difference.

It did make a difference. The colonel's demeanor changed to a so-this-is-the-infamous-Shatto look.

Nolan began speaking in that same guttural language Indy had heard before. There were a lot of hard d's and double vowels making it a harsh-sounding language with none of the flow of the European languages.

As he spoke, Shatto yanked up on the dead Indian's cartridge belt, lifted him off the pinto's withers, and let him drop to the ground at his horse's hooves. His reply to Nolan's question was short, his voice deep and resonant just as Indy remembered.

"What did he say?" the colonel asked impatiently.

Not taking his eyes off Shatto, Nolan translated. "He says these are some of Chie's warriors—part of the band who attacked the mail detachment. He says he has brought them to you to punish as you see fit."

The colonel's expression became suspicious. Scowling, he asked, "What does he want in return?"

Though she couldn't understand a word, Indy listened intently as the captain related the question and Shatto replied.

"He says he wants you to know that not all Apaches want to fight and kill the bluecoats. He says that Chie is an enemy to bluecoats and Apaches alike—that he makes much trouble."

"So these are Chie's bucks." The colonel moved off to the side to have a better look. "Sergeant Moseley, untie those prisoners and take them to the guardhouse and take this body away and have it buried. Outside the camp's cemetery," he added pointedly.

"Yes, sir," said Moseley, saluting.

Shatto said something else to the captain who nodded but didn't translate.

Loudly, Prudence sucked in her breath and squeezed Indy's arm. "He's something of a puzzle, isn't he?"

Indy swung her head around. "What do you mean?"

"They say that he's been given a special power that protects him against his enemies."

"Surely you don't believe in Indian superstition. He's just a man." Indy had guessed Prudence to be several years her elder, but looking at her now, with her face flushed a becoming pink and her china-blue eyes bright with excitement, she looked like a schoolgirl—a very smitten schoolgirl.

Prudence smiled, her smooth cheeks dimpling prettily. "Yes, isn't he though? A rather magnificent man, don't you think?" She dipped her head and looked at Indy from beneath her dark, spidery lashes. "Look at him, Indy. How many Apaches have you seen who look like that? For that matter how many white men have you seen who look like that?"

"I— Well—"

"My point exactly. I'll tell you what, Shatto can attack me anytime and I won't so much as lift a finger in protest!"

Indy gasped in shock. "Prudence Stallard. That's a shameless, unladylike thing to say."

Prudence gave a low, throaty laugh. "Yes, I know, but that still doesn't change how I feel."

Indy deigned not to comment, hoping her silence would be disapproval enough.

Because of Prudence, Indy missed the ending of the conversation between Shatto and Captain Nolan. Next thing she knew the Apaches had turned their horses around and were moving across the parade ground, heading toward Officers' Row.

Prudence broke away from Indy's side and moved out into the track where the horses would have to pass. It would serve her right if she got her foot stepped on or shoved aside, Indy thought meanly. She considered turning around and going back inside but changed her mind at the last moment, afraid that such an action might be taken as an affront. So she stayed where she was, trying to look like a normal spectator, hoping that Shatto's purported *powers* didn't extend to knowing what she was thinking . . . and feeling.

The riders approached. With an air of proud reserve impressed upon his hard, handsome face, Shatto rode slightly ahead of the others. If she were a superstitious person, she might actually believe that he possessed some magical power that made him impervious to bullets and arrows. When he saw Prudence standing in the middle of the track, hands on hips, smiling at him invitingly, his mouth quirked up at the corners, an almost imperceptible movement that Indy wouldn't have caught had she not been watching him so closely. Her temper flared and she felt a sudden, fierce resentment toward Prudence Stallard that prompted her to step forward and grab Prudence's arm. "If you don't get out of the way, they'll run over you."

Prudence's head swung around. "Don't," she said, her blue eyes snapping with sparks of anger.

Indy let go and stood back. God! What had possessed her to do such a thing? It wasn't for her to be concerned about how Prudence behaved. Let her fall at his feet in front of the whole camp. Let her make a fool of herself!

Deciding she didn't care what Shatto thought or how big a fool Prudence made of herself, she

turned and started back into her quarters. She
was just about to close the door when he passed
by. His dark gaze pinned Indy where she stood
and held her there, unmoving—not even breathing—until he and his braves had ridden around
the corner.

To get her mind off the morning's event, Indy
sat down at the table and began making a list of
supplies and food she would need. She looked up
when her father and Captain Nolan entered.

"Afternoon, Miss Taylor. Nice to see you looking so well," said the captain as he removed his
hat. He gave her a warm, friendly smile that she
was glad to return.

"Thank you, Captain, and same to you. But
shouldn't you be back in bed?" She stood up and
gathered her paper and pencil. Obviously her father had brought the captain to their quarters for
a purpose, probably to have a private discussion,
and she didn't want to be in his way.

"Doc says it's okay as long as I don't do anything too strenuous." His gaze slowly traveled
from her face to her hair, which she had let down
and braided into one long braid.

"Sit down, Captain," the colonel said abruptly.

Indy could tell that her father wasn't in the
best of moods. She thought it prudent to take
her pencil and paper and go sit down in the far-
thest corner of the room where she could be as
inconspicuous as possible.

The colonel spoke without preamble. "All right,
Captain, I'm tired of veiled suggestions and innu-

endo. You obviously have something to say, so say it."

"May I speak freely, sir, man to man, rather than captain to colonel?"

"You may," was his harsh reply.

"I know you read Major Clarke's reports upon your arrival so you're aware that he was making some progress with Cochise prior to his death."

"I am aware of his efforts, yes."

"I can only assume then that you are also aware that the Apache situation has worsened since you took command of Camp Bowie. Desertions are higher than ever before and the morale of the entire camp is at an all-time low. As much as I hate to say it, sir, your by-the-book methods and tactics are unsuitable for the frontier and for Apache warfare."

Indy stared at the items on her list but didn't see them. Pulling a breath and holding it, she waited for her father's reply.

"Is that all, Captain? Aren't you going to say something about my incompetency or my inability to command my men?"

"No, sir." Nolan handed him a piece of paper. "I've been asked to give you this. It's a petition to the War Department asking that you be removed from command here. Nearly every man has signed it."

The colonel took the proffered petition and read it over, then looked up, his face a stone mask. "I didn't come here to win friends, Captain. I came because the War Department made a mistake. I was supposed to have been assigned to the President in Washington."

"I'm sorry, sir."

The colonel leaned his head back and glared at the man across from him. "Yes, I'm sure you are. You think this command should have been given to you, Captain?"

"No, sir," came the quick reply. "But I do think the command should have been given to someone with experience in dealing with Indians."

In a level voice the colonel said, "You risk a great deal talking to me in this manner, Captain. I could take offense and have you charged with insubordination. It could be the end of your career."

"Yes, sir. I'm aware of the risk but am willing to do whatever it takes to save lives."

Indy dared a sideways glance. They were glaring at each other like two warring bulls. The friction between them could have ignited a fire.

"You're a brave man, Captain Nolan," the colonel said at length. "Few men would dare say the things you've just said to me."

"There's a lot at stake, sir. Not just Bowie, but the future of the Arizona Territory."

There was a long pause. The colonel gazed out the window, seemingly lost in thought. But Indy knew better. He never lost himself in thought. A minute later he said, "Suppose you tell me what I should do to make sure that petition never finds its way to the War Department."

Nolan looked uncomfortable with his role as mediator. "Throw your rule book away. The only way to control the Apaches is to fight them on their ground, and to do that you have to think and act as they do." At the colonel's quizzing look, he went on to explain. "They rely on concealment and surprise. The other day was the first time in four years I've seen them *before* they attacked. And I'm sure I saw them because they wanted me to, though I don't know why. You need to employ an Apache scout to—"

"Scout?" Colonel Taylor shook his head vehemently. "That would be putting every man, woman, and child at Bowie at risk. You can't trust a man who would go against his own."

"Begging your pardon, sir, but I was about to say that you should employ an Apache scout to train a select group of our own soldiers to travel, attack, and fight like Apaches. Once trained and properly outfitted, it would be like having a whole company of qualified scouts. They would know Apache tactics, desert survival skills, tracking, and a hundred other things that are a warrior's way of life. Those skills combined with Army discipline, arms, and ammunition would give *us* the advantage for once. Do you see what I'm getting at, sir?"

Indy pressed her lips together. How could her father not see? It was all so logical and reasonable. Never in her life had she wanted so badly to speak up, but she had promised her father that she would not interfere.

"I'm not blind, Captain. I admit I do see some merit in what you are saying, but I can't say I wholeheartedly agree with you. There's a lot more to solving the Apache situation than what you've outlined. A lot more."

The captain leaned back against his chair. He

looked tired, pained, and, Indy thought, defeated. She knew exactly how he felt.

"The idea I just expressed, sir, is not mine alone, but Sergeant Moseley's and some of the other men—veteran Indian fighters." He started to get up. "The mail goes out day after tomorrow." He took back the petition, folded it neatly, and stuck it in his pocket. "The men hope you'll consider what they've asked me to say, sir."

"Blackmail, Captain? Or mutiny?"

"You asked me what you could do to stop the petition from being sent. I've told you, sir. If you choose to think it's mutiny or blackmail, that's your prerogative."

"And if I agree to employing a scout, who would I get?"

"There's only one man for the job. Shatto."

Indy snapped her pencil in half and looked up.

The colonel gave an ironic chuckle. "Shatto again."

"Yes, sir. Shatto again. His coming here today only proved what we all suspected anyway—that some of the Apaches want peace and are willing to fight other Apaches to get it. Shatto has the skills we need, sir. He's cunning as a fox and as deadly with a knife as any longshoreman. And there isn't an animal or human he can't track."

Indy turned her eyes on her father and awaited his reaction with a pounding heart.

She didn't have to wait long. He stood up and pushed his chair back, the legs screeching as they scraped the floor. "Shatto." He ran his fingers through his hair, then walked away from the table. "I don't like it, Captain. I don't like it at all. What kind of man would train others to fight and kill his own?"

"Begging your pardon, Colonel, but you don't understand the Apache structure. The tribe is broken up into divisions, bands, and family groups—each of them having their own leader or chief who makes the laws for his people. Their loyalty doesn't reach to the other units. In that way, they're no different than we are."

"How's that, Captain?"

"The Yanks and the Rebs, sir. People of one race fighting against each other."

"I'll give the matter some consideration."

"Yes, sir. I'll tell the men."

Chapter 5

Shatto.

All of Bowie was talking about him—the soldiers, the women, even the half-dozen children. They recounted every story they knew—the time Shatto had given the puppy to the Clarke boy, the rescue of the mail detachment, his bringing Chie's braves to the colonel for punishment, and others.

They wondered. They speculated. And they placed bets on the colonel and on Shatto.

Indy was just as eager to learn of her father's decision as everyone else, though she couldn't see he had any choice but to agree, what with the threat of the petition being sent to the War Department. How utterly humiliating. A petition! Signed by nearly every soldier at Bowie! She had expected him to rant and rave, but he had said nothing and went about his business—getting up this morning, acting as if nothing had happened.

Midmorning she packed up the stew pot, pie dish, and gingham bread cloth and paid a call on Ava Burroughs. She was delighted to find Aphra and Opal there too. The three officers' wives sat in a triangle, a large patchwork quilt spread between them. All the while they talked they never missed a stitch, except once, when Indy mentioned Prudence.

"I've always felt sort of sorry for Prudence," said Ava. "To go from the social position of a major's wife on Officers' Row to a widow working as an Army laundress. It's such hard work for so little pay."

Indy was incredulous. Her face drained of color.

Ava, looking up from the quilt and seeing Indy's surprise, apologized profusely. "I'm sorry, Indy. I thought she would have told you."

Indy shook her head. "No, she hasn't said anything about being married."

"Well, it wasn't much of a marriage," Ava returned, bending her head back to the quilt. "Major Stallard was nearly twenty years older than Prudence. He found her working in a Nogales saloon and offered to marry her if she'd make a decent home for him."

"Some bargain," Opal said sarcastically. "All she did was drive him crazy with her wanton ways. And then—the poor man—hardly married a year when he up and died. Just like that!" She snapped her fingers and rolled her eyes. "Mercy! What a stir that caused."

"How did he die?" Indy asked.

Aphra giggled.

"Aphra!" Opal scolded. "Behave."

In spite of the warning, Aphra giggled again.

Indy looked over at Opal. Opal looked back, smiled, then set about rethreading her needle. "Doc Valentine said he'd never known a man to die . . . *like that* . . . in his bed and all. He said his heart just gave out. Thought it must have been the excitement."

This time when Aphra started to giggle, she put her hand over her mouth to make it look like she was coughing.

Finally, Indy realized what Opal was saying. "Oh," she said at last. "I see. How awful." With some difficulty she maintained her composure.

Opal pushed her needle into the quilt. "You'd never know Prudence was a widow—the way she goes about flaunting herself and flirting—like she did yesterday with that Indian. Next thing you know she'll be jumping on the back of his war pony and riding off with him to his wickiup."

"Opal! You shouldn't talk like that in front of Indy. Whatever will she think?" Ava asked.

Opal snorted. "I just hope Prudence has the good sense to stay away from Shatto if he does come here to train the men."

"What do you think your father will decide, Indy?" asked Ava. "Of course, our husbands are all in favor of it, but it's your father who has to make the decision."

Indy studied her hands. "I really can't say one way or another. He doesn't talk to me about Army business, you see."

All three women looked up at her at the same time.

"That's too bad," said Aphra.

"Yes, indeed," added Opal.

Indy had felt uneasy with the gossip about Prudence but now that they had turned their full attention on her, she felt even more ill at ease.

She suddenly realized she could be making better use of her time organizing her kitchen and learning how to use the cook stove.

She rose. "If you ladies will excuse me. I really have to be getting back. I haven't begun to organize my kitchen yet." She started for the door.

"Oh, wait a second. I just remembered something," Ava called out. "I meant to tell you yesterday but with all the goings-on I forgot. Julie Myers—she's the young woman whose husband was killed the other day—well, she's leaving for San Francisco day after tomorrow to join her family, and she's looking to sell most of her belongings to pay transportation costs. I thought you might be particularly interested seeing as how you don't have much furniture yet."

Indy stared off at nothing in particular. The young widow's sad face came to mind. "How awful to lose her husband, then to have to sell her things."

"They're just *things*, Indy. Army wives know better than to become attached to material possessions. Chances are she couldn't take them with her anyway what with weight restrictions and all. It's customary to hold an auction to sell things off. Anyway, if you're interested, it's tomorrow morning, just two doors down. She has some nice pieces. Mostly items she picked up from an auction a year ago from another Army wife."

At the door, Indy smiled and said, "Thank you. I *could* use a comfortable reading chair and a few other pieces."

After leaving Ava's, Indy walked around behind Officers' Row. Each of the officer's quarters had its own small, detached kitchen, set approximately thirty feet back from the main building as a fire precaution.

She was thinking about Prudence—feeling sorry that she'd had such a hard life. Then Opal's comments about Prudence's wanton ways nullified that sorrow and brought back the resentment she had felt yesterday.

"Any word on whether Shatto will be coming?" Indy gave a start. Suddenly Prudence was standing in front of her, holding a basket full of neatly folded laundry. "No, nothing yet." She felt like screaming the answer, but instead she opened the kitchen door and stepped inside.

Prudence stood on the other side of the threshold. "You will tell me as soon as you know, won't you?"

"I'm sure you'll hear before I do." She started to pull the door closed. "I'm sorry, but you'll have to excuse me. I've got to put this kitchen in order." She closed the door and leaned against it, half expecting Prudence to try to open it. When she didn't, Indy breathed a sigh of relief. She threw open a cupboard and jumped when the door banged against the wall. Chips of adobe broke loose and fell on top of her shoe.

"Oh, fiddlesticks!" She shook the adobe off her shoe and stared down at the floor. Prudence wasn't even trying to hide her excitement about Shatto coming to Bowie. After what Opal had said, it seemed to Indy that Prudence was asking for trouble by allowing her fascination for the Apache to show. Certainly no good could come from it. Just that one instance yesterday—and already there was talk and speculation. Didn't Prudence care what everyone thought?

Anger gave her speed and she put the kitchen to rights in no time, then returned to her quarters, just in time to see a courier arrive. He went directly to the adjutant's office.

Not ten minutes later her father came storming in the front door.

"How dare he do this to me? First he denies me the assignment I apply for, then he sends me out to this poor excuse of a fort—the biggest joke in the Army—and now—now this!"

"Father, for heaven's sake what happened?"

From his pocket he withdrew a small bottle of whiskey. He upended the bottle and took several large swallows. He wiped his mouth on his sleeve, shocking her with his crudeness. "I've just received a message from our esteemed President that I am to be *visited* by one of his newly appointed Indian commissioners." He plucked the letter out of his pocket and began to read. " 'IT HAS COME TO MY ATTENTION THAT THE SITUATION THERE AT CAMP BOWIE HAS BECOME CRITICAL. NUMEROUS COMPLAINTS HAVE BEEN RECEIVED REGARDING YOUR DENIAL OF MILITARY ESCORTS FOR CIVILIANS THROUGH APACHE PASS. I AM ALSO APPRISED OF AN INCREASE IN RAIDS ON OUTLYING RANCHES, FREIGHT WAGONS, AND TRAVELERS, WHICH HAS RESULTED IN GREAT MONETARY LOSS AND A NUMBER OF DEATHS. I ASK THAT YOU PLEASE COOPERATE WITH MR. MORELAND SO THAT HE MIGHT RECOMMEND NEEDED CHANGES AND IMPROVEMENTS.' " He stopped and looked down at Indy, then wadded the paper and threw it against the wall.

Indy didn't know what to say. It seemed peculiar that the President would send a man—a civilian—who had absolutely *no* military experience to scrutinize the methods of a career soldier.

The colonel took another long swallow and sat down at the table by the window. "If it weren't for me Grant would have never made it out of West Point. The only thing he was good at was horsemanship. As far as his studies . . ." The colonel glanced up at the ceiling and guffawed.

Indy knew her father had always resented Grant's rise to success. He could never understand how a tanner's son could achieve what he, the son of a well-educated politician, could not.

She took the seat next to him. "Perhaps it would be wise to take Captain Nolan's advice and invite Shatto to come and train the troops. I know it's against everything you believe in, but it's very different here than what you're used to, and it's true that you aren't dealing with civilized men who fight by rules. At the very least, with Shatto here, you could show the Indian commissioner that you're making an effort to improve the situation."

He stared at the whiskey bottle that he held in front of him on the table. "I wish Justice were here. He'd know what to do."

"He'd tell you the same thing I'm telling you, Father. I know he would."

There was a long pause during which Indy watched her father's face undergo any number of emotions and expressions: anger, petulance, contemplation, and finally elation.

"Perhaps he would," he said, a slow, devious smile playing about his lips.

Indy knew that look. It made her uneasy.

"If the troops were properly trained," he said musingly, "there's no telling what they might be able to accomplish. Who knows but they might be able to find Cochise's stronghold. If I could capture Cochise . . ." He looked up at Indy with an oddly smug expression that told her he was thinking ahead of himself, to what might be gained by such a feat. He stood up suddenly and walked toward the door. Speaking to her from over his left shoulder, he said, "You're right, Independence. Justice would have indeed suggested what you just suggested. Thank you for pointing it out." With that he opened the door and walked out.

Word of Colonel Taylor's decision was out within an hour after he had left his quarters. All the gamblers who had correctly bet on the decision were promptly paid and new bets were laid on everything from whether or not Captain Nolan could find Shatto and convince him to come back with him, to who would and wouldn't be picked for the special training.

Still, it was several days before Captain Nolan was given the go ahead to travel, and even then he had to wear his left arm in a sling to limit movement so the shoulder wound could heal properly.

At reveille, ten days after Indy's arrival at Bowie, Captain Nolan took twenty men and left to find and make contact with Shatto. The detachment was equipped with enough food, water, and ammunition to last several days. The whole garrison turned out to watch them leave . . . and then they waited.

It was hot. The unusually cool September weather had disappeared the morning Captain Nolan left. The sky was calico blue and cloudless. A swift shadow shot over the stables, causing Indy to look up. It was a large hawk. He began flying in a big circle, tilting and turning his wings against the sky as he watched the ground below. He was a magnificent sight to behold—all grace and beauty. She couldn't take her eyes off him. He dove suddenly, straight as an arrow, stretching taloned feet to brake against the air, and disappeared behind the corral. Barely an instant later he winged upward holding a wiggling, screaming rodent in his talons and soared away.

Indy grimaced as she watched the hawk fly over the mountain behind the camp, then continued on her way back to her quarters, anxious to get out of the heat. She had barely stepped inside when she heard the distant pounding of hooves. Turning, she squinted into the bright sunshine. The detachment was returning. The entire body appeared in the form of a single mirage, an undulating watery image that shimmered and sparkled.

They rode in a neat column, two by two at a slow canter. Indy crossed her arms nervously. Anticipation that had been simmering inside her since the detachment left now burst into full boil. The Apache rode out in front beside Captain Nolan. He appeared the same as she remembered him, yet different in some inexplicable way. The past and present came together making her stomach muscles twist and knot.

Wearing a light blue, loose-fitting shirt, slashed down the front, he sat straight and tall on his pinto—an imperious desert nomad—one sun-dark, sinewy hand loosely holding the reins, the other at rest atop his leg.

He was as unlike the slouching troopers he rode with as a horse was to a burro. It didn't have so much to do with appearance as with bearing. It was common knowledge that the Apaches were a proud people, but this Apache brave carried his pride before him like a war shield for all to see.

A faded red headband was wrapped around his forehead and he'd rolled his sleeves to just below his elbows. Around his lean waist was the leather cartridge belt Indy had seen that other time; the sun glinted off the bright brass bullets now as it had then. His legs were encased in snug-fitting buckskin breeches painted with yellow and green stripes and symbols, and his feet were thrust in tall moccasins.

The main body of troopers veered off and headed for the stables, while the captain and Shatto continued on, cutting diagonally across the parade ground to the adjutant's office, east of Officers' Row. They dismounted, tied their horses to the hitching post, and walked inside.

The sound of running footsteps dragged Indy's attention away. "I knew Nolan would bring him back," Prudence said, panting from her exertions. Her cheeks were apple-red and her eyes shone like bits of colored glass. "I'd give anything to know what enticement he used. He must have promised him something, made some sort of bargain. Of course, you'll tell me when you find out, won't you?"

"Well, I—I don't know," Indy stammered. "It really isn't any of my—"

"Oh, come on now. We're friends, remember?" Prudence wheedled.

Resentment doused the fire of excitement. "What makes you think I'll find out?"

Prudence sighed with impatience. "Because you're the colonel's daughter, for heaven's sake! I doubt there's very much going on around here that your father doesn't tell you."

From the corner of her eye, Indy saw Shatto come out of the adjutant's office, Captain Nolan and her father right behind him. The three of them started walking toward Officers' Row. "I'm sorry, Prudence," she said without a trace of sorrow, "but as you can see, I'm about to have some guests." She pointed in the direction of the adjutant's office, and while Prudence's attention was diverted, she moved inside and closed the door.

Trying to think what to do first, she stood in the middle of the parlor and stared at the far wall. Then she hurried to her bedroom. There wasn't time to change her dress—a mint-green muslin with white trim around the sleeves and collar. It wasn't the dress she would have chosen to greet guests in, but it would have to do.

Bending toward the mirror that she'd hung over her toilette table—two calico-covered crates salvaged from the quartermaster's—she fussed with her hair. As usual, the sides had escaped from the knot at the back of her head. No matter how long her hair grew, they came loose and fell over her ears. With shaking fingers she smoothed the traitorous wisps back and tucked them into the knot, then she pinched her cheeks, which, she noticed too late, were already flushed, as apple-red as Prudence's had been. The heat, she thought, placing the fault where she willed it to belong rather than where she knew it belonged.

She heard Captain Nolan's voice and started for the parlor, then stopped before reaching the bedroom door. "You can't go out there and greet them until you've composed yourself," she told herself in a whispered warning. She stared at the door and took several deep breaths, which had no effect at all. Next, she tried closing her eyes and leaning her head back, but that too failed to bring her the desired calm she sought. At length she gave up, realizing it was useless.

"Ah, there you are, Independence," said the colonel, walking toward her. "I was wondering if you had come back from the quartermaster's."

"Y-yes, just m-minutes ago." Her voice croaked like a frog. She hoped nobody else noticed.

"So Prudence Stallard told me." He stood directly in front of her, blocking her from seeing the two men behind him. "I wanted to be able to speak to Captain Nolan and our guest in private. My office has grown ears as long as an Army mule's. You will, of course, make certain that we aren't disturbed?"

She knew he was referring to the last time he'd conducted business in quarters and she had stayed in the parlor. "You needn't worry, Father," she said flatly. He nodded and turned away.

"Afternoon, ma'am," said the captain, removing his hat as he stepped farther into the parlor. It was covered with trail dust, which sifted to the floor when he turned it over.

"Good afternoon, Captain. I see you were successful in locating Shatto."

"Yes, ma'am. That I was."

Her father had already sat down at the head of the table and was thumbing through a sheaf of papers. Indy motioned for the captain to take the seat on her father's left.

She had discreetly avoided looking at the Apache since he'd come into the parlor, but she had *felt* him—felt his strength, his power. It pulled at her like a magnet and though she had been able to resist at first, she couldn't now. *He* wouldn't let her.

He had appeared incredibly tall to her before when she had been sitting in the ambulance, but he seemed even taller now that she was standing near him, and she had to lift her chin to meet his gaze.

It was a mistake, an unavoidable one, but a mistake all the same. His head was tilted at an arrogant angle, and he was watching her—had been watching her all along, since the moment he'd stepped inside. He was like that hawk that had circled the sky to watch the rodent.

And worse than simply being watched was that he seemed to know she was avoiding him. She was certain of it. She could see it in his expression. It was as if he could read her mind . . . and see into her heart. She forced a smile, praying she was wrong. "You can sit there," she said, indicating the chair at the other end of the table. When he didn't make a move to seat himself, she remembered that he didn't speak English. She walked over to the chair and pointed her index finger at him. "You," she said, then moved her hand down and patted the air above the seat. "Sit."

With the barest hint of a smile he moved toward the chair.

The captain swiveled around. "Ah, Miss Taylor? I think you should know—"

"It's all right, Captain," she cut in, assuring him. "He understands me now."

Shatto brushed her arm as he walked past to take his seat. Her nostrils flared at the scent of him, a wild and heady combination of earth and fire. It was a purely masculine scent, yet she knew it belonged only to him.

She stared at him long after he sat down. It was only when her father cleared his throat that she remembered her manners. "Perhaps you would like some refreshments? Coffee? Lemonade?"

"Coffee's good," said her father.

"Yes, I'd like a cup of coffee," agreed the captain.

Indy looked at Shatto, then back at the captain. "I'll get him some coffee too." She hurried out the back door.

Never in her life had she been so relieved to vacate a room. She picked up her skirt and ran as fast as her legs would carry her the thirty feet to the kitchen where she leaned against the door and breathed a sigh of relief.

Indy prolonged her kitchen duties for as long as she could. By the time she reentered the parlor, her father was well into explaining the difficulties he was up against in his efforts to control the Apaches. She pitied the captain who would have to translate his windy oration. Keeping as quiet as possible she moved across the room and set the coffee tray down between Captain Nolan and Shatto. With a thick towel wrapped around the metal handle, she poured a cup for her father and pushed it toward him, then a cup for the captain. Last, she tilted the pot over the Apache's cup and started to pour.

"Your hands are shaking."

She lifted her gaze from the pouring spout to Shatto's face. "I beg your pardon?"

"I said, your hands are shaking."

Her face blanched. She stared at him, her eyes as big and round as the rim of the coffee cup. It wasn't what he'd said that surprised her, it was that he'd said it in English—perfect, unaccented English!

Coffee sloshed over the rim of his cup onto the table. Quick as a cat, Shatto sprang to his feet and moved back, out of the way of the steamy, black flow.

"In-de-pendence!" the colonel roared.

Startled by her father's loud voice, she dropped the coffeepot and towel. There was a terrible clatter as it hit the table. Without thinking she reached out and caught it between her hands before it could topple over and spill its entire contents. Later, she would wonder what had come over her, why she had continued to hold on to the pot when it was burning her hands, but at the moment she couldn't think what to do with it—hold it, drop it, or set it down.

Shatto crossed the space between them in a single stride, jerked the pot away, and set it on the table. When he turned back, he saw the way she was holding her hands. "You burned yourself, didn't you?"

She was too baffled by the fact that he'd spoken English to feel the pain. She ignored his question. "You speak English," she stated, repeating what was in her thoughts.

"It would be difficult to live among the Apaches without speaking their language." Shatto's hand reached out quick as a rattlesnake and grabbed her arms. "Give me your hands," he said when she tried to pull away. He turned them over and shook his head. Her palms were an angry red and growing redder by the second.

She leaned her head back and stared up at him. "I'm not sure I understand. Are you saying that you live with the Apaches but you aren't an Apache?" she asked tentatively.

"No, I'm not an Apache," he said between his teeth, then exploded with anger. "What the hell were you thinking, holding on to that coffeepot like that?" he demanded.

Anger pushed the questions of who, what, and why out of the way. "I was *thinking*," she ground out, "that you had spoken English! I was under the impression that you spoke only Apache. It surprised me. No. It shocked me. You could have said something before . . . to let me know."

"And missed your first attempts at sign language? Not on your life."

She gasped and was even more outraged when he raised dark mocking brows.

"You let me make a fool of myself!" She winced when he ran the pad of his thumb across her palms. "Don't! That hurts!" She tried to pull her hand back but he held on to her, refusing to let her go.

He cut her an impatient look. "Would you be still. I'm trying to see if it's going to blister."

Captain Nolan moved up beside them for a close look. "My God. You've literally branded yourself with the pot handle. Maybe I should get Doc."

"There's nothing he can do," Shatto said. "I've got some salve in my gear." He glanced across at Nolan.

"I'll go get it." Nolan was out the door in an instant.

"Do you have any water in here?"

Indy inclined her head toward her bedroom. "In there. In the pitcher." She assumed he would go get it and bring it back. Instead, he put an arm behind her back and hurried her through the door.

"Maybe you should sit down on the bed. I don't want you to faint."

"I prefer to stand, thank you. And I assure you, I will not faint," she replied with firm conviction.

He poured water from the pitcher into the

basin, then pushed her hands beneath the water line. Indy gritted her teeth but didn't cry out.

"The cool water will stop the burning from doing any more damage. It'll also relieve some of the pain by reducing blood flow through your hands." He glanced at her, his eyes penetrating through the long curling wisps of hair that had fallen around her face.

"I suppose next I'll find out that you're a doctor."

"My grandfather was a doctor."

"How stupid of me. I should have guessed. And I suppose your father was a statesman."

"Independence Taylor! You're being rude and impertinent." The colonel stood in the doorway, his eyes hard as flint. "It was bad enough that you came to Bowie against my orders, but now you insult a military guest. You go too far, miss, and I will not tolerate it. I insist you apologize this instant."

Indy sucked in her breath, then stubbornly clamped her teeth down on her lower lip. She felt herself turning scarlet with humiliation and embarrassment. Tears smarted at the back of her eyes but she willed them not to come. Not now. Not in front of her father. And certainly not in front of Shatto.

"An apology isn't necessary," Shatto said, turning to confront the colonel. "If anyone should apologize, it's me for not telling her that I wasn't an Apache or that I speak English."

No one had ever stood up to her father for her, not her mother, not Justice. She wasn't sure what to think, what to feel; it was too new an experience, but one she knew she would never forget.

Chapter 6

Captain Nolan returned minutes later and stopped short at the bedroom door. He peered nervously inside, obviously uncomfortable with entering a lady's bedroom. "Where's Colonel Taylor?"

"He said he'd be out back," Shatto stated without elaboration. His dark gaze lowered to Indy's, though all he did was look at her, there was an unspoken promise that the scene between her and her father would not be mentioned.

She might have told him she was grateful, but stubborn pride forbade her. He didn't deserve a single word of thanks. It was a mean, unforgivable thing he'd done—letting her believe he was an Apache when he wasn't. He should have told her as soon as he'd halted the runaway team and come to the back of the wagon. It would have saved her a great deal of fear and despair. And if—for some reason—he couldn't tell her then, he could have told her when he'd come into the parlor with her father, as could have Captain Nolan. Instead, they had let her make an absolute fool of herself.

Smarting from humiliation and anger as much

as from the burns, she pulled her hands from the basin. "Oh, my," she said, heaving a sigh at the bold red stripe that ran across her right palm. She started to turn away, but Shatto snagged her wrists.

"Put your hands . . . back . . . in the water." His voice was low, dangerous, as if he might actually do her bodily harm if she didn't follow his instructions. She looked at the strong fingers circling her wrists and knew he could break them as easily as he could break a dry twig, although somewhere deep inside, she instinctively knew he wouldn't.

Captain Nolan stepped forward with the salve. "As soon as the colonel returns I'll talk to him about getting a striker to help out here for a few days. Or maybe Prudence would—"

"No!" Indy's chin snapped up and she pulled her hands out of Shatto's grasp. "I don't want a striker, or Prudence, or anybody helping me! I am perfectly capable of taking care of things, burnt hands or no!"

Captain Nolan was staring at her like she had gone crazy. Maybe she had, she thought, preferring that as an explanation to her emotional upheaval over any other. Her anger abated somewhat when she reminded herself that he was only trying to be helpful; he was a gentleman. "I'm sorry. I didn't mean to yell. It's just that Father nearly had apoplexy after Prudence came to clean and rearranged his things. I thought he would never recuperate. I don't want to put him through that again. He has so much on his mind these days . . ."

Nolan nodded his head with understanding, handed Shatto the salve, and left the room.

"You should feel some relief in a few seconds," Shatto said, startling her. Somehow, incredibly, in the midst of her panic over the captain's proposal, she had forgotten he was standing next to her. Did she detect a slight hesitancy before he bent his head to the task of spreading the salve over the burns? No. Must be her imagination. He'd pulled an arrow out of Captain Nolan's shoulder without a flicker of hesitation. If that didn't bother him, certainly a minor burn wouldn't.

His touch was light, but she winced all the same when he began smoothing it across her palm. It seemed odd that a man like him—more savage than civilized—was capable of such gentleness.

Indy tilted her head back and was startled to find his face so close to hers. She stared, fascinated in spite of herself, at the strong line of his jaw and chin, faintly beard-shadowed; the evidence—so plain to her now—that he was not of Indian blood. A muscle ticked his cheek near his mouth, drawing her attention there, to his lips, firmly set in concentration.

Her nerves quivered at his closeness and when she made a move to compose herself, her shoulder touched his arm. It was only a touch—sleeve brushing sleeve—but it made her senses spin like a top, and somehow she knew that no matter how hard she tried, she would never be composed in his presence. He was more man than she was used to—his masculinity too overwhelming for someone who had never experienced more than a friendly kiss. She felt an urgent need to get as far from him as she could, but was stopped from moving by that same magnetic power she had experienced before. And now, to her dismay, she felt it pull her toward him.

It was his breath warming her face and stirring her hair that took her out of herself to some far-off place. She closed her eyes for a scant second and imagined what it would be like to lean against him, to tuck her head beneath his chin and nuzzle her cheek into the front opening of his shirt against his skin.

"Feeling better yet?" His voice vibrated through her body and her mind like a small earthquake and jolted her back into reality.

She stiffened her spine and stood straight as a flagpole. "Yes, much better, thank you," she said in a tight, stilted tone. "I'd always been told to put butter on a burn, but whatever is in that salve is much better. What is in it by the way?" She hoped the chatter would help get her mind off him. It didn't.

"An old Apache recipe of bear grease and a few herbs. Nothing out of the ordinary." He set the salve aside, then cradled her hands in his, palms up. Indy was startled at the contrast. His hands were nearly twice as large as hers and his skin was dark and rough where her's was soft and white.

"Your skin is going to draw tight as a bowstring, but once it blisters and breaks, it'll loosen up. Don't try to help the process along. It will be raw underneath and you'd be opening yourself up to infection. I'll leave you the salve. Use it until it's gone."

Indy nodded, not trusting herself to speak for fear of saying something stupid. She didn't like the effect he had on her; the way just being near him wreaked havoc on her emotions and made her senses spin out of control. She'd never experienced that kind of reaction before; it was unnerving and, she had to admit, a little frightening.

Captain Nolan came back into the room. "I'll go out back and tell the colonel we're ready to resume the meeting."

"That's all right, Captain, I'll tell him," Indy volunteered hastily. She hurried away before either of them could protest, desperate for the chance to go outside where she could clear her head.

She found her father outside standing in the shade thrown off by the building.

"Father? They're waiting for you." He took a step toward her. "I wanted you to know how sorry I am for my clumsiness. I didn't mean to cause such a disturbance. I promise you it won't happen again."

"You don't *mean* a lot of the things you do, miss, and yet you do them anyway. It's because you don't think. You never have." His innuendo was, she knew, in reference to her mother's and brother's deaths. He threw his cigar onto the dirt and ground it down with his booted heel. "You shouldn't have come to Bowie, Independence." His cold, gray eyes sent a chill down the back of her neck and as soon as he walked away, she moved out of the shade into the sun.

*   *   *

With a frown drawing his lips in the same downward arch as his mustache, Colonel Charles Taylor came back into the parlor. "I apologize for the interruption, gentlemen." He strode across the room and stood behind his chair. "If you'll take your seats we can get on with this. I have a meeting with the quartermaster a little later."

Nolan promptly sat down.

Shatto ignored the request and walked over to the hearth where he studied the books standing between two cone-shaped rocks that served as bookends. Mahan's engineering textbook was there, as he'd expected. He could recognize a West Pointer from a hundred yards. It was something in the bearing and behavior. He picked up the book and leafed through it. After a few moments, he returned it to the mantel and took his seat, blatantly disregarding the colonel's example of correct posture by crossing his arms in front of him and leaning back, balancing his chair on its rear legs.

Indy opened the back door and slipped inside and walked quietly across the parlor to her bedroom, careful not to bring any attention to herself as she passed the table where the three men were seated.

With only one small window for ventilation, her bedroom was unbearably hot. She sat down on the edge of the bed, wondering how to occupy her time while their conversation was going on. Then, she noticed the latest issue of Godey's *Lady's Book* lying on her bedside table. Prudence had lent it to her. She was about to reach for the book—a weighty two-pound tome—when she heard her father's voice and looked across the room at the door, thinking she must have left it open. It was closed, but there might as well have been no door at all for her father's voice sounded like he was sitting beside her.

"Captain Nolan and Sergeant Moseley have reported that you and your men were responsible for the safe return of the mail detachment."

"You lost three men, Colonel. I wouldn't call that getting your detachment back safely." The cold sarcasm in Shatto's deep voice made Indy shiver with apprehension. No one had ever spoken to her father in that tone before—no one would have dared. He must be seething with anger, she thought, imagining his red-faced scowl. She leaned forward, turning her ear to the door, expecting to hear his angry reply, but instead he seemed almost affable.

"We could have lost more, including Captain Nolan, but for your quick medical attention." There was a long pause. "Anyway, on behalf of the 1st Cavalry Regiment and the United States Army—thank you."

Indy couldn't believe her ears; thank you's came hard to her father. He almost never thanked anyone for anything—unless he wanted something . . .

"The incident did serve a purpose, however, as it brought you to my attention. Captain Nolan has told me that you've lived with the Apaches for a number of years, and you're familiar with their way of living and thinking. Frankly, I need a man like you to help me subjugate the hostiles in this area. Your knowledge and skills combined with your military background makes you eminently suitable to train my troops."

"Dammit, Nolan! You lied to me—" Shatto slammed a fist on the table.

"Now, Jim, don't go jumping to conclusions." Behind her door, Indy held her breath. She could almost see the captain leaning forward and raising his hand in his own defense. "We've been friends a long time and you know damn good and well you can trust me. I didn't lie to you. I just didn't tell you everything because I knew you wouldn't come if you thought the colonel knew about your past. You can hit me later if you want, but do yourself a favor and listen to what he has to say."

"Shatto, or rather, Major Garrity, Captain Nolan has explained your situation. He told me about the four men you killed, your court-martial, your sentence to hang, and your escape. I gave my word that I would not have you arrested . . . regardless of the outcome of our talk."

"An extremely wise decision, Colonel. I don't take well to confinement."

With a gasp of surprise Indy bolted to her feet. He killed four men? And he'd been sentenced to hang? Dear God, what kind of man was he?

"I'm sure Captain Nolan has already told you what the situation is here at Bowie—"

"The situation, Colonel, is obvious. You've got more trouble here than you know how to handle. You can't get supplies in or take troops out without running into an attack and losing a couple of men. The Apaches have a name for you, *doo goyaa da, bini'edih,* which, simply translated, means fool. They laugh at you and make jokes. You've become quite a source of entertainment for them."

"You're impertinent, Major Garrity."

"Call me whatever you want. I am what I am, and I speak my mind."

There was a hard edge to his voice that made Indy think her father and Captain Nolan would do well to tread cautiously. After all Shatto or Major Garrity—whatever he called himself—was a convicted murderer.

"I'm going to ignore your impertinence, Major. But let me make something clear. As soon as Grant won the election, I applied for a post in Washington. The War Department, in their infinite wisdom, made an error and sent me here to this flea-bitten post. I know nothing about the frontier or Indians other than what I've read in Army reports and newspapers. My expertise is in civil engineering, though I did successfully lead a regiment in the Army of the Potomac. But that was an altogether different kind of warfare. Nothing like this. I expect I'll be reassigned soon, but until then I have a duty to perform and I find myself embarrassingly unable to perform it. Therefore, I'm in a position to make you a bargain."

"A bargain, Colonel? Money? Land? No thanks, I'm not interested."

"Would you be interested in having all charges dropped against you? A full pardon, Major. That's what I'm offering."

"You'd be free, Jim," Captain Nolan put in

quickly. "You could go home, see your family. See Tess. You wouldn't have to live like an outlaw anymore."

Tess? Indy's eyes bored holes into the door.

"Not good enough, Colonel."

"Jim! For God's sake. He's offering you the chance of a lifetime. I thought you'd be pleased. Jesus! I thought you'd be beside yourself. What the hell's the matter with you anyway?"

"Goddammit, Aubrey. I'll tell you what's the matter with me. I'm not guilty. I don't want just to have the charges dropped. I want to be proven innocent, and I want those men found guilty."

"But you killed them—all four of them. Not even the United States Army can bring charges against dead men."

Indy could feel both Shatto's and Captain Nolan's frustration.

"Gentlemen, please. Major Garrity, I understand your need to be exonerated. If I were in your position, I imagine I would want the same thing. But the problem, as I'm sure you already know, is finding the evidence, and after this late date . . . well . . ."

"I provided them with all the information they needed, but it was never even brought up at the court-martial. They didn't want to hear the truth."

"I'm not without influence, Major. President Grant and I went to the Point together and I often visited his home at White Haven and he at mine. I'll ask him as a personal favor to have your case looked into."

"I want my rank reinstated with all its benefits

and privileges. I want the word deserter stricken from the muster rolls."

"If you agree to train my men, it's as good as done."

Another pause, this one seeming to last an eternity. Indy held her breath and waited.

"What you're asking, Colonel—these skills you want your men to acquire—you can't expect them to learn them overnight. From what I've seen it'll take several weeks just to get your men in decent physical condition."

"Not everyone will be participating, Major. I'll only choose the twenty best men."

"No, Colonel, *I'll* choose the men."

"You'll choose them? But you don't know them."

"Neither do you, but one doesn't need to know them."

Indy could almost hear her father grit his teeth.

"All right. *You* choose the men."

"And the horses, the weapons, the ammunition, and the clothes they wear. They'll be under my command. They won't eat, sleep, or breathe without consulting me first . . . and interference from you will not be tolerated."

"Be serious, Major. You're taking this a little too far. What you're asking is out of the question."

"Those are my terms, Colonel. I do it my way or I don't do it at all."

A chair leg scraped the floorboards.

"All right. All right. We'll do it your way."

"Another wise decision, Colonel."

* * *

Shatto rode east, away from Camp Bowie through Apache Pass. He was careful to cover his trail on the chance that the colonel had sent someone to follow him. In spite of their bargain, which would take him back to Bowie in four days, he didn't like or trust Colonel Charles Taylor, and he thought the Apaches' name and estimation of his character were remarkably accurate.

Hours later he cut deep into the rugged Dos Cabezas Mountains, zigzagging along a trail that an untrained observer could not have recognized. Mammoth boulders, stark and sterile, towered arrogantly above him on either side. Near sundown, the trail descended sharply and he rode into the Valley of Thunder, his home and the home of Toriano's group these past six years.

Home. He thought suddenly of another home with a green expanse of lawn, an orchard with trees laden with fruit, and a pond that grew the biggest and tastiest catfish east of the Mississippi. He'd been happy there, living with his grandfather, and even happier when his parents had come there to live as well, their days of running stage stations in the territories behind them.

He mentally compared the locations and was about to ask himself which of the two he preferred when he reined in his thoughts. The Apaches had taught him that there was beauty, harmony, and power in all land; that the desert should not be likened to or measured against the mountains, or the valleys to the canyons.

His mouth drew up in a smile as he rode into the little vale that was crowded with shrubs and trees. It wasn't as green and lush as his other home, but it was beautiful all the same. Among the pine trees sat a dozen brush-covered wicki-ups, sturdily built to withstand the seasons. Toriano and his people, almost all relatives by blood and marriage, had made the Valley of Thunder a permanent campsite. Both water and game were plentiful. They had no need of moving from place to place as did most of the other groups within the central band.

Above him, from a point that overlooked the valley, a vedette screeched like a hawk to announce his arrival. At the lookout's call, three young boys came stampeding across the valley floor to meet him, whooping and hollering. They were followed by a half-dozen women, who gathered at the camp's edge, waving at him, as if he was an honored warrior returning from a successful raid. Toriano and his brother Luga and their cousin Eskinyea set aside the sinew they had been wrapping around their arrows and came to stand near the women.

The smell of game roasting over a slow-burning fire made Shatto's mouth water. He was glad to come home, but was not eager to tell Toriano and the others—his second family—about his visit to Camp Bowie and the bargain he'd struck. Though they were all anxious for peace, they would not like the road they would have to take to get there.

Toriano's straight black hair swung forward over muscular shoulders as he moved ahead and took the pinto's reins. "My heart is glad to see you, but could you not have come later, after the meal? The buck was a young one—very small—and you have a big hunger. I do not think there is enough for all of us to share." The glint in his eyes belied the seriousness of his tone.

Shatto raised his brow and cut Toriano a sharp sideways glance. "But I am very hungry," he said, patting his stomach. "I smelled the meat as soon as I reached the summit. Are you sure there is not enough?"

Toriano shrugged his shoulders. "I am sure."

"Well then, if as you say, there is not enough"—Shatto pulled the reins out of Toriano's hands—"I will have to go hunting. My story of the bluecoat colonel will wait until I get back." He reined sharply to the right and kicked the pinto into a trot.

Toriano's expression turned to disbelief. He broke from the group and sprinted after the horse. The women and children laughed and shouted with excitement at the game between the two warriors. Their shouts turned to screams of encouragement when in a sudden burst of speed Toriano reached the pinto's left flank and grabbed on to Shatto's leg.

Shatto whooped with surprise and released the reins. Had the attack come from an enemy he would have kicked the pinto into a gallop and dragged his attacker over the ground. Instead, he succumbed to Toriano's hold and slid off the pinto's back. He hit the ground hard but was quick to gain his feet and spring catlike at Toriano who lunged at him at the same time. The two men locked in mock combat, rolling over and over in the dirt, grunting, snarling like mountain lions, and laughing like children, until they looked up and saw Toriano's wife standing over them, scowling like an angry she bear.

Darkness crept slowly over the mountains, softly veiling the valley in shadows. Shatto sat cross-legged several feet from Toriano's campfire. He had discarded his civilian clothes for the breechclout and moccasins worn by the other men. The buck had not been small as Toriano had said, but a large one, big enough to feed the entire group, which now numbered twenty-five: ten women, eight men, and seven children.

Shatto talked of his visit to Bowie and his discussion with Captain Nolan and the colonel throughout the meal. When he had finished, he talked of his vision of the People's future. "Every day more white men come here to these mountains and the desert." His expression was grave, his tone solemn as befitted the subject. "It is true some go beyond to the great water, but many stay here to build homes, plant seeds in the ground, or search for the yellow iron. They do not think of the land in the way the Apache does. To them, it is a thing to be owned—like a rifle or a horse." He stopped, giving them a moment to digest his words. Because the Apache did not believe that land could be bought or sold—that it was for all men to use—they would have difficulty understanding.

"They want *this* land," he said with a wide sweep of his hands, "because it is rich in gold, silver, copper, and lead. There is coal and salt and much more that the white men wants and nothing will stop them from coming and taking it, for they are greedy and they do not respect the land like the Apaches."

"Let them come," said Eskinyea. At eighteen, he was full of himself and his bravado. "We will fight them and send them away."

"Yes, you will fight them and some of them will go away, but more will come—always more will come. Not even Cochise and all his warriors can stop them. There are more white men than all the Apaches, Comanches, Zunis, and the Navajos together." The mood of his audience suddenly tensed and they stared at him through the flames, their expressions fierce.

Luga, Toriano's youngest brother, was of a surly disposition and tended toward being argumentative. He grunted now and shook his head. "There may be many as you say, but they are weak, like women. I see this with my own eyes."

Stretching his arm across to Luga and grabbing his shoulder, Shatto said, "Am I weak?"

Luga did not flinch. "No, but you are—"

"No different than they," he finished for him. "Not all white men are weak or fools like the bluecoat colonel. Not all Apaches are strong like Luga." Turning back to the others, he continued. "The day when the Apaches could move about like the wind is no more." His hand left Luga's shoulder to slash through the air.

"We have talked of this before," Toriano spoke out, his voice carrying to everyone around the campfire. "Shatto's vision is greater than ours because he is a white man and knows the white man's ways and the Apache ways. He has guided us in the past. We must listen to him now and believe."

Toriano made an excellent chief; he was diplomatic and openminded—like Cochise had been until he was unjustly accused of abducting the son of a Sonoita Valley rancher. The ramifications from that affair—eight years ago—had begun a long and bloody war—a war that would have no winner, no victory.

In language they could understand, Shatto went on to explain President Grant's proposed Peace Policy, as told to him by Captain Nolan. It would be a system that would concentrate all Apaches onto reservations, where they would be educated, civilized, and taught the principle of agriculture so they could feed themselves. He didn't expect them to like the idea of being confined. He sure as hell hadn't liked that month he'd spent in confinement in a military prison. But he had to make them understand that the reservation system or something equally as bad was inevitable.

"You would be wise not to resist, because you cannot win." In the end, the braves sat staring morosely into the flames, their spirits going the same way as the sparks that died once they left the fire. "I have made a bargain with the nantan at the soldier fort." He explained what the colonel had offered and what he had agreed to do in return. "I have thought long on this and have decided that it is right that I should do this."

Luga stood, fire in his eyes. "You say we should not fight the white eyes—that we should be herded together like cattle and live on their reservation, where they will treat us like dogs." He spat into the fire. "I say no! I say it is better to fight and die than to live on the white man's reservation!"

"Luga!" Toriano rolled to his feet. "Your tongue is quick like the snake but your eyes do not see what is before you. We are here in this valley because we chose not to fight the white man as Cochise wanted us to do. We are here because we chose not to die. Cochise, Juh, Victorio, Chie—they will never agree to the white man's peace. Shatto is right in what he has agreed to do. Helping the white man will save Apache lives. Now, go from this council and ask the Great Spirit to take the blindness from your eyes."

Shatto knew that Luga would never understand and neither would he humble himself by coming back to the fire. "My heart is sad for Luga, for me, and for all Apaches."

Much later, when the moon was high, Shatto left the council fire and went to his wickiup where he laid down among the animal skins that made his bed. He didn't want to think about the days and weeks ahead. It was all he could do to make himself believe that he had not made a devil's bargain—that what he had agreed to do was for the good of the People—that he was not betraying them, but helping them by bringing a quicker end to the fighting.

Even if Grant didn't initiate his Peace Policy and the reservation system never came about, it was still only a matter of time before the white man ran the Apaches from their homes and off their land. A few years at the most, he thought. Regardless, the great Apache nation was destined to become a memory—a notation in the annals of history.

He clasped his hands together beneath his head and stared up at the sky through the smoke hole in the wickiup's center. There was much about the Apache way of life he had come to love, but he had to admit, there were a few things from his old life that he missed and looked forward to enjoying again, even though he knew it would only be temporary, for he was sure that he would want to live out his days within these mountains.

Independence Taylor reminded him of the good times before the war, before he'd been accused of murder and gone into exile. Her scented hair and velvet soft skin brought to mind fancy military balls and lavish midnight suppers. Her soft touch and hazel eyes made him think of long carriage rides around the square with Tess. Tess, who had sweet-talked him into getting engaged when marriage was the furthest thing from his mind. Tess, who had professed her undying love, then turned her back on him when he asked her to visit him one last time before they hanged him.

Tess was as unlike Independence Taylor as Camp Bowie was to West Point. Tess had known exactly what she wanted and how to get it. She had seen him as a means to wealth and position. Her sexual appetite had been voracious and he'd been willing to accommodate her every wish because they were his wishes too.

As far as he could tell, Independence Taylor wasn't looking for wealth and position; she was looking for love—from her father. Having met the colonel, Jim was certain she would never find it. The man was incapable of that particular emotion—the man was a fool. As to Independence's sexual appetite—he'd bet his skinning knife that she had never experienced a man. He knew by the way she reacted to him whenever he got close or touched her—an odd mixture of fear, curiosity, and desire.

He found the combination interestingly arousing.

He laughed at himself for entertaining such a thought. He'd been celibate for six years, since the last time he'd been with Tess. He hadn't thought all that much about it until he'd met Independence; there had been other things to keep his interest and give him contentment. Now, however, he couldn't seem to get his six-year-long celibacy or Independence Taylor out of his mind.

Her name came to him on the breeze that moved the light flap covering the entry. He imagined he was back there in Indy's bedroom holding her small, delicately boned hands in his. He could feel her trembling and it made his blood race through his body down into his groin. He swore softly when he felt the involuntary quickening, the kindling. It had been so long he'd almost forgotten what it was like—that surge of excitement for a special woman.

The trouble was—he was here and she was tucked in her bed at Camp Bowie. Not since his youth had he succumbed to bringing about his own relief and he wouldn't do so now.

"Damn you, Independence Taylor," he muttered raggedly. "I knew you'd be trouble the minute I laid eyes on you!"

Chapter 7

An unnatural peace filled the parlor that evening in the wake of Shatto and Captain Nolan's visit. Indy sat at the table by the window, watching the parade ground as two troopers lowered the flag and folded it while the bugler blew taps. Glancing over her shoulder, she saw her father sitting in a wooden rocker, making notations in his journal. He looked content as a cat in a creamery.

Considering all the pressure he had been under from the soldiers' petition and the impending visit from the Indian commissioner, Indy thought his look of contentedness odd, but obviously he was confident that the bargain he'd struck with Major Garrity would resolve everything. The soldiers' complaints had been shelved once word had gotten around about the training, and with them the petition. And when the Indian commissioner arrived, he would tell him he had reestablished the military escorts through Apache Pass and was sending out details to check on local ranchers. Those things should convince the commissioner that Camp Bowie was in fact in good hands.

Turning back and looking down at her hands,

Indy thought about Shatto. She had felt all along there was something different about him—something that set him apart. And now she knew what that something was. He wasn't an Apache. Prudence had felt it as well, she recalled, and by now would have heard the news. Indy could imagine Pru's elation upon learning that Shatto was indeed a white man and not an Indian.

"Independence. In-de-pendence!" The colonel's autocratic voice broke into her thoughts. She looked over at him. "I want you to put together some sort of welcome reception for Major Garrity. Do you think four days will give you ample time?"

She stared at him, surprised by his request. "A welcome reception?"

"Yes. You know. Like the one we attended at Fort Montgomery last year. Only on a much smaller scale and without all the formality—since that would be impossible anyway."

Indy couldn't believe what she was hearing. "Well, y-yes, of course I can," she stammered.

"What about your burns? Won't they be a significant hindrance?"

"Not to any major degree. I won't be able to lift and carry things for a few days, but I can do all the planning and arranging." Seeing his dubious expression, she quickly offered, "I could ask some of the officers' wives to help me. I know they would be delighted. It would give them something fun to do for a change. That is, if you're agreeable."

"Yes, of course. Ask whomever you think would be of help."

Indy was afraid to show her delight. It wasn't just the planning of the reception that excited her so much, but that her father was entrusting her to do it. It had been years since he had asked anything of her. That he had now gave her hope that the day of forgiveness was forthcoming. The trip to Bowie wasn't a mistake after all.

"Everyone is to be invited," the colonel proceeded with uncommon enthusiasm. "The officers, enlisted men, and all the women and children. Make certain there's plenty of food and drink, and not just lemonade if you get my meaning. Put somebody in charge of that who knows what they're doing." He stood up. "And music and dancing," he added. "The men haven't had any entertainment since before I arrived here. It will be good for them. Boost their morale." He threw his head back and chuckled. "Yes. God, yes, that's exactly what it will do. Boost their morale!"

Indy had never seen him so exuberant. "I'm sure it will," she agreed, somewhat bewildered by his peculiar behavior but pleased by it as well. It was a rare occasion. Not one to be scrutinized or questioned.

"Then I'll leave it to you," he said, again implying trust, but when Indy started to get up he called her back. "Independence." He waited until she was looking at him before speaking. "You won't let me down, will you, daughter? This is *extremely* important to me . . . and to my career."

"No, Father. I won't let you down. I know exactly what needs to be done. It'll be a grand reception. Don't worry. I'll make you proud."

*   *   *

Indy started out early the next morning, going first to the auction, where she accidentally outbid herself by fifty cents on a chair she wanted.

Ava, Opal, and Aphra were there, and after the auction, Indy drew them aside and asked if they'd like to help work on the reception. Ava declined, her advanced state of pregnancy being her excuse. Aphra and Opal were, much to her surprise, anything but eager to lend a helping hand, but they did agree, which eliminated having to ask for Prudence's help.

On the morning of the reception, the bugler sounded the nine o'clock drill. Soldiers came running from all directions to line up, two deep, within their own companies around the perimeter of the parade ground. They stood straight as broom sticks, arms close and stiff against their sides, awaiting orders.

Indy had gotten up at reveille to prepare her father's breakfast. The burns on her hands were healing nicely but she had to take care with everything she did and that made her slow at performing her tasks. She heard the clip-clop of a horse's hooves and ran to open the front door, instinct telling her it was Major Jim Garrity's big pinto.

The early morning air seemed to crackle with excitement as the high-stepping horse came trotting along the western boundary of the parade ground, then slowed to a walk in front of Officers' Row. Today, the major was to be introduced to the entire garrison, look over the facilities and the men. Tonight, he would be the guest of honor at the welcome reception. Tomorrow, he would make his choices among the men and begin the training.

As in the past, he had a galvanizing effect on Indy, throwing all her emotions into chaos so that she felt like she had been turned inside out. Emotions, for the most part, could be hidden, she thought. She hoped.

The pinto tossed his massive head in impatience and played with his bit, but kept to the walking pace his rider had set. The major nodded, acknowledging her presence. His dark eyes flickered with some secret thought and the side of his mouth lifted impudently as he gazed down at her.

Indy had no idea what could have provoked such a look but it made her feel susceptible, like he knew something about her that she didn't even know. She stayed where she was until he passed by, then she dropped her hands and was about to turn around and go back inside when Prudence came around the corner.

"What in heaven's name was all that about?" Prudence asked.

"All what?" Indy had avoided Prudence these last four days, knowing she would be confronted with a gamut of questions.

"That *look* he gave you."

"Look? I don't know what you mean," she said impatiently. "You'll have to excuse me, Prudence. I have to—"

"Independence Taylor! If I was a suspicious sort, which I am not, I'd think you and Shatto—I mean Major Garrity—had something to hide. Really now, tell me what's going on between you two. No man looks at a woman like he looked at you unless . . ." Her voice trailed off suggestively and she gave Indy a speculative look.

Indy had had about all the strange looks and innuendo she could stand from the officers' wives. "Unless what?" she demanded, wanting to know what Prudence had seen that she had not.

Prudence's eyelashes fluttered as she laughed. "Well, if you don't know, then you obviously aren't hiding anything. I must have imagined it."

"Imagined what?" Indy was at the end of her patience. She searched Prudence's face for the answer but found nothing to tell her what she wanted to know.

Without warning Prudence changed the subject. "I should have known all along he wasn't an Apache," she said with a wistful sigh as she watched the major ride into the parade ground. "There was just something about him that didn't fit with the other Apache bucks I've seen." She placed her right hand over her heart. "But what a surprise to find out that he's not only a white man but an Army major. That changes things considerably, if you know what I mean."

"No. I don't know what you mean. Suppose you tell me," said Indy, bristling now with indignation.

Seemingly oblivious to Indy's ire, Prudence explained, "Well—you know. It's like I said before. About what would happen if he wasn't an Apache—how all the women would dream about him."

Indy had lied. She had known exactly what Pru

meant though she had pretended not to. Abruptly, and without thinking, she asked, "Have you considered the possibility that he might be married? He's lived with the Apaches for six years. He probably has a wife and a whole passel of kids." It was a mean-spirited thing to say since she had no idea if it was true or not, but she wanted to give Pru something to think about—to worry about. Prudence's mouth dropped open just as Indy had hoped it would, and before Pru had a chance to question her, to find out exactly what she knew, Indy twirled around like a dancer and dashed away.

Everything for the welcome reception was as ready as it would ever be. For all that she'd had only four days to plan and prepare, Indy could not have been more pleased at the way it had all come together. Aphra and Opal had taken charge of the food and drink, soliciting a dish of some kind from every woman at Bowie. The result was a long, gingham-covered mess table laden with an assortment of tempting dishes and a large punch bowl full of lemonade.

Captain Nolan had been put in charge of the men's punch, and Indy had set the bowl a good distance away from the lemonade so there would be no mistake. God forbid that some poor, unsuspecting female should drink the men's punch—she would be shocked senseless.

The enlisted men had cleaned the mess hall, decorated it with flags, and hung twenty kerosene lanterns from hooks in the overhead beams.

Indy had recruited the musicians from enlisted

men and officers alike. The cacophony of sound
that came with the testing and tuning of their
instruments made her ears ache. She would have
been worried had she not heard them earlier in
practice, and knew they could indeed play
harmoniously.

The guests began arriving after dark. Indy
stood at the door and cheerily greeted each man,
woman, and child. She had come to know many
of them in the short time she had been at Bowie,
but with the exception of Prudence, Sergeant
Moseley, and Captain Nolan, she had not been
able to gain their friendship. Even Aphra, Opal,
and Ava, congenial as they had been, kept their
distance, offering her everything *but* friendship.
Indy suspected the standoffishness was due to
the animosity they all felt for her father, which
she understood because they were afraid that his
methods would do more harm than good, but understanding didn't fill the lonely hours after she
finished her chores.

Indy had thought her father would be by her
side to greet everyone, as the reception had been
his idea, but he had yet to arrive and neither had
the guest of honor. Minutes passed and the room
filled to capacity.

"Miss Taylor," said Captain Nolan, bowing
slightly, his hat in his hand as he stepped inside
and stood before her.

"Good evening, Captain." She looked around
behind him, but he was alone. "Have you seen
my father or Major Garrity? I thought they would
have been here by now."

"No, I'm afraid I haven't."

She sighed. "They probably got to talking and forgot the time. Maybe I should send someone to find them?"

A raised eyebrow indicated the captain's disapproval. "I don't think that would be a good idea. I'm sure your father wouldn't be late without good reason."

Indy's forehead furrowed with confusion, then smoothed as the meaning became clear. "Good reason, meaning some sort of strategy?"

"Perhaps."

She thought about it a moment. "Yes, I see your point." Of course, he was right, she realized, wondering why she hadn't considered it before. Arriving after everyone else would assure maximum attention. She glanced again out the door, then looked up at the captain.

His head was bent and he was gazing at her with an ardency that couldn't be misinterpreted. "You should be proud of what you've accomplished on such short notice. Everything looks and smells wonderful. The entire garrison is grateful for your efforts." He paused a moment, as if to prepare himself for some difficult task. "I don't think your father realizes how lucky he is to have you," he said unsteadily, his voice growing thicker by the second. "I—I feel lucky just knowing you. And . . . if you wouldn't think me too presumptuous—I'd like to call on you, that is if you're agreeable, and with the colonel's permission, of course."

Flushing, Indy glanced away. She didn't know how to respond. No one had ever asked to call on her before. She would have been wildly ecstatic if she felt something more for him than friendship. "Captain, I—"

"Aubrey. Please," he insisted. "We've been Captain Nolan and Miss Taylor long enough, don't you think?"

She gave a nervous laugh. "Captain, I hope you won't—" She broke off when, out of the corner of her eye, she saw a glint of metal—and turned to see her father and Jim Garrity walking across the parade ground. "There they are," she said, her voice flooded with relief.

The two men were walking side by side. Jim Garrity's stride was long, loose, arrogant—the gait of a man who always knew where he was going because he had been there a thousand times before. It wasn't the first time he had given her that impression along with a sense that he had seen too much and experienced too much of the world.

He was a head taller than her father and considerably broader of shoulder. He was dressed in light-colored buckskin pants and a loose white shirt, similar to what he'd been wearing when he rode in. The only significant difference in his appearance was his hair, which he had neatly pulled back away from his face; its length tied in a leather thong at the back of his head. His hair and the absence of the headband made him look like a very different man from the near naked warrior who had vaulted into the ambulance and pinned her to the floorboards. Then, he had been Shatto—an Apache—a dangerous savage. Now, he was Jim Garrity—a major in the United States Army—a gentleman, she thought, then took it back, remembering that in spite of his staunchly proclaimed innocence, he had been convicted of murdering four men, court-martialed and sentenced to hang!

She gave an involuntary shiver. No, he wasn't a savage and neither was he a gentleman. But he was definitely dangerous. In more ways than one, she suspected.

In her study of Jim Garrity, she had all but forgotten the captain and the question she had been about to answer. With alarm she realized that while she had been staring at Jim, he had been staring at her. Nothing could have been more sobering or more disquieting. Suddenly she knew how that poor rodent had felt when the hawk flew over the camp.

"Father," she called out, then quickly made her way toward him. "We've been waiting for you."

He continued walking toward the mess hall. "We were unavoidably detained," he answered stiffly, his eyes narrowing critically as he looked her up and down, from head to toe, as if conducting a uniform inspection.

"It's the only special occasion dress I brought," she explained defensively. She hadn't been sure the dress—a pale yellow lawn with a tier of three organdy ruffles around the hem—would be suitable for the occasion. But having seen how the other women were dressed, she felt confident in spite of her father's critical eye. Twining her arm around his, she walked alongside of him, chattering like a monkey about the food and the musicians, all the while acutely aware of

Jim Garrity's discerning gaze watching and studying her.

Once inside, and after the formal salutes, the colonel surveyed the room and everyone in it. Indy searched his face, looking for something in his expression to tell her he was pleased. His gaze swept the room and rested on the flags artfully draped over the fireplace mantel. His mouth thinned, then formed a grimace of distaste that stayed with him as he continued his survey.

That told it all, Indy thought, sighing inwardly with utter disappointment. Everyone had worked so hard to make it a nice reception. And it was— by anyone's standards except, obviously, her father's. She had no idea what specific thing displeased him—maybe everything.

Again, she had gotten her hopes up for nothing, and again she felt the pain of defeat.

With false cheer, she took her father's arm and signaled the musicians to begin playing the Grand March.

"I would prefer that Major Garrity lead you out," said the colonel, pulling away from her.

"Oh, but, Father, you know that protocol demands that the commanding officer lead—"

"Protocol?" he flared at her, his eyes cold as the steel saber dangling from his hip. "I set the protocol here, daughter."

Jim Garrity came forward, stepping directly in front of the colonel. "Miss Taylor, I'd be honored if you would allow me to escort you through the Grand March." He bowed, his dark eyes intent upon hers. The sophisticated formality so contrasted with everything she knew about him that she was momentarily stunned. *He's not a gentleman,* she reminded herself. *Don't be fooled. He's dangerous.*

"Thank you, Major," she said, moving toward him. As long as she remembered who he was and what he was, and stayed within her father's sight, no harm could come to her. Lifting the sides of her skirt, she made a small curtsy. Jim proffered his right arm, crooked at the elbow, for her to grasp on to, then led her out onto the floor.

"Major James Garrity will lead out Miss Independence Taylor in the Grand March," Captain Nolan announced in a stentorian voice that effectively silenced the crowd. In a matter of seconds everyone had claimed their partners and formed a line starting at the stone hearth.

Jim and Indy took their places in front of the hearth and awaited the signal to begin. Indy felt conspicuous standing next to Jim. Not only was he the talk of the garrison, but he was the only man not in military uniform. It seemed to Indy that every eye in the room was watching them, which made each second an eternity. Her emotions ran the gamut: embarrassment, confusion, unease, fear.

Feeling the need to say something—anything to break the chain of her thoughts, she said the first thing that came to mind. "It's been a long time since I've done the Grand March," she confided, raising her chin to look up at him. He was so tall, too tall as far as she was concerned. She could imagine all sorts of awkward predicaments a couple of what respective heights would en-counter. "I hope I remember the steps." He *had* to sense her nervousness. She couldn't hide it. But hopefully he would attribute it to her father's reprimand and not to himself.

The music began with slow, introductory notes. Jim tilted his dark head and gave her a consider-ing look. "It will come back to you, but just in case, I suggest you hold on to me a little tighter. I wouldn't want to lose you in the turns." Until then her hold on his arm had been purposely light, but his warning had merit so she tightened her fingers and felt the tensing of hard male mus-cle. "I assume your burns have healed and you're no longer in any pain."

Disconcerted by the awesome power that lay just beneath the surface of his skin, she found she couldn't form an answer and shook her head instead.

Finally, the drummer gave the signal. Arm in arm, Jim and Indy marched down an invisible path through the center of the room. At a point just short of the music dais, Jim stopped, step-ping in place, while Indy picked up the side of her skirt and made a quick curtsy. Without missing a drumbeat, he led her out again into a sharp right curve and they marched back, past the line of couples who had yet to reach the dais. Returning to the point where they had begun, they met up with Sergeant Moseley and Prudence Stallard, who were returning via the left loop.

With the first round behind them, and while continuing to step in place, Indy took time to catch her breath and sneak a glance at her partner, who, in spite of his lack of uniform, was an impressive figure and looked every inch a proud military man. She wasn't the only one who thought so. Prudence hadn't taken her eyes off of him, nor had a half-dozen others, though they, at least, were more discreet with their admiring glances.

Of all the women present, only Prudence seemed out of place because of her ruby-red satin gown, a style the likes of which Indy had never seen before in polite society. Why Prudence would choose such a gown Indy couldn't fathom; it was decidedly inappropriate with its dangerously low bodice that left little to the imagination. Then she remembered: Prudence's husband had rescued her from a saloon—which explained the gown—a saloon girl's gown.

Indy could see the officers' wives' disapproving stares and couldn't help but feel sorry for Prudence, though it didn't appear that Prudence was overly concerned. Quite the contrary, she seemed to be thoroughly enjoying herself, as if she didn't have a care in the world.

As soon as the last couple had made the turn, Jim and Prudence linked arms. Now, four across, they marched to the dais, made the loop, and returned to join with the other foursome coming from the opposite direction. The cycle repeated with eight across, then ended, everyone breaking with their partner and applauding.

With the march out of the way, it was time for Jim and Indy to lead out the first dance of the evening. A polka. Everyone moved back to clear the floor. Jim bowed and Indy curtsied. Anticipating his actions, she raised her hands into position. He moved up a step and pressed his left hand against her right hand and bent his fingers over the tips of hers as if to say he was in complete control. His other hand wound around her back, pulling her closer than she thought proper, but before she could say or do anything about it, he was dancing her across the room.

Indy hadn't danced since her seventeenth birthday, a few weeks before her mother and brother died. The polka was her favorite of all the dances, but how much she enjoyed it depended on the skill of her partner. Jim Garrity was an excellent dancer, which, after the Grand March, didn't surprise her. But it did make her wonder about what kind of man he was. He'd lived in two worlds, as different from each other as night and day. He had fought in the war and risen to the rank of major. Other questions presented themselves. How had he and Captain Nolan come to know each other? Why had he killed those four men? And why had he chosen to live with the Apaches? Surely there had been other choices.

Something told Indy that even if she had all the answers, she still wouldn't *know* Jim Garrity. She doubted anyone did. He was like a maze with so many twists and turns that one could spend an entire lifetime exploring him.

After completing three circles around the room, they were joined by a dozen or more other couples and the dance floor was filled with light-hearted conversation and laughter. Then Sergeant Moseley came onto the floor with Prudence Stallard. Envious of Prudence's nonchalance, Indy decided she too deserved to enjoy herself and promptly threw herself wholeheartedly into the dance, putting everything and everyone except her partner out of her mind.

Too soon the dance ended and Jim led her off the floor. She hadn't enjoyed herself that much since—she couldn't remember the last time, it had been so long ago. She was breathless and hot, and it felt wonderful. Unconsciously, she plucked her lace handkerchief from her sleeve and pressed it against her forehead. She was about to tuck it back away when Jim took it from her hand.

"You missed a spot," he told her, then gently wiped the handkerchief over her right temple. The unexpected gesture paralyzed her. She felt his cool palm brush against her cheek and his fingers touch her hair. The contact sent a tremor of longing through her body and a singing into her ears. She found herself fighting the urge to look up at him, to gaze into his eyes, afraid of what she would discover there. Instead, she stared at his mouth and saw an almost imperceptible smile. Then it was gone, and he was putting the handkerchief back into her hand. "I'll go get us some punch," he said, bending close so she could hear him above the voices and the music.

All she could do was nod. The moment he started across the room she expelled the breath she had unconsciously been holding. She watched him wend his way around the fringes of the dance

floor. It didn't surprise her that people stepped
out of his way when they saw him coming, but
what did surprise her were some of the loudly
whispered comments that followed in his wake.
The two women closest to Indy seemed not at all
concerned that they might be heard.

"Yes, four men! The only reason they caught
him was because he was wounded. They court-
martialed him and sentenced him to hang, but of
course, as you know, he escaped."

"My goodness. I won't be able to get a decent
night's sleep as long as that killer is here."

Indy shut out their voices. How could they be
so cruel as to talk about him like that as soon as
his back was turned? Weren't they two of the
women she had seen flashing him smiles only
minutes ago?

Desperate to get a breath of fresh air, Indy
moved closer to the window. She hated gossip
and gossipers. She would never forget what her
own so-called well-meaning friends had said
about her after her mother's and brother's deaths.
Their cruel gossip was one of the reasons she had
withdrawn from society.

She leaned her shoulder against the windowsill
but found no relief. The outside temperature had
yet to significantly cool down and there wasn't a
hint of a breeze. Beyond the window, in the shadows of the building, she heard a man's voice.

"I don't know if it was such a good idea bringing him here or not. Even if he was wrongly accused—he's lived with those damn savages all
these years, playing Indian. Could be he even has
a squaw or two—you know how those Apaches

are—just like the Mormons! Hell! You can believe what you want, but I don't trust him. Not for a minute. You watch. I predict that the first chance he gets he'll lead a detail out into the middle of the desert and set Chie or Cochise on them. No, sir. I'm not volunteering. I'll desert before I do that."

"Lemonade?"

Indy jumped at the sound of Jim Garrity's voice. She hadn't seen him coming back through the crowd, but then she hadn't been looking; her gaze had been on a dark silhouette outside the window.

"Yes, thank you." She reached out to take one of the two glasses he was holding and saw that her hand was shaking. "It feels like rain, don't you think?"

He stood in front of the window and looked directly at the man she had overheard speaking. "This is the time of year for it," he said. "The Apaches call this the time of the big harvest."

From that the conversation could go off in a dozen different directions, none of which Indy was inclined to take. "I wanted to ask you," she said suddenly, before she had actually thought the question through, "wherever did you learn to dance the polka like that?" It seemed a harmless question.

"At the Point," was his blunt reply.

Surely she had heard him wrong; there was so much chatter going on all around her. "You don't mean West Point, of course." It was more a statement than a question, but no sooner had she said

it than she realized how priggish it sounded and
wished she could take it back.

His mouth twisted wryly. "I don't?" He left the
question dangling as he lifted his glass to his lips
and stared at her over the rim while he downed
the contents.

"I'm sorry. That came out all wrong. You *do*
mean West Point, don't you?" She was so embarrassed she could die. In an attempt to turn the
conversation she said, "My father went to West
Point. He was in the same class as President
Grant. My brother, Justice, went there too. He
was number three in his class," she told him
with pride.

Still staring at her, brown eyes now darkened
to black, he set his glass down on the windowsill.
"Why does it surprise you so much that I went
to West Point? Don't I look like typical West
Point issue?"

She flinched at the sarcasm in his voice. "You
know you don't," she said, being honest. And she
knew he knew it too. She supposed he was teasing her, trying to embarrass her more than she
already was.

"What *do* I look like, then?" he challenged.

Her eyes widened at the question—an impossible question, because he looked different every
time she saw him. Again, she visualized the dark-
eyed rider who had daringly halted the runaway
team. The tall, broad-chested warrior whom she'd
thought bent on raping and killing her. The ruthless Apache leader who had brought his captives
to justice. And now, tonight, the buckskinned
major-scout. All different, yet all the same. The

two constants being his dark good looks and an aura of danger that would always be an inherent part of him no matter what he wore or how he combed his hair.

An utterly impossible question to answer.

"Miss Taylor?" Sergeant Moseley interrupted to Indy's great relief, for she had no idea what she was going to say. "Sorry to intrude, ma'am, but Miss Stallard here begged me to bring her over so she could formally be introduced to our guest of honor."

Indy turned to see Prudence standing behind the sergeant, her expression overtly eager. She felt a sinking feeling within her breast. Next to Prudence Stallard's radiant beauty she was as plain as a mouse. "Yes, of course," she managed, then moved to bring Prudence into the fold. She hurried through the introductions.

"I've heard a great deal about you, Major."

"A pleasure to meet you, Mrs. Stallard," Jim replied, his voice low, deeply resonant. "I remember seeing you last week when I was riding out."

Prudence's pert chin lifted, and she flashed him a dazzling smile. "Yes, I remember too." Tilting her head she blatantly examined him from head to toe, and unwittingly, Indy found herself doing the same thing, as if Prudence might see something she had missed. "But you look so different than you did that day. I hardly recognized you at first." Clamping her teeth together, Indy turned her head sideways and lifted her gaze heavenward. Who did Prudence think she was fooling? Hardly recognized him indeed! Prudence would have recognized him if he had been tarred and feathered! "My late husband, Major Stallard," Prudence went on in a voice so silky that Indy could hardly bear listening to it, "used to speak very highly of you. He claimed you even saved his life once."

"The major was a good man and a good soldier," Jim told Prudence. "I was sorry to learn of his death."

Prudence bowed her head, the first display of bereavement Indy had seen her make. "I miss him very much." Prudence sighed convincingly, then peeked up at Jim from beneath her long, sooty lashes. "I'm afraid widowhood doesn't suit me very well. I found I enjoyed having someone to pamper and care for."

"Maybe you should get a dog," Indy suggested.

Prudence's head swiveled around, her disgust evident in her stricken expression. "A dog!"

Sergeant Moseley pulled a face. "Funny you should mention that," he said earnestly. "My old Bess had a litter of nine pups last week and they'll all be needin' homes here before long." To Prudence he said, "I'll bring them by tomorrow evening so you can take a look see."

"I—well—" Prudence faltered. "I really don't know that I want a dog exactly."

"Maybe a cat then?" Indy ventured.

"No—" She cut a sharp glance at Indy, then slowly her expression began to change. "I do need *something*," she said, turning her gaze on Jim, "but I haven't decided just exactly what yet." The provocative innuendo drew a frown from Indy. "What do you think, Major Garrity? Should I get a dog to keep me company during the day? Or a cat to cuddle up with at night?"

Indy blinked in astonishment. Now, she knew what Opal had meant by Prudence's *wanton ways*.

Enough is enough, she decided. If Jim Garrity and Sergeant Moseley wanted to stand there listening to Prudence's talk about dogs and cats—which translated to something entirely different—it was fine with her, but she had better things to do.

Chapter 8

Dark clouds hid the stars and the moon and distant thunder rattled across the sky heralding the storm to come. Indy kept herself busy straightening up and removing empty dishes from the long plank table, all the while trying to ignore Prudence and Jim Garrity, who at last glance were still dancing.

Nearly a half hour later she had done everything she could and was looking for something else to occupy her time, when Captain Nolan came up and solved the problem by asking her to dance. Glad for the timely invitation, she stepped up in front of him, placed her left hand on his shoulder, and went quickly into his arms.

A smile spread over his face as he drew her to him, his hand firm against the curve of her waist, guiding her smoothly onto the dance floor. "I've been waiting all evening to dance with you," he told her as he moved them into the circle of dancers, "but you've been so busy."

"Yes, well—" she hesitated, looking for a valid excuse but finding none.

"You don't have to explain, Indy. I think I know how important it is to you that the evening go especially well."

He surprised her with his understanding, but it worried her that she was so transparent that he could see right through her.

"By the way, there's something I've been meaning to say to you." His steps slowed and she sensed his nervousness. "During the attack—after I took that arrow—if you hadn't come for me and pulled me down into the wagon . . . I owe you my life, Indy. There aren't words to tell you . . ."

She shook her head, stopping him from continuing. "It was no more than you would have done for me. But if you don't mind, I would really prefer not to talk about that day. It's still very upsetting to me."

"Of course. I understand."

"There is one thing, though . . ." she said on a rising note.

"What's that?"

"After Shatto, I mean Major Garrity, halted the team . . . why couldn't he have told me that he wasn't an Apache or that he didn't intend to . . . to kill us?"

His shoulder muscles tightened beneath her hand. "You should probably ask Jim about that, Indy. No one can speak for Jim but Jim. All I can tell you is that he has been wanted by the Army for six years for murder and desertion. There is a very large price on his head. If he had revealed himself to you, he would have put himself in jeopardy, don't you see?"

Yes, she did see, but she was loath to admit it. Considering how badly he had frightened her, it didn't seem quite fair that his actions should be so easily explained away and made to seem logical and just. "I suppose so," she conceded reluctantly, feeling cheated. "However, that doesn't excuse you, Captain!" she said, chiding him more gently than he deserved. "*You* could have told me who he was on any number of occasions prior to that day you brought him into my parlor. Instead, you—both of you—let me make an absolute fool of myself!" Just the mention of that meeting brought a fiery blush to her cheeks.

The captain stopped dancing and stared down at her, his light blue eyes studying her expression as if to determine whether she was truly angry or just venting her frustration. Either way, he had the good sense to look suitably repentant.

"I admit it, I'm guilty," he confessed. "I have absolutely no defense other than it never even occurred to me to mention it to you." He shook his head. "All I can do now is tell you that I'm sorry and ask that you accept my apology." He ended on a questioning note.

Men! she thought. "Apology accepted, Captain."

He seemed genuinely relieved, although his smile was still a bit uncertain as he picked up the dance steps and led her around the floor.

Among the waltzing couples Indy saw her father, partnered with Opal. Not even in dancing did he relax his stiff military bearing, she realized, watching the way he executed each step, as if it had some strategic purpose. If he was enjoying himself, it was his secret.

Indy was startled out of her thoughts when she heard Jim Garrity's deep baritone nearby. Without looking toward the sound of his voice, she strained to catch a word or two but the music and the chatter of the other dancers made it impossible to make sense of what he was saying, though his low, intimate tone told her it was definitely a private conversation and not one for public address.

When Prudence began to laugh, Indy's thoughts were confirmed. With sudden, inexplicable resentment, she flashed a disapproving glance at Jim and was horrified to find his gaze on her. He must have overheard her question to the captain and was amused that she was still so upset. He arched an eyebrow and slowly lifted the corner of his mouth in a mocking smile.

Indy felt the blood drain out of her face and was glad for the captain's sturdy shoulder. Stiffening with outrage, she returned the look with a mutinous glare to which he had the audacity to laugh.

What arrogance! What nerve! she thought. Oh, but to have the opportunity to relive that moment when she had dropped the coffeepot. She pictured it falling near the edge of the table, and the coffee—steaming, scalding, and black— spilling into the center of his lap!

Putting a stop to her imaginings, Indy turned her attention elsewhere—to the expectant couple standing by the punch, his arm lovingly around her shoulders. Ava and her lieutenant husband seemed very much in love.

"Everyone seems to be having a good time, don't you think, Captain?" Indy asked, surprising them both with the abruptness of her question.

He glanced around at the dancing couples and

nodded. "It's especially good to see Jim enjoying himself again." His pointed gaze rested on Jim and Prudence. "I was beginning to worry that he'd forgotten what it was to enjoy himself. There was a time, believe it or not, when he thought of little else."

"Well, I'm sure if anyone can get Major Garrity to enjoy himself again it's Prudence Stallard," Indy said without thinking.

If Captain Nolan noticed her small indiscretion, he didn't let on. "Actually, Mrs. Stallard looks an awful lot like Tess." He stared across at Prudence, his eyes squinting in the yellow light.

Indy recalled the captain's mention of Tess as an added incentive to strike the bargain with her father. She had thought at the time that whoever Tess was she must be someone special, but in light of the rest of the conversation that day, she had all but forgotten the name.

"Tess?" she queried now, cautious not to sound overly interested.

"Jim's former fiancée. Coincidentally or maybe ironically, their wedding date was the same date the court sentenced him to hang. I didn't know it the other day, when I brought up Tess's name, that she had refused his request to see him the night before the sentence was to be carried out."

"She refused? But they were to be married! How could she have been so unfeeling? What kind of woman would—?" She stopped abruptly having heard the fiery passion in her own voice.

"I guess you would have to know Tess," he said, as if that explained it. "Now, of course, Jim has decided it was a good thing that she refused him. If she hadn't, he wouldn't have gone into a rage and he wouldn't have found a way to escape. And now, with your father's help, he might be able to prove his innocence. He *is* innocent, Indy," he added with strong emphasis.

"You obviously know him very well?"

"We grew up together. We were like brothers. I trust him implicitly."

Indy danced a second time with Captain Nolan, then with one partner after another until, much to her surprise, her father claimed her.

He was not an easy partner to follow; his movements were quick and sharp, like the way he barked orders to his men.

"Captain Nolan is taking care of the men's punch, I take it?"

Indy nodded. "You haven't said whether or not everything is to your satisfaction. There wasn't much to work with as far as food, drink, and music, but we all did the best we could."

"As you say—considering what there was to work with, I suppose it was the best that could be done," he said in a tight voice.

"Yes, it was," she replied sadly, bending her head to hide her hurt. Again she had hoped for a kind word and again was hurt and disappointed.

"Where's Major Garrity?" the colonel asked.

She looked up and glanced around but didn't see either the major or Prudence. "I have no idea. He was here, dancing with Mrs. Stallard a short while ago."

The music ended and he abruptly dropped his hands to his sides. "When you see him, tell him

I said he should begin the selection of the trainees right after breakfast call."

"Surely you could tell him. I'm certain he's here somewhere."

"No, I could not. I'm retiring for the evening. I've been wanting to sit down and read Justice's letters." He started to turn away but Indy caught hold of his sleeve.

"But, Father, you can't leave. Not yet. It wouldn't be right. What will people say? Besides, you've read those old letters a hundred times before. I don't understand . . ."

His nostrils flared in sudden anger and the look he turned on her was as sharp as the cutting edge of his sword. "No, of course *you* wouldn't understand," he seethed between his teeth. "Your mother didn't understand either—the bond between Justice and me. But at least your mother— God rest her soul—had sense enough to know her place and not try to come between us. But not you. You looked for every way you could to break us apart. And you finally found a way, didn't you?"

Unconsciously, she raised her arms and steepled her hands in front of her face. "I didn't know it was smallpox. All I knew was that they were children, Father," she reminded him with a fervent plea for compassion and understanding—as she had so many times before. "They were orphans. No one wanted to help take care of them. I couldn't refuse. You know that. They needed—" Her voice broke preventing her from finishing.

His mouth was set in a thin line. "If they needed you so much, why didn't you stay there with them! Your mother and Justice would be alive today if you hadn't come home. You killed them just as surely as if you had stabbed them to death. And you dare wonder why I read and reread Justice's letters? Those *old* letters are all you left me of my boy—my life. They give me comfort, as nothing else does." He stood glowering at her, his gray eyes stone-cold and narrowed with hate, then turned on his heel, and marched off.

Too stunned to move, Indy held her breath as she watched him leave. After a moment she became aware of people staring at her, and gathering what was left of her pride, she slowly turned to meet their curious stares. "Excuse me," she mumbled to no one and everyone as she threaded her way between couples to the door, where she escaped into the dark of the night.

You killed them just as surely as if you had stabbed them to death. You killed them— Killed them— Killed! Killed!

She walked aimlessly, blindly, with no idea where she was going. She had barely reached the end of the building when someone stepped out in front of her and clutched her upper arms.

"Where the hell do you think you're going?"

She had opened her mouth to scream, then recognized the voice. Him! Jim Garrity!

"That's the second time you've scared me half to death!" She put her hand to her breast, trying to still her pounding heart.

"Better to scare you than let you go off half-cocked into the desert where you could get yourself killed."

Breathless and growing angrier by the second she came back at him. "I really don't think . . . it's any of your business where I go." She would have said more if she could have caught her breath.

"It's not safe for you to go beyond camp," he told her in a low, even voice that might have sounded reasonable to anyone else's ears, but not to Indy's.

"Thank you for the warning. Should anything happen to me, you can tell them you did everything you could to stop me." She struggled against his iron hold, but his grip was firm, inflexible. She dropped her arms to her sides, pretending resignation.

"Believe me, Indy, I *will* do everything I can to stop you. Even if it means hurting you. So don't test me," he warned. Hard and implacable, he was as frightening now as when she had first seen him.

She shivered at the memory—still so vivid. So terrifying. It was that memory that gave her an uncommon surge of strength. With a violent jerk that caught him off guard, she broke free and started to run.

"Indy! Don't!" His hand reached out whiplash quick, grabbed her around the waist, and pulled her back with an economy of movement and speed that both surprised and baffled her. "Did you really think I'd let you go? You don't take advice very well, do you?"

She was trying to catch her breath. "Advice, Major? Funny, it sounded more like a threat to me."

"Call it whatever you want. It makes no difference. You still aren't leaving this camp!" Overhead the moon peeked between the dark clouds allowing her to clearly see his features. His eyes were diamond bright. Diamond hard. His gaze cut right through her.

Before, she had been bent on a walk to escape the curious stares and to soothe her wounds. But now, her only thought was to escape Jim Garrity! But how? She was willing to try anything. Fighting. Crying. Screaming. Intimidation . . .

Drawing herself up, stiff and straight, she assumed a haughty pose. "It seems you have forgotten your place, Major. May I remind you that I am your commanding officer's daughter? If you don't let me go this instant, I'll have my father charge you with insubordination and he'll have you thrown in the guardhouse!"

He did release her, but she could see in his challenging expression that she was far from free. He stood staring at her, his long, lean body negligently poised, legs apart, arms now folded across his chest, clearly not the least bit intimidated.

"The guardhouse, huh? Too bad. I was actually looking forward to riding the cannon."

Her mouth fell open. "Why would you say—? How did you know—?"

"Let's just say the colonel is an easy man to figure."

"You really *are* impertinent!"

"Among other things," he replied with cool mockery.

"Yes, among other things," she agreed, glaring

at him. "Arrogant. Insolent, Rude. Despicable. Shall I go on?"

"Whatever you want. You'll find me most accommodating," he said, raising her ire to the boiling point. "You could try mean, hateful, insolent— Oh, no, you already used insolent. How about—?"

"How about offensive and contemptible?" she supplied, fussing with the lace edge of her bodice. "That should pretty well cover it, though if I think on it awhile longer I'm sure I'll come up with a few more."

"Indy. Listen to me. You didn't come out here to quarrel with me and I sure as hell don't want to quarrel with you. If you'll calm down a minute, there's a thing or two I'd like to tell you about what I overheard that bastard father of yours say to you inside." He hesitated when he saw her chin jut out in anger and defiance.

"I'm not interested in anything you have to say, Major. Especially when you call my father a bastard!"

"Stubborn as an Army mule, aren't you? Too bad you don't have a mule's savvy."

Her chin snapped up. "What's that supposed to mean?" she demanded, ready to begin doing battle all over again.

"It means that a mule is smart enough to know when to quit, unlike his cousin, the loyal and trusting horse, who will run himself to death trying to please his master."

"Horses! Mules! You're talking in riddles." Militantly, she crossed her arms in front of her and spun around, presenting him with her backside.

"You know damn well what I'm talking about."
He moved up behind her and gripped her upper
arms. "When was it that your mother and brother
died? Seven years ago? All that time you've tried
every way you could think of to earn your father's
forgiveness. But you've wasted your time. He'll
never forgive you. There's too much hate in him."
Strong hands squeezed her tender flesh but she
wouldn't give him the pleasure of letting him
know that he was hurting her. "It's time to come
to terms with the fact that you can't make him
forgive you or love you. It's time to quit trying
and start living your life."

Every muscle in her body stiffened in defiance.
"How dare you say this to me!"

"I dare just about anything I damn well please,
lady! I always have and I always will."

She tried every means possible to hold back
the tears but nothing worked. They filled her eyes
and slid slowly and silently down her cheeks.

"Indy." There was an unspoken message in the
way he whispered her name that told her he re-
gretted having spoken so harshly. She tried to
choke back a sob but the effort was beyond her.
She was weary of hiding her hurt, tired of pretending that there was still a chance that her
father would eventually forgive her. He was right.
It was time to face reality. Time to give up—to
quit.

She shuddered with the force of her pain and
Jim pulled her back against him, fitting her
curves solidly against his hard length. His arms
bound her in a tight knot of muscle and sinew.
There was comfort within his arms. Comfort.

Shelter. Compassion. All the things she had longed for. All the things she had never had.

"What I wanted to tell is that I've seen a lot of smallpox, in the Army and out here. Once it starts it spreads like wildfire. Whole Indian camps, wagon trains, even towns have been wiped out—all from one person passing it to another. It can't be helped."

She shook her head emphatically. "Father was right, if I had stayed there at the orphanage—if I hadn't come home—" she broke off, unable to continue.

Bending his head, he rested his chin on her crown. "If. If. If. You don't know that for a fact, Indy." His warm breath stirred her hair and sparked a sleeping fire deep down inside her, causing her to shudder. "The children in the orphanage—they weren't the only ones in town with the disease, were they?"

When she didn't answer, he moved her slightly to the right and bent even lower so his mouth was at her temple. "Come on now, Indy. Answer me. There were other cases in town, weren't there?" Lifting a hand he took her chin between his thumb and index finger and brought her head around so that they were face-to-face and eye to eye. His warm, moist breath, smelling faintly of brandy, intoxicated her as if she had consumed it herself.

"I—I think so," she managed, but just barely. "Yes, there were other cases." She blinked her eyes and swallowed down her anxiety.

"Don't you see, Indy? That means that anyone entering your home, a friend, a servant, a merchant, anyone—even your father—could have brought the disease into the house."

Her eyes widened. "Father?" She pondered the idea, thinking back, but so much time had passed her memories were dim and the way Jim was holding her, touching her, was making it impossible to concentrate. She wondered if he had any idea what effect he was having upon her.

"Anyone," he stated.

She stared up at him. "I— That never occurred to me before."

"You got sick too, didn't you?" At her nod, he added, "But you survived. And now every time he looks at you he's reminded of what he lost. He's the kind of man who has to put the blame on somebody and you have always allowed that somebody to be you."

His look of arrogant self-assurance was gone. In its place was a look of . . . She hesitated to give it a name thinking she had to be misreading it, that it was her imagination, and it didn't really exist.

He let go of her chin and ran his fingers down the side of her neck and stopped at the base of her throat, his thumb resting on her pounding pulse. He *had* to know what he was doing to her, touching her like that, she thought. He had to be able to see the desire in her eyes, the wanting. Closing her eyes she wet her lips and let herself imagine what his lips would feel like against hers.

"Indy—?" His mouth came down over hers, smothering his words. The imagined kiss was nothing like the reality. This—this she couldn't have imagined without some former knowledge and even then . . . She had seen couples kissing and experienced a chaste kiss or two herself, but nothing had prepared her for the excitement and depth of emotion that he was causing her to feel.

She felt his hand move back up her neck, then across her cheek to wipe away the trail of tears. His thumb tickled the corner of her mouth, coaxing her lips apart.

She didn't understand his unspoken request, but she didn't object to it, at least not until the moment when he slipped his tongue between her lips and plunged deep inside her mouth to taste and explore her. Shocked and bewildered, she tried to close her mouth but he refused to let her, and then after a moment she gave in to the awesome sensations he was arousing within her—sensations she had never felt before, never even knew existed.

Still kissing her, Jim slowly turned her around so she was facing him. With a low moan, that to Indy sounded like he was in pain, he wrapped his arms around her and deepened the kiss.

Unsure of herself, she lifted her arms and tentatively placed her hands on top of his wide shoulders, then little by little moved them until her arms were around his neck and she was clinging to him.

A jagged bolt of white lightning sliced through the clouds illuminating the night. It seemed a fitting symbol of how he made her feel—like she had been struck by lightning. She raised up on her toes and strained against his hard, flat length and every nerve in her body stood up too and danced a jig.

Suddenly he pulled away, leaving her confused, lost. "Come on," he said in a hoarse voice, and before she knew it, he was leading her around the corner of the building.

"Jim—I really think maybe I should go—"

"No, it's too dangerous." He walked to the end of the next building, away from the people going to and leaving the reception.

The walk gave Indy's head a chance to clear so she could think. It had been a mistake to let him kiss her and an even bigger one to kiss him back—no matter how right it seemed—no matter how good it had felt. She had been upset and vulnerable and he had taken advantage of her susceptibility.

Where he was leading her she didn't know, but she knew she couldn't let him kiss her and get her in that position again. Major Jim Garrity was far too persuasive and powerful a force for her to control.

"Jim! Please. Stop!"

"We're here," he said, halting abruptly, and before she could make a word of protest, he pulled her around and backed her up against the building, catching her hands between their bodies, and brought his mouth down on hers in a hard, savage kiss that took her breath away and made her weak-kneed. She couldn't move; she was literally trapped between two walls, one of adobe brick and one of hard male muscle.

He held her face between his hands to prevent her from turning her head to the side. Where before he had been tender, now he was almost cruel in the way his tongue pillaged the inside of her mouth, and when he was done there, he moved down the curve of her throat, his lips hot and wet, his tongue a flaming torch that set something inside her on fire.

At last, she worked her hands loose but her plan to use them to gain her freedom was gone and instead—as if they had a mind of their own—they found their way around his neck and clung.

He groaned then and his mouth moved even lower, to the soft swells of her breasts that rose and fell rapidly with her heavy breathing. His hands were there now too, outside her dress below her breasts, lifting and squeezing them as his mouth worked over their tops.

Suddenly he straightened and his mouth came back to hers with an urgent demand that she felt in his hands too as he grasped her hips.

"Indy— God, woman, if you had any idea how long it's been . . . and what you're doing to me." Then he showed her exactly what she was doing to him by pressing her flat up against the adobe and pushing his lower body into the folds of her skirt.

"No. My God, no," she protested, feeling his hardness, and afraid of him now that she understood what he was doing and what he wanted of her. Afraid of herself too because she didn't really want him to stop. But her complaint died under the onslaught of his kiss and she felt his hips grinding mercilessly against hers, spreading the fire of passion throughout her body.

Off in the distance, a lone coyote called out to its mate and she felt his muscles contract and become tense. It came again a second later and he lifted his head to listen. He stared down at her, his expression agonized. It seemed to Indy that he looked to be in a great deal of pain as if he had been wounded.

"Indy, listen to me," he whispered close to her ear. "Don't make a move or say a word. We've got some uninvited guests."

Alarmed and frightened she stared into his eyes, hoping he would tell her they weren't in any danger.

"Who—?"

"Apaches. There's three of them, maybe four. I'm going to reach my hand down between us and get my knife, so don't make a move."

"No. I won't," she whispered, barely moving her lips. Looking down, she saw his hand remove the wicked-looking blade from the sheath attached to his belt, then slowly bring it up between them.

"Now, as soon as I make my move, I want you to run back to the reception and get Nolan. Don't stop for anything or anybody. Understand?"

She gave an imperceptible nod and he placed a quick kiss upon her trembling mouth.

"Now!" He pushed her away.

She ran like she had never run before. Behind her she heard that frightful cry. Shatto's cry.

"Hai-eee! Hai-eee!"

Chapter 9

Indy ran as fast as she could, driven by the knowledge that Jim would need help to fight off the Apaches. She hadn't run more than a few dozen yards when a bolt of lightning slashed across the sky and struck the roof of the butcher's building directly in front of her. Wood and adobe splintered in every direction sending Indy to her knees, screaming. She tucked her chin into her chest and covered her head with her hands to protect herself from the flying debris and from the deafening explosion of thunder that accompanied the lightning.

The ground beneath her vibrated with the sudden fury of the storm.

It seemed that the world was coming to an end.

The first drops of rain fell cold and hard upon her neck and arms. Like a turtle peeking out of its shell she raised her head and looked about. The butcher's building was on fire; tongues of flame escaped from the roof and through the windows, carrying with them the overpowering smell of roasting beef.

Then she saw him. An Apache warrior. Cold fear washed over her and her heart pummeled

her chest like a blacksmith's anvil. She pushed
the hair away from her eyes and strained to see
through the rain and smoke. He seemed to have
come straight out of the inferno—a demon from
hell. And now he was riding directly toward her,
his horse bearing down hard upon her.

Shaking, she struggled to her feet and stood as
if bolted to the ground, unable to move so much
as a muscle.

Nearly upon her now, the warrior bent low over
the galloping horse's neck and leaned off to the
right, stretching his arm toward her. At the last
possible second instinct took control. She darted
away, avoiding the Apache's reach by a scant
inch. She picked up her skirts and ran toward
the burning building, her screams following her
like a pennant.

If she could get past the fire, she could make
it to the mess house. She saw herself dashing
through the doorway into the middle of the reception and announcing that she and Major Garrity had been attacked by Apaches.

The next second changed everything.

The Apache's horse came galloping up from
behind. She could hear its hooves pounding the
hard ground but had no idea how close or far it
was. Glancing over her shoulder she saw the
horse gaining on her. She knew she couldn't out-
run it, but neither could she change her course.
She had to go on. Jim's life depended on it and
so did hers.

She had no sooner turned back than the horse
came up even with her, then abruptly swerved.
By the time Indy saw what was happening it was

too late. She couldn't stop soon enough. She hit the horse's flank and bounced backward. The ground rose up to meet her and everything went black.

Indy blinked her eyes open and groaned. When she tried to take a breath she realized that the wind had been knocked out of her. She panicked and clutched her throat.

Hovering over her, watching her like a hungry vulture, was the Apache. He made some sort of guttural sound that drew her gaze. He had frightening eyes, shiny like bits of volcanic glass set deep into his face. His features were ugly and his skin thick and scarred. But most fearful of all was his mouth—a sharp, narrow-lipped gash that split his face.

When he bent down to reach for her, blessed air came rushing back into her burning lungs. She gasped and gasped again, each breath deeper and stronger than the one before. Each breath filling her with the dusty-wet odor of him. Each breath possibly the last.

She winced when he jerked her to her feet. He half dragged, half carried her across to his mount. Then he tossed her onto the animal's back and vaulted up behind her, capturing her legs beneath his to hold her while he quickly removed his headband and tied her wrists together behind her back.

She hurt too much to put up a fight and besides she knew it was useless; he was twice her weight and half again her size, a giant of an Indian. His arm whipped around her middle eliciting a small, pained cry, which he ignored.

Taking his reins in his left hand, he snapped them over the horse's withers and the animal moved forward. They had ridden only a short distance when they stopped. Indy saw that it was the same place where she had left Jim a short time ago.

In a matter of minutes it had become a battle-field. One dead warrior lay faceup in the mud, rain falling into his sightless eyes. A second warrior knelt beside a boulder, trying to hold back the stream of blood that poured from his stomach. Cloudy-eyed and expressionless, he stared at Indy.

She couldn't bear it. She turned her head to the side and tucked her chin into her shoulder. The wounded Apache made a grunt of noise and when she turned back, he had slumped down in front of the boulder. Dead.

Her captor's only apparent reaction to the warrior's death was that his arm tightened like a cinch around her waist. Again she cried out and again was ignored.

"You're hurting me." She twisted her shoulders this way and that trying to make herself understood. After a moment he took his arm away. "Thank you," she said automatically and realized a second later, when he poked the tip of his knife into her spine, how very foolish she had been to think that he had responded to her plea with kindness.

He said something to her in Apache and pricked her. She didn't understand his words but she did understand his meaning. She wasn't to make a sound or he would do more than prick her. Again, he touched his heels to the horse's flanks, signaling it to walk forward.

Just ahead, through the rain, Indy saw a young warrior, naked but for his breechclout, and Jim, who had stripped off his shirt. They faced each other across a distance of several yards. The orange-yellow glow of the fire reflected off Jim's rain-wet body, accentuating the rippling, fluid muscles in his back and arms. Watching him closely, she saw that he was clearly the more skilled of the two, the more sure of himself and his capabilities. Crouching down, his legs spread wide, he thrust and jabbed his long-bladed knife, tempting and teasing his opponent. In his left hand, he held his shirt, which was twisted around itself like a thick rope. He used it like a whip to lash out at the warrior's legs.

He was Shatto now, not Jim Garrity, she realized. The thought made her as uneasy as the knife poking into her spine. And Shatto was as much of a savage as his rival and as her captor.

With dismay she recalled that only a short while ago he—Shatto—had been holding her, kissing her, touching and kissing her breasts. She had all but surrendered herself to him and the newly awakened passions he had aroused.

Shatto—Major Jim Garrity—one in the same, no matter how he dressed or what language he spoke. A dangerous adversary who wielded a knife as easily as he reined a horse. A savage who could kill a man without a bit of remorse. And a man who had the power to turn her inside out and make her feel things that no respectable woman should feel.

Thunder rumbled overhead and the horse blew out of his nostrils. The noise must have reached Shatto's ears for he glanced around at Indy. Then, without warning, he raised his left arm and lashed out at his opponent's face with his shirt-whip. Blinded, the young warrior reeled back-ward, rubbing his eyes. Shatto seized the opportu-nity and closed the distance between them and threw him to the ground.

Indy felt the tensing of her captor's hard-muscled thighs against the backs of her legs. His reaction seemed to indicate his anxiousness over his com-panion's fate. But, if that was true, why didn't he get down and help him? Perhaps it was a matter of custom or pride with the Apaches not to come to the other's aid. What other explanation could there be?

"Let the woman go, Chie," came Shatto's deep authoritative voice. He had knelt down beside the young warrior and was holding a knife to his throat.

"No. The woman is mine."

Indy's heart sank. She had not realized that her captor was Chie, the warrior who had led the attack on the ambulance the day she came to Bowie. Since then she had heard any number of stories regarding Chie. Apparently he was an outcast even among his own people.

"No. She is not yours. Let her go now or I'll kill this brave," Shatto warned, his eyes mirroring the flames of the burning building in the distance.

"Kill him. He is nothing to me."

"If he is nothing to you, why didn't you ride

away and take the woman with you when you had the chance?" Shatto challenged. When Chie did not answer, Shatto taunted him with "Is it because this foolish brave is Chie's son?"

Indy knew by the way Chie stiffened that Shatto had hit upon the answer. Was it a guess or did he know?

"Shatto has eyes of the hawk but sees only what is before him. If you kill my son, I will kill the woman." To make his point he jabbed the knife into Indy's back.

Indy gasped but otherwise tried to hide her pain and her fear.

"We will make a bargain," said Shatto in response. "I will spare your son and give him back to you if you let go of the woman."

Chie then said something in Apache that Indy took as an agreement. Next thing she knew Chie was slicing through her wrist bindings and was putting her off his horse. She moved away quickly, running toward a boulder, thinking he might change his mind.

"You all right, Indy?" Shatto called to her.

"Yes." It was all she could manage as she tried to rub some feeling back into her hands.

Like Indy, the young brave had also gotten away as quickly as he could. He had dashed across to where his father sat upon his horse.

It was over, Indy thought. She breathed a sigh of relief, then cringed when she heard Shatto's taunting words.

"Chie is a woman who sends old men and boys to fight Shatto."

Chie's chest expanded with an indrawn breath

of rage. "Chie is not woman. Chie is great Chiricahua warrior with much power."

"If Chie is so great a warrior why does he not
fight Shatto himself?" Shatto mocked.

Oh, God, Indy thought. Why? Why did he have
to insult Chie? Why couldn't he just let them go?
Angry and afraid all over again, she considered
abandoning him and running back to camp to get
the help she had sought in the first place. Only
she couldn't do it. She couldn't move.

Chie dismounted and tossed the reins to his
son. "Shatto is a fool like the bluecoat *nantan*."

Indy held her breath as the two men moved
toward some invisible central point and stopped.
It seemed an interminable time that they did
nothing but stare at each other.

A tremendous burst of light illuminated the
sky. Fiery fingers of lightning streaked across the
sky, linking heaven to earth. Chie's horse bolted
and ran off in a panic toward the camp.

The relentless rain combined with the lightning
flashes made it difficult for Indy to see. Reluctantly she came out from behind the boulder.

Like dancers, the two men moved in a sort of
circle, reaching, thrusting, jabbing, each testing
the other's skill and agility. Chie was the more
graceful, but Shatto was faster and his superior
skill with a knife was immediately evident. He
lunged forward and slashed the tip of his blade
across Chie's upper arm.

Indy was repulsed by the sick excitement she
felt at Shatto having drawn first blood. She chastised herself yet could not turn away.

Long minutes passed as the two went back and

forth, left and right, lunging and retreating. It seemed to Indy that the fighting would go on forever because neither man could get enough of an advantage to best the other.

She was wrong. In the blink of an eye, Shatto grabbed Chie's right arm and twisting himself around so that his back was against the Indian's midsection, he pulled Chie over him and threw him on the ground.

Chie rolled away and came up covered with mud. Like an enraged bull, he charged Shatto, who adroitly stepped out of his way.

Indy's hands clasped and unclasped. Her teeth clenched. She could hardly tell who was who, both were so black with mud.

Their arms locked. Bodies twisted and strained, dodged and ducked until, at length, Shatto drew his knife arm back in a half coil and thrust it forward, driving his blade between Chie's ribs all the way to the hilt.

All was silent for a moment. Shatto moved back, his chest rising and falling with exertion. He glanced at Indy and frowned.

Holding his side, Chie managed to sit up. The rain was like a silvery curtain separating him from Shatto. Mud ran down from his head into his eyes and mouth. "Shatto is not Apache," he accused.

"No," Shatto conceded. "I am not Apache. I am white eyes."

Chie nodded slowly, his body beginning to slacken. He fell forward and splashed facedown into the mud.

Immediately Shatto turned to Chie's son, who

stood staring down at his father, his face a pitiless mask. "You will go to your camp and tell your father's braves that Shatto has taken Chie's power. Tell them to return to Cochise."

Without a word, the young warrior ran off into the hills.

Through the curtain of rain Jim stared across at Indy. Then he crossed the distance between them and took her in his arms. She was stiff and unyielding and he knew it was because she was afraid of him. She had seen him fight and kill a man; she had seen him at his worst and he could imagine how he must have looked to her. A savage.

And maybe he was. Maybe six years of living with the Apaches had changed him more than even he had realized. Maybe he wasn't fit to be with his own people anymore.

He felt a painful gnawing deep inside his gut at the thought of what might have happened if his strength had not held out, if he had been wounded or killed. There had been moments when he seriously doubted he would last. The only thing that had kept him going was knowing what Chie would do to Indy once he got her away from Bowie. Rape was the least of it. Chie's brand of revenge demanded the worst kinds of torture that kept his victims alive and suffering for days.

He had no idea how long he had been standing there holding her. He only knew that he couldn't seem to hold her close enough, and that he would kill anybody who tried to take her from him. Even that damn father of hers. The rain came down in torrents, yet Jim couldn't bring himself to let her go. The minute he did he would have to return her to camp, which would mean he would have to take her to her father, whom she had been trying to escape in the first place.

He could guess at the colonel's reaction to their sodden appearance and his inappropriate dress. Questions were inevitable, and it was up to him to answer them since he was responsible. But what could he say? That he had been so desperate to get Indy alone so he could make love to her that he had misplaced his good judgment?

He had been a fool, he thought bitterly. If he had heeded his own warning and stayed inside the camp's perimeters none of this would have happened.

Taking hold of her arms he moved her away from him. "I guess I'd better get you back to camp," he said, more sternly than he had intended. It was hard to know what to say to her. The fact that she wasn't crying surprised him and concerned him. Any other woman would have become hysterical long ago. "Are you all right? Did he hurt you with his knife?"

"Just a little prick. Nothing to worry about." She took a step back.

"Dammit, Indy. You don't look all right."

She took a deep breath and he sensed her frustration. "I'm tired," she said, clenching her hands.

But she was more than tired, he thought, his brows drawing together in a frown. She seemed spiritless, world-weary, and he was partly to blame.

He had started them heading back to camp

when a group of soldiers came running toward them, and another group toward the butcher's building. They stopped and waited.

Sergeant Moseley slid to a stop and saluted. "I've been lookin' all over for you, Major. I wanted to report an Indian pony wanderin' around the parade ground, and I—" He halted midsentence, his eyes widening in alarm when he recognized Indy. "Beggin' your pardon, sir." He sounded embarrassed. "I didn't realize you were— Miss Taylor?" He leaned forward to get a closer look. "Is that you, ma'am?"

"Yes, Sergeant, it's me," she answered, her voice strained.

Jim realized how she must have looked to Moseley. Half-drowned, her hair soaking wet and hanging straight down her back. Her pretty yellow dress all mud-covered and clinging to her slender body like a second skin, showing every curve, every hollow—curves and hollows he didn't want every soldier at Bowie to see.

"We ran into a little trouble, Sergeant, and Miss Taylor here has had quite a scare. I was just taking her back to her quarters."

"Trouble, sir?"

Jim gestured a hand behind him and Moseley went to investigate. It was a moment before the soldier spoke. "What in God's name happened here?" He heeled around and came back to Jim and Indy, looking for an answer.

"I'll make a full report in the morning, Sergeant. Get a detail to bring the bodies into camp, then lay them out under the flagpole."

"Lay them out, sir?"

"You heard me right, Moseley. Lay them out just as they are and don't cover them up. Furthermore, they're to stay there until I give the order that they're to be buried. I want to make sure every soldier at Bowie has a chance to see what dead Apaches look like."

Moseley's forehead wrinkled in confusion. "But, sir—" he started and stopped in two steps. His brow smoothed and a slow smile drew up the corners of his mouth. "Yes, sir! Wise decision, sir. I'll take care of it." He saluted, then shouted orders to his men to go back into camp and get a wagon.

Jim didn't bother saluting back. He couldn't care less about military protocol. Right now the only thing that he did care about was getting Indy back to her quarters.

Moments later they were at Indy's door. When Indy reached for the doorknob he said, "I'm coming in with you, Indy. I need to talk to your father."

"I can tell him what happened," she offered.

"No. I'll tell him."

"Is that an order, Major?"

"Yes." He reached around in front of her, opened the door, and let them inside.

Colonel Charles Taylor looked up from the letter he had been reading. His eyes slowly narrowed with suspicion as he took in the bedraggled couple before him. "What's going on here?" he asked in an accusing tone. He put the letter down on the table next to his chair and rose to his feet, tightening the belt of his burgundy satin dressing gown.

"Father, I—"

"Go to your room, Indy," Jim interrupted. "I'll explain to your father."

"Now, wait just a minute here," the colonel protested, reaching out for Indy's arm as she passed by him. She didn't stop. "Independence!" he shouted, taking a step toward her, but was brought up short when Jim moved in front of him barring the way. "I beg your pardon, Major."

"You can beg it all you want, Colonel, but Indy's been through a lot tonight, thanks to you and me."

Colonel Taylor's eyes darkened to the color of lead. "By God— If you molested her—"

"Would you care?"

"What kind of question is that?"

"A simple one. With a simple yes or no answer."

"I don't think I like your attitude."

"No. I don't imagine you do. You're not used to people challenging your authority."

"Must I remind you who you're talking to, Major? I happen to be your commanding officer. Speaking to me in such a manner could warrant me charging you with in—"

"I know." Jim almost laughed. "Insubordination. And, let me guess, for punishment you'll have me ride the cannon." Jim clenched his hands to his sides, and for one rash, unthinking moment, he considered pulling his knife and jabbing its tip beneath the colonel's chin just to scare him. Nothing would give him greater satisfaction than to see the man quiver like a frightened rabbit.

The colonel must have read his thoughts; his face paled and there was a flash of fear in his eyes that Jim found immensely gratifying. "Why don't you sit down, Colonel, sir?" It was more of an order than a suggestion, but the colonel did indeed sit down. "Now then, like I said, Indy has been through a lot tonight because of you and me."

The moment Indy stepped into her bedroom and closed the door tears filled her eyes and her knees started to quiver. A delayed reaction, she thought, putting her hands over her mouth to stifle her sobs so that neither Jim nor her father would hear.

Weary to the bone, she moved cautiously across the room and grabbed on to the back of the chair and slowly began to remove her clothing, tossing each item into the corner.

Out in the parlor, Jim and her father were arguing. Jim had no regard for her father; she had guessed as much the day she burned her hands on the coffeepot and Jim had defended her rude and impertinent behavior. Now there could be no doubt about Jim's feelings; his tone of voice evidenced his aversion along with the way he mocked her father about riding the cannon. As far as Indy knew, no one had ever talked to Colonel Charles Taylor in such a manner. Maybe if someone had, long ago, he wouldn't have become such a tyrant.

Indy was actually surprised her father didn't order him out. Then she remembered: he needed Major Jim Garrity. Needed him badly. First to salve the troopers' complaints so they wouldn't send in their petition. And second because the Indian commissioner was due to arrive any day. Without Jim's training her father couldn't show that he was making significant changes in his handling of the Apache situation.

No, Indy thought, he wouldn't order Jim out, and he wouldn't press any charges against him, or order any form of punishment. The consequences of Jim not performing the task of training the men would undoubtedly mean the end of her father's military career, a career he had devoted his entire life to.

Within minutes the arguing stopped and Jim began a detailed explanation of how the fire had started and of Chie's thwarted kidnapping plans. That Jim believed Chie had come specifically to capture her so he could use her against her own father to get what he wanted was just one more shock to add to the others she had received tonight.

Her father asked a number of questions but none of them required revealing why she and Jim had gone beyond Bowie's perimeters. Nor did he again ask if she had been molested.

By the time Jim had finished relating the story, Indy was finished washing. She desperately needed a bath but it would have to wait until tomorrow. Choking back a sob, she turned her back to the mirror and looked over her shoulder to see what damage Chie had caused with his knife. There were a couple of bloody spots, little pricks, but nothing serious. Holding a wet cloth and reaching around behind her back, she wiped the area clean, then put on a freshly laundered nightdress.

Rain was still coming down in torrents when Indy finally crawled into bed. It had been a long day and an even longer evening and she was glad for its end. She lay flat on her back, hands clasped over her stomach, staring at the ceiling.

Jim had left a few minutes ago, and now she could hear her father moving around in the parlor. The rustle of paper told her he was refolding Justice's letters and putting them away. His beloved letters that meant more to him than anything else.

She half expected him to knock on the door and insist to speak to her, to chastise her for blatantly disregarding his authority and turning her back on him. But he didn't. Instead, he went into his room and closed the door.

All was quiet now except for the rain, which didn't show any sign of letting up. The September rains were legendary and in spite of bringing relief to the droughtlike conditions that had existed since the middle of May, they were not something to look forward to, according to Ava, Aphra, and Opal, all of whom had been in residence at the first Camp Bowie. Indy recalled their description of the horrors they had suffered from leaking roofs, mold and mildew, herds of insects, spiders, and other creatures seeking shelter from the rains.

In the glow of the lamplight, turned down low, Indy didn't see any signs of the roof leaking. She couldn't imagine anything worse than having to set out pans and buckets to catch the drips, then running around all night long checking on them to make sure they didn't overflow.

"Oh, God!" she groaned, grabbing one of her pillows and holding it close. Who was she fooling? There were things a lot worse than rain and leaks and tending overflowing pans and buckets! There was knowing that she had caused her mother's and brother's deaths. There was her father's hate. There was the fear of being raped and tortured to death by Apaches. And now, there was falling in love with a man who was more savage than civilized.

Like the rain, Indy's tears came in a torrential downpour, wetting the pillow she clung to. She should never have come to Bowie. Not only had she made matters between her and her father worse, so that now there was no hope for reconciliation, but she had indirectly caused the deaths of three soldiers and God only knew how many Apaches and had jeopardized the lives of several others including Captain Nolan and Jim Garrity.

The wisest thing to do would be to catch the first stage back to St. Louis where she was a danger to no one. And once there, she should pack her things and move out of her father's house. It wasn't as if she depended on him for anything. The inheritance her mother had left her would more than provide.

Tomorrow, she promised herself. Tomorrow she would find out about the next eastbound stage.

Chapter 10

Jim Garrity walked down Officers' Row until he came to Aubrey Nolan's quarters, which he and Aubrey were to share during the next few weeks. He stood outside for a few minutes before going in to let the rain wash the mud from his body and clothes.

Aubrey's quarters reminded Jim of his West Point days. The rooms were square and stark, devoid of any furnishings, wall hangings or pictures, curtains, or bric-a-brac of any kind other than what was absolutely necessary. He had to laugh. Even his wickiup had more appeal than this.

Nevertheless, Jim made himself at home. It had been a long time since he had poured water out of a pitcher into a basin to wash himself. A long time since he had smelled lye soap. He stripped naked and washed himself clean. When he had dried off, he opened his saddlebags and took out his only other pair of buckskin trousers, put them on, and stretched out comfortably on the bed and let his mind drift.

He had been out hunting the day the colonel arrived at Bowie via the same ambulance that had later carried his daughter. He had observed him through his field glasses, a remnant, like his saddlebags, from his soldiering days. It was obvious that the man was a martinet, a career officer, who paid more attention to adhering to detail, forms, and methods than to caring about his men. Jim had seen his kind too often during the war and had come to recognize the type before he was even introduced.

Since that first day's observance, there had been several other occasions that he had seen the colonel from afar and had watched, with interest, the way he handled his troopers, leading them out on patrol into the broiling desert heat in their heavy uniforms to look for the enemy Apaches the same way he might go looking for a detail of Rebs in the hills of Tennessee. It might have been amusing if it wasn't so pathetic.

The man was a fool. Even the Apaches thought so. Jim neither liked nor respected him, not only because of the way he treated his men but also because of the way he treated his daughter.

An image of Indy's ravaged expression as she had left the reception after her father had gotten through with her came to mind and he reached for his knife, picking it up off the bedside table. He studied the blade.

There was something else about the colonel that he didn't like. He couldn't pinpoint it exactly, but it had something to do with his posture when he talked to people; his arms were always straight down to his sides and his fingers curled into his palms. It seemed to Jim awkward and unnatural and it made him uneasy.

If it weren't for Aubrey and their long-time friendship, he'd forget the bargain he and the colonel had made and walk away from Bowie, but he owed Aubrey, and he always paid his debts. For six years Aubrey Nolan had been his only link to the world he had left behind—the white man's world, his home, and his family.

Almost an hour had gone by before Captain Nolan returned to his quarters. "For God's sake, Jim. I've been looking all over for you," he said the second he opened the door.

Jim put the knife back on the table. He looked at Aubrey. "That's the same thing Sergeant Moseley said when he found me. Don't you soldier boys have anything better to do than chase after me?"

The captain carefully removed his hat and dumped the water that had collected in the crown into the washbasin. He guffawed. "If we could keep up with you maybe you wouldn't get into so damn much trouble. I've just come back from helping to clean up the mess you made and walked away from. Jesus Christ, Jim! It looked like a Goddamn massacre out there. Three bodies. One of them Chie. Nothing but blood and mud! And here you are . . . bright and clean as a new mirror and not even a scratch!"

Pretending to be grievously offended, Jim said, "Sorry about that. Next time I get attacked I'll make sure to get my throat slit or something equally as bloody."

"Very funny," Aubrey replied dryly as he bent his right leg and struggled to pull off the muddied boot. It came off with a whoosh of air and he tossed it near the door. The left one, however, refused to budge in spite of his efforts. He glanced up and saw Jim watching him.

"Need some help?"

The captain crossed the space between them and presented Jim his foot.

Jim sat up and wrapped one hand over the toe of the boot and the other behind the heel, then pulled back. The boot slid off as if the inside had been greased and hit Jim square in the chest, splattering mud all over his chest and arms.

Aubrey's brows shot up and his brown eyes flashed with amusement. "Sorry," he said, attempting to hide a grin as he reached for the boot.

"Yeah, I can see how sorry you are." Jim stood up and walked over to the washbasin and cleaned himself off for a second time. A moment later, looking composed as ever, he resumed his position on the bed.

Aubrey stripped down to his trousers and pulled a chair out from under the table and straddled it backward. "Are you going to voluntarily tell me what went on out there tonight, or am I going to have to pry it out of you word by word?"

Jim chuckled. "All you had to do was ask." His expression then grew somber and he launched into a detailed retelling of the entire evening from overhearing the colonel publicly accuse Indy of killing her family to his fight with Chie. He prudently left out the description of the intimacies he and Indy had shared.

Dumbfounded, Aubrey shook his head. "Sometimes I don't think I know you at all anymore.

Like the way you came into camp the other day with that dead warrior slung over your horse, and tonight—My God, Jim! If anybody else had told me what you just told me, I would have called him a liar. One man against three Apache warriors! Armed with only a knife!"

"Four," Jim corrected him.

"Four what?"

"Four warriors. That is if you count Chie's son. I let him go."

"What do you mean you let him go?" Aubrey was incredulous.

"Hell, he was just a kid. Seventeen. Maybe eighteen. I told him to tell his people to go back to Cochise."

"What makes you think he will listen to you?" Aubrey wanted to know.

Jim hesitated. For all that he and Aubrey had remained close friends these last six years while he was living in the Valley of Thunder, he had never talked to Aubrey about the Apache way of life, their customs or beliefs. Most white men had trouble accepting the importance that the Apaches attached to their religious ceremonies and superstitions, just as the Apaches considered many of the formalities that the soldiers deemed necessary to be pure foolishness—like lining up for formal roll call instead of just getting started, or riding two by two in a line, or carrying flags.

"Because—when I killed Chie, I took his power."

"Power? What power?"

"Apaches believe that when a man dies he gives up his power. When one man kills another, he may take the dead man's power and add it to his own. The more men he kills, the more power he gains."

"That's ridiculous." Aubrey made a sour face.

"To you maybe, but not to them. It's what they believe," Jim affirmed. "The Apaches are a superstitious people. Chie was thought to have a great deal of power because he had killed many men. That qualified him as a leader among his people."

Aubrey appeared to give the information consideration. "So now . . . you have Chie's power . . . and that added to your power makes you . . . what? Their leader?" Doubt and confusion contorted his face.

"No. Let's just say that they'll think twice before they challenge me."

Aubrey stood up, took a bottle down from a shelf, uncorked it, and poured himself a whiskey. "Here's my power. Join me?"

Jim shook his head. He wasn't a drinker. He had never acquired a taste for whiskey. "You might be interested to know that Chie came here specifically looking for Indy." Aubrey choked down his first mouthful and met Jim's gaze. "I suspected he was after her that day he attacked the ambulance. You weren't carrying any supplies or anything else he would want—except Indy."

"But why would he want her? As a wife? I can't imagine that." Aubrey tapped his fingers against the side of the glass. "A slave maybe?"

"I think it was because she is the *nantan*'s daughter. He probably figured he could use her to bargain with."

"But, Jim. Women come through Apache Pass

all the time. How the hell would he have known that Indy was the colonel's daughter?"

"Didn't I hear you complaining about the condition of the mail coming through San Simon? That it looked like it had been tampered with?" Jim asked.

"Well, yeah, but it's to be expected what with all . . . Wait a minute. Are you suggesting that Chie intercepted the mail and read it? I never heard of an Apache who could read English."

"I'm thinking someone at San Simon reads the mail for him. Chie understands English well enough."

Aubrey stared thoughtfully at the glass he was holding. "That would explain a lot—like how the Apaches always seem to know when supplies are coming through. I'll have to investigate and find out who could be doing it."

"Good idea," Jim agreed. "The sooner the better."

Nolan started to pour himself another shot of whiskey when he stopped abruptly and did an about-face.

"Indy—she wasn't hurt was she?"

Jim gave Aubrey a considering glance. "No. She was scared half to death. Chie's horse damn near trampled her and he threatened her with his knife, but he didn't actually hurt her."

Intense relief washed over the captain's face. "Thank God." His expression abruptly changed to suspicion. "You didn't say what the two of you were doing out there so far from camp?"

Jim frowned. "Not that it's any of your business, but we were walking. I was trying to explain that she cannot be held responsible for giving her brother and mother smallpox when the whole town had it."

"I should have stayed with her at the reception," Nolan said guiltily, completely ignoring Jim's explanation. "I must have been out back rehearsing how I was going to ask the colonel for permission to call on her."

Jim came off the bed as quick as if he had discovered a rattler beneath his mattress. "Call on her? You mean as in court her?" He laughed out loud.

Nolan chuckled. "You think I'm joking? I'm not. I'm serious. I've been thinking a lot lately about getting married, settling down, and starting a family. A few weeks ago I was halfway considering taking a leave so I could go to California and look for the right girl—a girl who wouldn't mind following the drum. And then here comes Miss Independence Taylor. She's everything I would have been looking for. I don't think I could have found anyone more suitable."

"Suitable!" Jim spat the word back. "You mean because she's from a military family?"

Aubrey looked at Jim. "Well, that's just one of the reasons. There's others. She's pretty, well educated—"

Jim was incensed and he didn't know why. "Suitable!" he said again. "That's one hell of a reason to want to marry her if you ask me."

Aubrey frowned, yet his reply was cool. "Nobody's asking you."

"Just because she was raised in a military family doesn't mean she would want to turn around and marry a military man."

"And it doesn't mean she wouldn't either. What the hell is the matter with you? You act like—" Slowly, his mouth widened into a smile and a mischievous look lit his eyes. "By damn! I should have seen it before. You're in love with her yourself!"

Jim swung around, his eyes glittering lethally. "That must be some pretty bad whiskey to get you drunk that fast."

Aubrey persisted. "It's true. Admit it. You're in love with her, aren't you?" Jim bent down and started rifling through his saddlebags. "I wish to hell you would have told me so I wouldn't have gotten myself all worked up for nothing."

"You mean now that you think I'm in love with her, you won't call on her?" At length Jim found his shirt and put it on.

"Hell no! We're friends, Jim. We've been through a lot together. I like Indy. Even care for her. But I'm not in love with her. Not yet, anyway."

Jim stood up, surprised, relieved, and more uncertain about what he was doing than ever. "I need some air. I'm going out," he replied stiffly.

Aubrey smiled benignly. "You'll be back at reveille to pick the men and start training?"

"Haven't I always kept my word?" Jim asked as he opened the door.

Aubrey nodded. "As soon as things calm down around here, maybe after the Indian commissioner has come and gone, I'll put in for that furlough and go to Los Angeles or San Francisco and find me a *suitable* woman."

Jim glanced at Aubrey over his shoulder. "Do what you want. It makes no difference to me one way or another."

"Yeah, I can see that."

The rain had let up, but the sky was still dark with clouds. Disgruntled, Jim followed the well-worn footpath in front of Officers' Row. He walked all the way to the end and found himself standing in front of Colonel Taylor's quarters. The parlor was dark.

It was no happenstance that he had walked this way. He needed to confront his feelings and see if he couldn't make some sense out of the shock of emotion that had gone through him like a fiery arrow when Aubrey had talked of Indy as a suitable wife.

The last time he'd been that emotionally upset was when nobody would believe that those four men he had killed were Reb spies. It was the utter helplessness of being unable to prove it that had made him so violently angry.

The emotions weren't exactly the same. That much he recognized. The incident with Aubrey had made him feel like his heart had been torn out of his chest. With the idiot judge who had convicted him, it was just the opposite. He had wanted to tear the judge's heart out.

Definitely not the same.

So what were his feelings? he wondered. Was he in love with Independence Taylor? He had been attracted to her from the first moment he had laid eyes on her. She was a beautiful woman. As beautiful as Tess but in a different way. Tess was fire and ice with her wild red hair and bright blue eyes. Indy's was a more placid beauty, like a quiet mountain stream. Her light brown hair was soft and silky and had a clean, fresh scent that he couldn't identify. Her eyes were nearly the same color as her hair, but they were anything but quiet. She had by far the most expressive eyes he had ever seen. They told everything she was thinking and feeling. And he couldn't help but listen when they had told him that she liked him kissing her and touching her and that she wanted more.

She wanted him. But unlike Tess, Indy's wanting came from her heart as well as from her body.

He wanted her too. God how he wanted her. But did his wanting come from his heart or was it just a reaction of his body?

It had been a very long time since he had made love to a woman. He couldn't help but wonder if he had taken advantage of the opportunities that had been presented to him, if he would be in this situation now—standing in front of Independence Taylor's window like a lovesick boy.

"Christ," he swore softly. He sure as hell hadn't felt this way about Tess, and he had never fancied himself in love with her.

Then a new thought occurred to him. He wondered if Indy had talked to her father after he had left. And if she had, was she all right? She hadn't been all right the last time she and her father had talked. He was probably worrying over nothing, he thought, but just for the hell of it,

he decided to walk around the side of the building and see if the bedrooms were dark as well. If
they were, he'd leave.

A dim light still burned in Indy's room, but he
didn't see any movement. He walked several
paces to the left, then the right, looking into the
room from every possible angle.

Nothing.

He started to walk away, then stopped and
turned around. He couldn't leave now until he
knew she was all right, he told himself, feeling
better for having come up with a valid reason for
becoming a Peeping Tom.

Like a thief he stole up close to the window
and looked inside. The lamp beside Indy's bed
had been turned down low but not so low that
he couldn't see her. She lay on her side, turned
away from the window. She had kicked the quilt
off and it was on the floor at the foot of her bed.
Her thin nightdress gently hugged her womanly
curves, sloping into the valley of her waist and
rising up over her hips. The hem stopped just an
inch or so below her sweetly rounded bottom and
from there down he could see the bare backs of
her shapely legs.

Suddenly she turned over, dragging one of her
pillows with her and holding it close to her body,
like she had held him. His breath caught in his
throat and he ran his tongue over his bottom lip.
The fire that had flamed earlier and had been
banked by the attack ignited now and centralized
in his groin, causing him to grow painfully hard.

Again, he started to turn away, but at the last
second he saw her throw her leg over the bottom

of the pillow and he couldn't have turned away now if the whole Apache nation had started shooting arrows at him. Sweat broke out on his forehead and he felt like a randy youth who had never experienced a woman.

It was bewildering. Aggravating. And damn irritating.

He considered climbing into her window and just as quickly rejected the notion. It wasn't the threat of her father catching him that stopped him, it was the look of fear that he remembered seeing in her eyes after he had killed Chie.

She was afraid of him. Of what he was—a white man, who had lived with the Apaches for so long that he had become like them—savage.

Whatever he felt for Independence Taylor—love or lust—it didn't matter. He was what he was. He couldn't change himself.

He did turn around then, and slowly walked away, damning his body for having a will of its own and making each step pure torture.

Turning the corner to go back down Officers' Row, Jim unexpectedly ran into Prudence Stallard.

"Why, if it isn't Major Garrity. Where are you going in such a hurry?" She stretched her neck to look around behind him. "Or should I say, where are you coming from in such a hurry?"

"Just making sure everything is ready for tomorrow morning." He leaned his weight to the right, hoping to relieve some of the pressure off his groin. "Isn't it a little late for you to be out?" he asked, turning the questions back to her.

"It is late," she agreed. "I was just on my way

home. Maybe you'd care to walk with me? It's just across the parade ground."

He hesitated, then thought better of it. Maybe a walk was just what he needed to get his mind off Independence Taylor and her damn pillow! "Lead the way."

Prudence slipped her arm around his and crowded up beside him. "Whatever you say, Major."

The laundresses' quarters were similar to the enlisted men's except considerably smaller. They were some twenty feet away from the door when Prudence stopped and turned to him.

"I don't have to go in. It's not as if there's anybody waiting for me." Jim stared down at her, one eyebrow lifted. He was by no means deaf to her implied invitation or blind to her striking beauty. "I know a place close by where we could go and . . . talk."

What the hell? he thought. No one was waiting for him either. He'd be seven kinds of a fool to deny himself *this* opportunity, with a woman so warm and willing.

"I don't feel much like talking," he said in a low, rusty voice.

It was all the encouragement she needed. She led him to the next set of buildings, which was still partly under construction as was much of Bowie. "They're using this for a storeroom right now," she told him, "but later it will be a cavalry barracks." She opened the door. "The beds and bedding were shipped in last week." She made a sweeping gesture with her hand.

It took a moment for Jim's eyes to adjust to

the black interior but once they did he almost laughed. He could count at least twenty iron beds. The mattresses were piled on the floor as were pillows and standard-issue woolen Army blankets. Jim stepped inside while Prudence stayed at the door. He heard the door close behind him.

"Cozy, don't you think?" She came up behind him and slid her arms around his waist. He felt her body's tension, its heat.

"Very cozy," Jim replied nonchalantly. If there was one thing he had learned in his six years with the Apaches, it was never to reveal himself to a stranger. Prudence Stallard, though a very desirable female, was a stranger—a very appealing one to be sure but a stranger nevertheless.

Slowly, carefully, almost as if she were blind, she felt her way around him until she stood before him. At the same time her arms lifted and went around his neck, she pushed the length of her body against his. Jim heard her sharp intake of breath at the moment of contact.

"Well. Well!" She reared her head back to look up at him. "And I was beginining to think you didn't like me." Boldly, without warning, she moved her hand down between their bodies and wrapped her fingers around the hard source of her surprise.

Instinctively, he arched his head back, closed his eyes, and pushed himself into her hand. This was what he wanted, what he needed. *God, how he needed.* He started to reach his hand down to show her the movement, but quickly realized she didn't need any instruction; Prudence Stallard knew exactly what to do to please a man.

"I was right, you know," she whispered, straining toward his ear.

"About what?" He could hardly talk.

"I told that stuffy old Independence Taylor that there was something very different about you, something that set you apart from the others." She giggled. "And now I know what it is."

He reached down and grabbed her hand, stopping her motion. "You discussed me with her?" he asked.

She seemed surprised by his question. "You know how women talk, Jim."

His demeanor changed suddenly. He took a deep breath and backed up a step. "No, I don't. Why don't you tell me."

"I thought you said you didn't feel like talking."

"I've changed my mind."

"Well, there really isn't much to say other than she said you terrify her."

"And you? Do I terrify you too?"

"Do I look frightened?" She made a move toward him, but he stopped her with his hands.

"No, but you should be. I might hurt you. I've lived with the Apaches so long that I've forgotten how to act like a civilized man. Good night, Prudence."

Chapter 11

It was the fresh, clean smell of a new day that awoke Indy from her restless, nightmarish sleep. She opened her eyes slowly. Her bedroom window faced east, affording her an unobstructed view of the slopes of the Chiricahua Mountains, which even in the midst of summer were green with a variety of shrubs and cacti.

Each morning since her arrival, she had awakened in time to watch the sun come up and paint the blue sky with streaks of pink and coral. As long as she lived she would remember the glorious Arizona sunrises.

This morning, however, dark, rain-swollen storm clouds hid the sun. They heaved and churned like the bubbles in the slumgullion that the company cook had the audacity to call stew.

It was appropriate that the weather was so gloomy, Indy thought, sighing. It reflected her mood. It wasn't the thought of going home in defeat that saddened her, for she knew now that it could never have been any other way in spite of her efforts. Her father thrived on blaming her and hating her and would never allow anyone to take that away from him even though he may have been wrong.

It was the thought of Major Jim Garrity that saddened her, the thought that once she left Bowie, she would likely never see him again, yet she knew with a certainty that her mind, her heart, and her body would never allow her to forget him, that they would, in fact, find ways to constantly remind her of him. Torturous ways, no doubt.

She squeezed her pillow, burying her face into its feathered softness but found no comfort. She could see herself back in St. Louis, a moderately wealthy spinster living by herself with nothing to do, no one to love, and no one to love her. She would grow old with her memories of the handsome Major Garrity, the dark and dangerous Shatto. One man. One love.

Out in the parlor she heard the front door open and close and guessed her father was on his way to breakfast. In a short while the bugler would call the camp to assembly for roll call. Almost every morning since plans had been announced to train the troops, one less name answered the call.

Drunk with sleep and body-sore, she cautiously left her bed, put on her wrapper, and went into the parlor. From the parlor window she had a clear view of the parade ground. It was a sea of mud.

Beneath the flagpole, beside the cannon, lay Chie and his two braves. Indy pressed trembling lips together. For the rest of her life she would remember the way that brave had looked at her when he was dying, and the surprised expression on Chie's face as Shatto's knife plunged between his ribs. He had thought himself invincible.

"Rider comin' in," Sergeant Moseley called out in a stentorian voice that carried in the thin early morning air.

Indy's breath caught in her throat at the sight of Shatto. He almost looked exactly as he had that first time she had seen him riding up alongside the ambulance: tall, lean, and proud. He wore that same tan breechclout, knee-high leggings, headband, and cartridge belt that she remembered. And now, in addition, he wore a brown buckskin vest, open all the way down the front.

Her legs went suddenly weak and she quickly pulled out a chair and sat down. It was that same peculiar feeling of being turned inside out that she had experienced last night and it was just as bewildering now as it had been then.

Leaving the mess, Colonel Taylor, followed by the men of G Troop, First Cavalry, and Troop D, Thirty-second Infantry, assembled on the parade ground.

Jim dismounted near the hospital. No sooner had his feet hit the ground than an orderly appeared to take his horse off to the corral.

"Give him some grain," Jim said, stroking the horse's withers. "And rub him down good. We've had a hard morning's ride." Long before sunrise, he had ridden out into the mountains to be alone with his thoughts, all of which directly or indirectly concerned Independence Taylor.

From the first day he'd met her his life hadn't

been the same. It wasn't her fault that he couldn't stop thinking about her, he admitted. Until last night, when he had kissed her and she had kissed him back, she had given him no outward sign that she desired him. But he had known—right from the beginning. He had seen it in her eyes. If she had any idea how her eyes translated her thoughts and emotions, she'd hide them beneath a veil.

The short time he had spent with Prudence had been poisoned by thoughts of Indy. Prudence could have alleviated his body's agony had he not gone lame when she mentioned Indy's name. Exactly what that meant, he wasn't sure, but he sure as hell didn't like the implication.

Was he in love with her? he had reluctantly asked himself. He couldn't deny the passion he'd felt—also right from the beginning, and since then, thoughts of making love to her had caused him many a restless night. It impressed him too that he had become troubled by her relationship with her father because of the constant upset it caused her. Then, last evening, he had damn near gone crazy worrying that he'd be badly wounded or killed and wouldn't be able to protect her from Chie. And when it was over, and he had held her in his arms, it had hurt him to know that she feared him.

The depth of his emotions had been something of an unexpected surprise. He had never felt emotionally attached to any woman, not even Tess.

He had yet to resolve anything when he realized the hour and had to race back to make it in time for roll call. Meanwhile, he had decided that the best thing he could do was stay away from Independence Taylor. She would be the better for it and so would he.

Jim handed over the reins and started walking toward the colonel who stood by the flagpole, looking down at the three dead Apaches. He was acutely aware of the curious looks his clothing, or rather the lack of it, was receiving, especially from the colonel, who overtly scowled his disapproval. They'd all damn well better get used to it, he thought, irked. He sure as hell wasn't going to play Indian in a goddamn wool uniform. Not for anybody!

"Are these corpses lying here your idea of a joke, Major? Because if they are, I want you to know that I'm not amused." The colonel raised a gauntleted hand and waved Sergeant Moseley over. "Have these bodies taken away and buried immediately."

Jim had been watching him closely and consequently his reaction was delayed. "No," he said emphatically. "They'll stay where they are until I give the order to remove them." He would have said more in protest, but he needed to evaluate what he was seeing before it got away from him. The problem with the colonel's pose hadn't been his posture, Jim realized now, but a rigidness caused from the want of common hand gestures when he spoke. Yet, when he wore his gauntlets, as he was now, he made frequent and expressive hand gestures.

The colonel's head jerked up, his mouth pulled and thinned into a tight, angry line. "You'd do well, Major, to remember that you're an officer in my command and as such you'll take orders from me, not the other way around!" His right hand tightly gripped the hilt of his saber.

"Captain Nolan," Jim called over his shoulder in a voice meant to get all the troopers' attention. Aubrey Nolan came forward and saluted. "At ease, Captain." Jim waived a return salute, "Would you take a moment to refresh the colonel's memory about the bargain we made that you witnessed?"

Aubrey Nolan eyed Jim narrowly, obviously not convinced that humiliating the colonel in front of his entire command was the wisest tact to take. Nevertheless, he complied, as Jim knew he would, practically reciting word for word the terms of the agreement, which did indeed give Jim complete authority. Jim found a perverse pleasure in seeing the vein in the colonel's forehead swell with indignation.

"That will do, Captain Nolan," the colonel said acidly. "Your memory for details is commendable."

"Thank you, sir." The captain executed a smart salute and did an about-face and walked away.

Jim resisted a smile. "On that note, sir, I would like to begin looking over the men and making my selections."

The colonel looked ruffled, but maintained his uncompromising authority. "You have my permission to begin, Major."

To Sergeant Moseley, who stood only a few feet away, Jim said, "Call the troops to attention, Sergeant."

Moseley marched to the center of the parade ground. "Attention!"

Like puppets on a string, nearly a hundred troopers fell into formation, standing side by side around the perimeter of the parade ground. They butted their feet together, positioned their arms straight down and close to their sides, and focused unwavering attention on some theoretical object. Their uniforms were of standard-issue blue-black wool, with roll collar blouses, light blue trousers, and dark blue wool kepis for their heads. From Aubrey, Jim had learned that the colonel had flatly refused any individuality in dress, or, even when summer came upon them, to substitute the blue undress blouse for the lighter weight blue flannel shirt.

That would all change for the men he chose for training, Jim thought.

Jim began to walk in front of the men, glancing briefly at each face before going on to the next. Some he recognized as having seen from afar through his field glasses, others from that day Chie had attacked the ambulance, and still others from his visits to Bowie.

Captain Nolan joined him after Jim had made his first inspection. "So what do you think?" he asked in a low voice.

Jim nodded soberly. "I think I've got a lot of work to do," he confided.

"Then you'd better get started."

"I have," Jim said, challengingly. "The first man I'm going to choose is you. You've got all the qualifications that I'll be looking for in them." He slanted his head toward the men on the south side of the parade ground. Then in earnest added, "I want you with me on this, Aubrey. The men look up to you, respect you. It isn't going to be easy getting them to do the things I'm going to ask them to do. The Apaches didn't learn to become skilled warriors overnight; they were taught from childhood. We've only got a few weeks."

Aubrey's mouth tightened into a grimace. "Are you going to make me run around half-naked like you?"

"If it's necessary," Jim quipped. If he had thought for a moment Aubrey didn't want to be included, he wouldn't have asked him, but they had been friends too long, been through too much together, for him not to be sure of Aubrey's response.

Aubrey lifted his eyes and looked away. "What the hell! I'm with you, but only because I wouldn't want you to have all the fun!" he said, his index finger shooting out at Jim.

A smile appeared on Jim's lips but never actually reached his eyes. "I assume you've told the men all about me. I don't want my past rearing its ugly head and causing problems. They'll need to trust me, Aubrey. Their lives will depend on it."

"They know. I've told them everything. I don't think anyone here doesn't know what you were up against and why you chose to escape and desert. The only problem I foresee is a question of your relationship with the Apaches. I'd suggest you explain it to them as you did to me. They're not stupid, Jim. They'll understand. Many of them already do. Fact is, quite a few of them were instrumental in helping me formulate the plan that brought you here. I'll point them out to you as you make your selections. We have a lot of good, honest men here. Men who want to make Arizona a prosperous territory where people can start businesses and raise families. Most of them advocated the training. The ones that didn't— Well, you'll be able to pick them out," he said with confidence.

"Let's hope so," Jim said dryly as he strode toward the center of the parade ground. It had been a long time since he'd had his own command—since the war. His last order was the one that had ended him up in jail, accused of killing four Yankee soldiers. Only they weren't Yanks. They were Johnny Rebs, disguised in Yankee blues.

Hands on hips, legs spread slightly apart, he stood alone before them. If he was in their boots, he too would be wondering what kind of man would call the Apaches his friends, then teach their sworn enemies to fight them. He could see that a question of loyalty would arise. It had risen within himself and he had struggled with it.

Thanks to Toriano, he had overcome his misgivings about leaving behind his Apache friends and training the troopers. For all that he and Toriano were nearly the same age, there was in Toriano an age old wisdom that allowed him to see things differently than most men. He never said if a thing was good or bad, or tried to persuade Jim to think as he thought, only to help him to look at a thing from all sides so that he could make his own judgment and decision.

Toriano had long known that the day was coming when the Apaches would no longer be free to ride on the wind, go where they wanted to go, do what they wanted to do. He told Jim he saw the size of his world grow smaller with each new white man who came into the territory and claimed a piece of the land for his own. Apaches didn't understand why the white man needed to own land, why he couldn't just live on it and make use of it, but because they had this need, they would take and take until there was nothing left.

Jim had discussed the peace plans of the white eyes' new *nantan* in Washington and the concepts of the reservation system with Toriano, and both had agreed that it was inevitable that the Apaches would have to come to a decision, surrender or face extinction.

First things first, Jim told himself, getting his thoughts together. The men needed to know exactly where he stood and why. He couldn't expect them to trust him if they thought him a Judas.

As he opened his mouth to speak, he realized he was being watched from afar. He stole a glance at the austere line of adobe buildings that were Officers' Row. He knew it was Indy even before he saw her sitting in front of her parlor window. He had sensed her, felt her. It was curious how he had known. Quickly averting his gaze, he tried to think what he had been about to say before she had distracted him.

"The Apaches have a saying," he began, somewhat uncertainly. "It's better to be dead than be tamed." He paused to add emphasis to his words, then went on to explain what his position had been with the Apaches and what it was now. He told them that he felt that the use of trained scouts would ultimately end the Apache wars and save lives. He made a complete circle as he spoke, studying their reactions. Everything from respect to contempt was reflected on their faces.

That out of the way, he said, "As many of you already know, last night, while you were busy enjoying yourselves, dancing and drinking, Chie and three of his braves paid Bowie a visit. They shouldn't have gotten anywhere near camp without somebody sounding an alarm. That's called negligence." He pivoted and his gaze rested briefly on Colonel Taylor. "I will not tolerate carelessness, idleness, or cowardice." Among the men there were many long, sad faces. "Sergeant Moseley," Jim said brusquely. "Order the men to parade slowly in front of those corpses. I want them to see that Apaches are flesh and blood like everyone else, and that they can be killed—like everybody else." As soon as he had spoken, he walked to the flagpole and casually leaned against it.

Sergeant Moseley gave the order and the men tramped slowly through the mud, splashing the men in front of them and the men behind them. Jim watched each man's face as he looked down at the bodies. Any man who flinched, he ordered out of line. From a total of ninety-eight troopers, he eliminated twelve and returned them to their normal morning duties.

After the men had resumed their positions, Jim again stood before them and told them what he would expect from them mentally and physically. He spoke of the rigors of the training he planned, of the hardships and adverse conditions they would undoubtedly suffer, the dangers they would face, and when he had finished, he clasped his hands behind his back and cut a glance to Aubrey who was staring at him like he didn't know him.

From the west side of the parade ground, a freckle-faced infantry soldier stepped forward. Jim looked at his young face and imagined it face-down in the sand. "Do you have something you want to say, Private?"

"Yes, sir." His Adam's apple bobbed up and down. Clearly, he was nervous and scared. "You can label me a coward if you want, but I ain't riskin' my neck for no lousy thirteen dollars a month." He slapped his hat against his thigh and half ran, half walked away from the assembly.

"That goes for me too," said a veteran corporal. "I'm too damn old to go traipsing all over this godforsaken territory after them red devils. I've already killed my quota and I figure to take it real easylike till my enlistment is up."

As the corporal started to leave the parade ground, Colonel Taylor stepped forward and ordered him back.

"Let him go," Jim said, countering the colonel's order. "He's right. He is too old for this kind of duty. He couldn't stand up to it." Jim's hard-eyed gaze challenged the colonel to refute his authority. Wisely, he said nothing at all, but Jim knew his type well enough to know that someday, somehow, he would get even. Colonel Charles Taylor was a vindictive man.

In all, eighteen men abandoned the parade ground, which left sixty-eight, and of those Jim knew another twenty would be found unsuitable for one reason or another after closer inspection.

Impressive was the word that came to Indy's mind as she observed the way Major Garrity handled not only her father but the entire garrison. Throughout her life she had met dozens of Army officers and had come to realize that they were not all made of the same stuff and too many of them ended up martinets like her father.

Major Jim Garrity, though obviously a leader, who would demand obedience and punish disobedience, would never be more concerned with the methods of soldiering than with the soldiers themselves.

It had startled her when he suddenly glanced her way. His gaze, though brief, was profound. She had been staring at him, remembering how he tried to convince her that she wasn't responsible for her mother's and brother's deaths. His words had given her succor, and his arms had provided comfort.

He had *felt* her gaze upon him, she realized, the wonder of it making her breathless. She knew it as surely as she knew she had fallen hopelessly in love with him.

She got up immediately after he turned back to his men, defending her actions by telling herself that she needed to get dressed, fix herself something to eat, and then see if she couldn't find someone who could tell her when the next eastbound stage would be departing.

A short while later she stepped outside and adroitly avoided a pothole that had become a small pond. The sky loomed dark and forbidding and looked to open up and release its reservoir of water at any moment. It was odd, but instead of trying to identify the new smells brought on by the rain, all she could think about was that for the first time since she had come to Bowie she didn't smell dust.

She had gone but a few feet from her door when Prudence called her name. "May I speak with you a moment?" she asked.

There was a look of sadness in Prudence's china-blue eyes that made Indy curious as to what was on her mind. Maybe she was going to apologize for last night's bold behavior. "Yes, of course, but could you do it as we walk? I need to make inquiries about when the next stage leaves for the East."

"You're leaving? But I thought—" She made a small sound of distress that alerted Indy.

"You thought what?" Indy asked, frowning.

Prudence turned her back on the parade ground and partially covered her mouth with her hand. "I thought you and the major—" she said in a half whisper.

Another half-said sentence! It was annoying. "Me and the major what?" Indy probed, determined to find out what she was inferring. It started to drizzle. Reluctantly Indy suggested they go inside before they got wet. "Now then, you were going to explain?"

Prudence's hands could not seem to keep still. "It's just that I assumed you and Major Garrity had become . . . more than just acquaintances."

Indy felt her cheeks grow hot. Obviously Prudence had observed her after she had left the reception and Jim had stopped her. At least she hoped it was then and not later when things had become a bit more intimate.

"You mean because of last night when Jim kissed me outside the mess?" she asked, trying to confirm her suspicions.

Prudence pulled a chair out from the table and sat down. Indy did the same and then waited.

Gazing out the window at the parade ground, Prudence said, "Well, you have to admit, it would indicate that you were more than just friends."

"I can see where you might think that, but it isn't so. I was overwrought about what my father had said, which I'm sure you must have overheard, as did everyone else. I went outside and was going to run as far and as fast as I could, but the major stopped me, realized how upset I was, and refused to let me go. Next thing I knew he was kissing me."

"I see," said Prudence.

"No you don't. It was just his way of comforting me, nothing more, and then . . . Well, you know the rest." She drew a deep breath, then sighed and focused her concentration outside on the parade ground.

Prudence's hand covered hers and Indy gasped in surprise and scooted her chair back a few inches.

"You really are naive, aren't you, Indy?"

Indy resettled herself. "In some things, yes, I suppose so. In others, I'm wiser than Moses," she said with heavy sarcasm. "What does my naïveté or lack of it have to do with anything? What is all this about for heaven's sake?"

Prudence sighed wearily. "Part of me, the jealous side, says I shouldn't tell you what I know and the other part of me, Major Stallard's widow, says I should because you're the only one who's been nice to me and who hasn't gone around talking about me behind my back."

"Prudence—"

"No. Please. No interruptions. You may have something very different to say to me after I've finished saying what I have to say."

Indy sat back and braced herself.

"Late last night, very late, after everything had calmed down, I was on my way back from"—she cleared her throat—"visiting a friend, when I ran into Jim. He was coming away from the east side of this building, where your bedroom window is, I think. He said he was making sure everything was ready for this morning, but I didn't believe him. He was looking real unhappy, like he'd just lost his prized stallion. I asked him if he'd walk me back to my quarters, thinking that once I got him all to myself, he would make . . . Well, you know," she said, waving her hand dismissively.

"Yes," Indy said blandly. She felt benumbed, hurt. But she would force herself to wait until Prudence had finished her tale before making any judgment or drawing any conclusion. As if that was really possible!

"Of course, you've known all along how I felt

about Jim. Even before I knew that he wasn't an Apache."

"Yes, you managed to make yourself perfectly clear." Resentment had a firm grip on her already.

Prudence pointed her index finger at Indy. "But *you* never made yourself clear. You were as taken with him as I was and you never said a word."

Indy opened her mouth to speak but nothing came out. Her first thought was to deny it, but she knew that Prudence would know she was lying. "No, I didn't," she admitted at length, but was loath to say anything more. Enough had been revealed already.

"You can't leave Bowie, Indy," Prudence said with fervor. "You love that man and he loves you." She chuckled. "He may not know it, but he does. Men are slow to know their feelings."

It took Indy a few seconds to recover herself. "Do I dare ask how you know this?" she ventured, half afraid to learn the answer.

The answer was a long time in coming. Head bent, eyes cast downward, Prudence said, "I know Aphra, Ava, and Opal have told you about me and what I was doing when Major Stallard found me. I'm not denying what I was: a saloon girl. I made my living off of men. That qualifies me to understand them better than most, so when I tell you Jim Garrity is in love with you, you can count on it." She stood up. "You don't believe me. I can tell. You're going to make me tell you exactly how I know, right?"

Indy did nothing more than raise an eyebrow.

"All right. I didn't figure it out myself until

after he had left and I thought about what happened." She hesitated, evidently not quite sure she was doing the right thing by telling. "When I ran into him, I think he must have just come from looking in on you. Maybe to make sure you were all right. Whatever he saw caused him to become . . . Oh, God, Indy. Tell me you know *something* about what happens to a man's body when he wants a woman."

Indy looked away, so embarrassed she could feel the blush heat climbing up her neck into her face, even her ears. "I have sort of an idea," she managed, choking out the words. She remembered now with vivid clarity when Jim had pushed her against the adobe building and she had felt his rigidness pressing into her skirts.

Prudence wiped invisible perspiration away from her brow. "What I'm trying to say is that it was you he wanted. Then I came along and thought it was me he desired, right up until the second I said your name. I've never seen a man turn cold like that before. Do you get my meaning, Indy? I hope you do because I sure don't want to have to get any more detailed than that."

Indy nodded her head emphatically. She couldn't bear hearing any more of the vivid details. Quite enough had been said.

Prudence moved toward the door. "This really isn't what I came to tell you. I'm leaving Bowie as soon as I can manage it and going back to doing what I do best, being a saloon girl. I thought I'd try my luck in Tucson. I wanted to thank you for being kind to me." She had one foot out the door when she turned back briefly

and said, "And by the way, I've never told anyone
this so don't you go telling anybody, but I really
loved that old coot I married."

The moment the door closed Indy slumped in
her chair, as if the air had gone out of her.

In the theater of her mind, she saw the entire
performance as Prudence had described it from
the time she and Jim had run into each other:
the two of them walking together in the cloud-
dark night, talking low so their voices wouldn't
disturb, going into each other's arms with fevered
kisses and hands reaching, caressing, touching.
Touching everywhere. All the forbidden places,
the places that longed and yearned and . . . An-
gered by what she saw, she dropped the curtain
on the play, and when she pulled it up for the
second act, the understudy, herself, had taken
Prudence's place.

The imagined warmth of Jim's touch still lingered when she lifted her gaze and looked out the
window. She saw Sergeant Moseley and Captain
Nolan moving slowly down a line of men. They
each had a canteen from which they poured a
small amount of liquid into a tin cup. After the
soldier had drunk it, he handed it back and
started running around the perimeter of the parade ground.

For the life of her Indy couldn't figure out what
they were doing. Jim was nowhere in sight and
her father was heading for the sutler's store at a
fast pace, looking for all the world like a man
with a bad toothache.

"You love that man and he loves you," Prudence
had said. Was it true? she wondered. Could it be

that Major Jim Garrity was in love with her, as she was with him? Had he looked in her window because he'd been worried about her? It must have been after she had fallen asleep. How long had he watched her? But more importantly, what had he seen that would cause him to become aroused? She didn't think she wanted to know how Prudence knew that.

She had been sitting there in front of the window, still and silent for nearly an hour, when suddenly she remembered what she had been about to do before Prudence had confronted her. The stage schedule.

Even if what Prudence said was true and Jim did love her, they could never have a life together. There was no common ground between them; they were from different worlds.

Besides that, there was her fear of him. She wasn't sure exactly where it came from, but it was there, deep inside her, and it manifested itself every time he came near her.

She needed a quiet man, a placid man. A nice staid banker, perhaps. Or a merchant. Major Jim Garrity—Shatto—was too volatile, too unpredictable and given to impulsiveness. She would never have the peace of mind of knowing how he would react in any situation. He was as wild and untamed as the Apaches he had lived with. He could never be domesticated and made completely civilized.

With those thoughts buried within her breasts, she jumped up and was out the door before she could change her mind about going home. In spite of her carefulness to keep out of the potholes and wagon ruts, her shoes were covered with slimy mud within seconds. The clerk behind the desk in the adjutant's outer office greeted her with a gap-toothed smile.

"I'd like to find out when the next stage will be heading east from San Simon please."

"You're not thinkin' of leavin' us already are you, Miss Taylor?"

Indy gave a half smile. "I'm afraid I have to get back home as soon as possible."

"Oh. I hope it ain't nothin' urgent, 'cause we got us a problem. Had a runner come in just a few minutes ago with word that Cochise has been terrorizing the whole San Simon Valley. All stage and freighting arrivals and departures have been suspended until the situation is improved."

"But that could be—"

"A long time," Jim finished for her, in a slow voice.

Indy swung around, then froze. He stood in the doorway, leaning against the jamb, holding a message in his hands. He glanced back down at it, ignoring her. She could see his fierce expression and wondered what had caused it. It was the same expression that he'd worn when he had challenged Chie, the same expression as when he'd plunged his knife between Chie's ribs. The blood in her veins turned to ice and she felt herself tremble in reaction.

"But— You don't understand," she said in a small voice. "I need to go home. I shouldn't have come in the first place."

He looked up at her with those dark, *killing* eyes. "No, Indy. You don't understand," he contradicted her. "The stage isn't running so you aren't going anywhere."

She gave a nervous laugh. "Well, surely there must be other routes, other stage lines."

"There's one that leaves out of Prescott once a week." At her expectant look, he added, "But in order to get you there, we'd have to send a detachment out with you and that's not possible, especially right now. The only men I would trust to escort you are going to be with me. I'm sorry, Indy, but you'll have to wait. Arizona just isn't a safe place to be right now."

"No, it certainly isn't," she retorted, giving his statement a different meaning altogether. When she started toward the door, Jim stepped aside, but only slightly.

"If there's anything I can do—anything you need, Indy. All you have to do is ask."

"You've done quite enough, thank you." She stepped outside. The troopers had stopped running and were again standing at ease. One by one they leaned forward and spat a mouthful of water onto the ground in front of them.

"It's a test," Jim explained without her asking. Again, he had come up behind her without her hearing him—like an Indian, she thought. "Each man takes a mouthful of water and holds it in his mouth while he runs twenty times around the parade ground, or approximately four miles. If he loses it or swallows it, he fails the test."

Indy frowned. "But what does it determine?"

"His ability to take orders, to concentrate—to do as well as an Apache boy."

Indy started back toward her quarters. "Seems

like a pretty silly test to me," she mumbled beneath her breath.

Jim's laughter followed her halfway across the parade ground. Indy, however, was not in the least amused for she realized that it would be up to Major Jim Garrity and his yet to be trained company of white scouts to make those improvements in the Indian situation that would allow the stage line to continue operation.

Chapter 12

By late afternoon the sun had burnt off the clouds and slowly moved across the western sky like a giant fireball, taking the temperature to well over the century mark. Beneath the sun's merciless rays the rain-soaked parade ground cooked. A vapor of steam rose out of the mud.

Indy was miserably hot. And sticky. Her simple calico dress clung damply to her back and she could feel perspiration trickle down between her breasts. The parlor was an airless oven that was sapping her energy. When she could stand it no more, she picked up her father's padded foot-stool, located the one and only parasol she had brought, of a dark serviceable material that would shield her against the sun, and went outdoors.

While trying to decide where the best place would be to set her stool, she noticed Aphra and Opal coming back from the sutler's store and felt a stab of envy for the close friendship they shared. Indy waved and they waved back, but as usual, they didn't give any indication that they would like to have her join them. They had each other and that seemed to be enough for them.

She placed her stool up close to the wall

beside the parlor window, sat down, and leaned
against the cool adobe. A small breeze, coming
through the mountains off the San Simon Valley,
made quick work of drying her dress.

Shaded by her parasol, she resumed watching
the activities on the parade ground. The original
ninety-eight troopers had been whittled down to
thirty. Those remaining looked to be capable of
most any task assigned them.

In making his selections, it appeared Jim had
not concerned himself to a man's rank, but instead had selected each man on his individual
merit. Ava's husband had been returned to duty
at the onset of the selection process due to his
impending fatherhood. Aphra's and Opal's husbands had been disqualified because of their ages.

Prior to her coming outside, a dozen horses
had been brought up from the corral and picket
pinned. All were lean and muscled. Their coats
shone with good grooming and health. Docilely
they stood by, swishing their tails at flies and
occasionally blowing dust out of their nostrils.

The last Indy had seen of Jim Garrity, he had
been walking with her father to the adjutant's
office. That had been an hour ago. It came to her
that with the exception of her talk with Prudence,
and this morning's jaunt to check on the stage,
she had done nothing all day long but watch Jim,
as if her eyes couldn't get their fill of him. No
matter who or what drew her attention away, her
gaze was pulled right back to him as if magnetized.

A question haunted her: Why had the mention
of her name caused him to so abruptly end his
late-night tryst with Prudence?

During Jim's absence, Captain Nolan taught the infantrymen, most of whom had no knowledge of horses or riding, how to clean stones and other debris out of their horses' hooves. "A stone, left in the hoof too long, can cause a horse to go lame," he explained. "Your new skills will be your most valuable asset when fighting the Apaches. Your horse is second, so take good care of him, treat him with the respect he deserves, and he'll bring you home."

Leaving the men to work on their horses' hooves, Captain Nolan hastily retreated from the parade ground. Beating his hat against the side of his leg, he made his way across to Indy. He was shaking his head as if there was something he just couldn't quite comprehend.

"Is everything going as well as you had hoped, Captain?" Indy thought he looked tired but exhilarated. He was certainly dirty, even dirtier than she had been last night.

He came up to stand in front of the hitching post and leaned against it. "Better than I'd hoped. We've got thirty able-bodied men, good men, who will give all they've got and more. There's probably a couple of troublemakers in the group, but there always are. It's unavoidable. Jim can handle them though."

During the welcome reception, Captain Nolan had talked briefly about his long friendship with Jim, but now Indy realized he looked up to Jim as well.

"Though I'm hardly qualified to judge, it seemed to me he was very hard on the men, demanding more of them than they were capable of doing." As soon as she had said it, she knew it wasn't so. It was just her own frustration coming out. Watching Jim Garrity all day long demonstrating various physical exercises to help the men build stamina had strained her ability to remain indifferent to him as much as Jim had worked and strained the hard muscles of his magnificent body—to nearly the breaking point. The result was that she had spent the day in a continuous state of physical agitation.

"There's different kinds of *hard*, the mean-spirited kind or the for-your-own-good kind. Those men's lives are going to depend on Jim teaching them all he knows of fighting and survival. They may grow to hate him and some of them may even want to kill him before this is over, but if he's too easy with them, they won't survive their first encounter with the Apaches."

"I don't mean to sound pessimistic, but how much effect can thirty scouts really have?"

"We're only going to be fighting the Chiricahua Apaches, Cochise's band. They have several strongholds within a few days ride. So far, they've made a complete mockery of our efforts, playing with us like a cat plays with a mouse. As far as they're concerned, we don't even qualify as worthy opponents. Once those troopers are trained and put out into the field, tracking down Apaches, sniffing them out of places they thought were inaccessible to the bluecoats, I think they'll have a tremendous effect.

"Ultimately, I believe the use of scouts, Apache scouts now, not white men trained to scout, will be the means to the end."

"It would have saved a lot of time if my father had agreed to let you hire Indian scouts, wouldn't it?"

"Yes, but it's not difficult to understand his thinking. Using Indian scouts in place of soldiers causes doubt about the capabilities of the regular troops, especially in the minds of the generals in charge. And besides that, there's a feeling that soldiers should be civilized men, not savages."

"Of course, you know, Captain," Indy stressed, "that assuming the scout company is successful, my father will take all the credit." She gave him a long, hard look, then added, "It's entirely possible that neither you nor Major Garrity will be recognized for your efforts."

He nodded. "I can't speak for Jim, Indy, though I'm certain he's of the same mind as I am. I'm not looking for accolades or medals. My goal is to bring this territory to peace with a minimal loss of lives."

"A very noble ambition, Captain. But then, I already had figured you for a noble man." The compliment came from her heart. Captain Aubrey Nolan was the kind of officer she wished her father was; someone to look up to, to be proud of.

He snuggled his hat onto his head. "If anyone is noble, it's Jim. He lived with the Apaches for six years. They gave him a home and called him their friend. He's bound to feel like a traitor even though the Apaches won't see it that way. Apparently they have a different way of looking at things than we do."

"I didn't think of that," she admitted. "It must

have been a very difficult decision for him to make."

"It was."

Frowning, the captain shifted his weight. "Forgive me for changing the subject so abruptly, but I wanted to tell you how sorry I am about what happened last night with Chie. Jim told me everything. It shouldn't have happened."

"It's over now, Captain," she answered slowly. "I wasn't injured. I'm hoping to be able to put it behind me."

"Well, just so you'll know it didn't get ignored, I checked into the matter and discovered that the sentries assigned to duty did a little celebrating of their own. I presented the men to your father and he's dealing with them."

"I hope not too severely. I wouldn't want to see anyone locked up in the guardhouse on a day like this."

"I don't know. It wasn't up to me."

Something—a feeling—a sixth sense—pulled her gaze away from Captain Nolan. She turned her head and squinted.

From out of the glare of the sun, Jim Garrity walked southeast across the parade ground toward Officers' Row. She would have thought that after observing him in his breechclout and open vest the whole day long, she would have grown accustomed to his near nakedness, to the breadth of his shoulders, muscled chest, and powerful thighs and legs. Every exposed inch of him was brown, not as dark as the Apaches, but shades darker than any of the other soldiers.

He exuded danger, like a predatory animal. But

was he a danger to her? She hated being afraid of him. She reflected upon those incidents that had frightened her. At no time had he threatened her. In fact, he had rescued her. Saved her. Twice from Apaches. And twice from her father.

It was the predator in him then, Indy rationalized, that was causing her to be afraid.

Men weren't born with predatory instincts or skills, they learned them.

Fear was also learned. And could be conquered.

For the last hour, the colonel had been questioning Jim about Cochise. Jim was surprised when the colonel told him that until several months ago, after receiving orders to take command of Camp Bowie, he had never heard of Cochise.

Jim thought everyone had heard of Cochise. He had been a prominent war chief since before the war. The letters Jim's parents sent him through Captain Nolan often expressed concerns over his association with the famed Apache chieftain. From time to time he even got newspaper clippings that dramatized some of Cochise's grander exploits, making him seem an almost invincible foe who commanded legions of painted and feathered red men.

Sometimes the articles were amazingly close to the truth.

Jim didn't object to telling the colonel what he could. He had been in Cochise's stronghold several times, smoked pipe with him, and learned as much about him as anyone could.

Upon the colonel's desk lay stacks of Eastern and territorial newspapers and a box of reports from the Commission of Indian Affairs. All were completely ignored while they talked.

"Tell me, Major. Have you thought ahead to the day the men are through with their training?"

"I have. I plan to send them all out together as one unit for a while. I have a feeling that once they're seen in action, word will get around to the various Apache bands that they're being hunted by white wolves. It should make them think twice before they go on another raid."

"White wolves, Major?"

"A wolf is a respectful term the Indians use for their own scouts. When I'm through with those men out there we'll have a company of wolves."

"I see. A Wolf Company. White wolves." It seemed to Jim he was testing the words to see how best to fit them together.

"Very good, Major. I don't like your arrogant attitude, but I do like what you're doing, and I guess that's what counts. I'll make a note in my report about your wolf company. But for the official paperwork to my superiors, I will call them Camp Bowie's Independent Scout Company."

At the onset of their conversation, Jim had reminded himself to be aware of the colonel's hands and gestures now that he wasn't wearing his gauntlets. His hands were balled into fists and his arms straight down against his sides, as if he had been called to attention. As to his gestures, he didn't make a one the whole time they talked.

It didn't seem natural, Jim thought, to talk without using your hands to gesture and express yourself. Yet, when the colonel was wearing his gauntlets, as he had been this morning, he used his hands expansively.

After leaving the adjutant's office, Jim went to see Doc Valentine to inquire about various conditions that might affect the hands.

"Doc's delivering a baby," the orderly told him, so Jim headed back to the parade ground to begin putting the infantrymen on horses.

Jim held his concerns and wonderings before him like an Apache war shield as he made his way across the parade ground. He thought about the colonel, his sudden interest in Cochise, the stacks of newspapers and reports, and the odd way he had responded to the mention of the company of wolves.

On that one last thought, it came to him what the colonel was thinking. Coalescing inside his head, he saw the bold, black lettering that was the headlines of an Eastern newspaper.

COCHISE CAPTURED!
APACHE WARS AT AN END!
COL. CHARLES TAYLOR LEADS WOLF COMPANY INTO BATTLE AT APACHE PASS
WEST POINTER AWARDED MEDAL OF HONOR FOR BRAVERY AND VALOR!
ARIZONA TERRITORY OPEN TO SETTLERS, MERCHANTS, FREIGHTERS

Jim reminded himself to tell Aubrey what he had discovered at the first opportunity. That way, both of them could be on the lookout for signs of trouble.

Ambition, Jim thought grimly, could be a powerful force within a man, especially if it got coupled with vengeance. And the colonel had plenty of that in him. He had made it plain from the beginning that the War Department had mistakenly assigned him to Bowie. In a way, Jim didn't blame him for his anger. Colonel Charles Taylor wasn't cut out for the hardships of frontier duty; he was a textbook soldier, whose expertise was in engineering, not Indian fighting.

Jim was sure what galled the colonel the most was that the mistake had yet to be corrected, which led Jim to wonder if it really was a mistake and not a sly reprimand for some military infraction that even he wasn't aware he had committed.

Jim's whole life had been the military, from the day he had turned eighteen and entered West Point until six years ago when he had escaped. In that time he had learned to expect the unexpected and count on nothing.

Aubrey was standing by the hitching post in front of Indy's quarters, waving to Jim to join him.

"Where have you been? The horses are anxious to teach these men how to ride." Aubrey had a jackass grin on his face, clearly anticipating a show.

Jim wished he could share his good humor, but he had too much on his mind. "Having a talk with the colonel. Remind me to tell you about it."

"I've been discussing you with Miss Taylor."

Glowering, Jim glanced behind him. He hadn't

acknowledged Indy when he'd walked up. The cursory glance was all she was going to get. She had become a fire in his blood, setting him to boil every damn time he was near her and looked into her eyes. Even those few moments this morning in the adjutant's office had done their work on him.

Damn her soft brown eyes, anyway! "I wish everybody would mind their own business and find someone else to talk about besides me."

"What's the matter with you? Did a snake crawl into your bedroll?"

Jim didn't dignify Aubrey's questions with an answer. Instead, he called Sergeant Moseley over and told him that it was time to get started. "Have the men who can ride help those who can't."

"Yes, sir, Major. This is going to be real interesting." The sergeant had abandoned saluting at the major's request but hadn't stopped the formal address. He headed back to the middle of the parade ground, briskly rubbing the palms of his hands together as though they'd been frostbitten.

Indy had pretended to ignore Jim's scowling glance and thought it was just as well; the less they had to do with each other, the better. Flashing him a look of disdain, she lifted her chin and focused her attention on the sergeant, wondering why he seemed so gladdened by lessons in horsemanship.

Even if some of the men had never ridden a horse before, they would learn quickly enough. There were some things men just took to naturally, the way women took to . . . quilting, she reasoned, although personally, she disliked quilting, or maybe she just disliked the gossip that always seemed to accompany it.

Sergeant Moseley stood before the company. "All right, you wolf cubs. We're gonna have us some learnin' in the fine art of horsemanship." Sarcasm dripped like tree sap from his words. "Untie them horses and get them in line."

"I've been waiting for this," Captain Nolan said. A look of mischief came into his eyes and a smile played at the corners of his mouth, reminding Indy of the first time she had seen him smile and how she had thought it flattered his face.

Out of the side of his mouth, Jim said dryly, "Don't take your eyes off that big roan. He's got a real unusual disposition."

Closing her parasol and leaning it against the side of the building, Indy got off her stool and went around the hitching post to stand next to Captain Nolan. She suspected that all of them were up to some kind of tomfoolery and found herself eagerly anticipating a good laugh. She remembered then the fan she had bought at the sutler's store and considered going back after it, but was afraid she would miss something.

In a voice loud as a trumpet, the sergeant blared, "Mount up!"

To a man, the infantrymen looked like the sergeant had lost his mind. "There's no saddles," one man braved.

"Is that a fact?" Sergeant Moseley thoughtfully rubbed his beard-bristled chin. "Well, I guess I'll have to see about that."

As if on cue, Jim moved to the invisible edge of the parade ground. "You heard the sergeant. Mount up. This isn't a cavalry unit; it's a wolf company. In case you haven't noticed, Apaches don't have saddles. Weights the horse down." When the trooper just stared at him, Jim said, "That's an order, mister!"

The young private scrambled to comply and ran to his assigned horse, grabbed on to his mane, and swung one long leg up onto the roan's back. Briefly, the look of victory lit his youthful face, then turned to horror when the roan reared up, sending him sliding willy-nilly off his back into the mud.

Indy let out a gasp of astonishment and looked to see that the young man wasn't hurt. Cursing like a teamster told Indy the only damage done was to his ego. She brought her hand up to stifle a giggle. Even as the private was picking himself up out the mud, his fellow troopers were making similar attempts to mount their horses, which resulted in more of the same.

Between the men sliding off sleekly curried backs, loud cursing the likes of which made Indy curl her toes, and several mounted riders whose rein-sawing made their horses go through all kinds of contortions, sidesteps, and turns, the scene on the parade ground had become a circus, complete with a ringmaster, clowns, trick riders, and dancing horses.

Indy had never laughed so hard in all her life. She laughed so hard her stomach hurt. Everywhere she looked horses were rearing and bucking, turning in circles and reaching their heads around to bite the men hanging on to their manes. There were plaintive whinnies and disdainful snorts. The men yelled, cursed, and called the horses such startling names that Indy was left openmouthed and gaping.

There was no time to recover herself from laughing at one thing before discovering something else even funnier. But for having to wipe stinging sweat from her eyes, she hardly noticed the heat or the way the sun beat down on her head.

Captain Nolan was beside himself, bent forward, slapping his leg with his hat, laughing in loud spontaneous bursts that had Indy laughing at him as well.

Even Jim was heartily amused, Indy noticed when she was forced to stop laughing long enough to catch her breath. Though more conservative than the captain's, Jim's laugh was a rich, full bass that gave her unexpected pleasure and she hoped she would have the opportunity to hear it again and again.

Laughter gave relief to Jim's dark, ruthless features and took the wariness from his eyes, allowing her a brief look at the man Captain Nolan had described as thinking about little besides enjoying himself. That had been before the war, before his court-martial, before Tess had deserted him, and before going into exile. Time and events had changed him, hardened him, wizened him. Some of his wounds were the invisible kind, but pained him still, she thought, unprepared for the surge of emotion that resulted.

Suddenly she knew that she wanted to be the one

to heal his wounds, to bring a smile to his lips and happiness and love into his heart. She would never desert him as Tess had done. She wanted only to be able to love him and care for him always.

She stood silent now, overwhelmed by the enormity of her thoughts and wishes, hopes and dreams, fears and desires. She stared bemusedly at the circus scene that had suddenly started to shimmer and shine. Frowning with annoyance, she blinked, then closed her eyes and raised a hand to wipe away the sweat. Upon reopening them, she was struck by a wave of dizziness that caused her to take a steadying step forward, but in fact added to her unbalance and started her to totter back and forth and from side to side.

"Captain? Aubrey?" Blindly, she reached out her hand . . .

Something warned him. He glanced her way and saw her sway and her eyes roll back in her head. Crossing the distance between them in two swift strides, he caught her as she was going down, just barely saving her from falling face-down in the mud.

Aubrey was there now too. "For God's sake. What happened?"

None too gently, Jim maneuvered Indy's limp, lifeless body into a position where he could pick her up in his arms rather than throw her over his shoulder like a grain sack.

"Must have been the heat," he said in as few words as possible as he curved his arm behind the backs of her legs. With an economy of movement he lifted her up, settled her within his arms, and started for her quarters.

Over his shoulder, he shouted, "Carry on, Sergeant, until they've got the hang of it, then dismiss them for supper call."

"Yes, sir! Hope the little lady's gonna be all right."

He didn't hear the sentiment. He was too busy wondering what the hell he was going to do with Indy once he got her inside. It wasn't that he didn't know *what* to do, he'd seen heat sickness before. It was more a question of *should* he do it? The person had to be cooled down however it could be accomplished. Since there wasn't a stream handy or even a water trough nearby, it would mean taking off some of her clothes.

Aubrey had run in front of him to open the door. He looked about helplessly. "Take her in her bedroom, I guess. I'll get some water."

"And some cloths. Lots of them."

Aubrey nodded. "Cloths," he repeated. "Lots of them." And hurried off to the back of the parlor.

Jim could scarcely squeeze the two of them through her bedroom door. Gently now, he laid her down on the bed. Trouble, he thought. She was nothing but trouble. He'd warned himself about her early on and just the other day he'd vowed to stay away from her—and he'd tried but he couldn't. She was everywhere he was.

Remembering the pitcher of water from the last incident, he went for it, but it was empty. "Damn. Of all the luck." And no telling when Aubrey would come back with the water and cloths.

He stood over her and heaved an exasperated sigh. "Well, I suppose they can court-martial me as many times as they want, but they can only hang me once! So, here goes." Leaning over her, he picked up the hem of her dress, put his teeth to it like he was biting off a piece of jerky, then rent it as far as it would go, which was to her waist, where the skirt was sewed to the bodice.

Once that was done, he contemplated the dozen or so pea-sized buttons that filed down the front of her bodice and decided to hell with it. Why bother undoing them? He'd already ruined the dress. What was one more tear? So thinking, he undid the top button and gave each side of the neck opening one quick yank that sent the buttons popping off and flying through the air like buckshot from a scattergun.

His sense of triumph ebbed when he realized an even bigger challenge faced him in getting her arms out of those long, tight sleeves.

He jerked his head toward the bedroom door. "Aubrey?"

No answer. It was as if he had disappeared.

Bemoaning the fact that he didn't have his knife, he set to work, pulling, tugging, wondering how the hell she had gotten into the stupid damn thing in the first place, and how, in years past, he'd gotten women out of their clothes so easily. The answer to that, he realized, feeling foolish, was that the women had helped him.

Finally, he got one arm out of one sleeve and that's when Aubrey walked in.

"Do you think you should do that?" Aubrey's

voice sounded unusually high and anxious. "Good God, Jim! What will her father say?"

"We need to cool her off."

"We?" Under his sun-browned skin there was a whitening.

"I'm not taking off anything else, if that's what you're thinking. I'm a lot of things but I'm not crazy! This will have to be enough," he said as he got her out of the second sleeve. "Set that bucket down and soak those cloths while I get rid of this damn dress." With one hand behind each rounded, white shoulder, Jim shimmied the dress down behind her back, then tossed the offensive garment across the room. "Jesus, that was worse than breaking jail."

"You should know," Aubrey replied jokingly.

Jim shook his head and chuckled. He never would have thought the day would come when he'd laugh at anything having to do with the time he'd spent in military prison. Maybe someday he'd even laugh about Tess.

"Start wringing out those cloths, but not too much. I want them good and wet." After a moment, while waiting to be handed the first cloth, he said, "If you're planning on taking a furlough to find yourself a *suitable* wife, you'd better be prepared to deal with all the female trappings, or you could run into a few problems." He folded the cloth and laid it across Indy's smooth, unblemished forehead.

"If she's *suitable* I won't have to deal with them."

A second cloth he laid on the bare skin just

above her milk-white breasts. "I didn't know you were such a model of propriety."

"Who said I was?"

"If I'm not mistaking, I think you just did."

Jim laid out more cloths on her shoulders, her arms, and, after lifting her petticoat up to her knees, on her legs as well. "That ought to do it. She should be coming to pretty soon."

In a rush of words, Aubrey said, "Well, that's about all anybody can do. I'm no help here. Think I'll get back to the parade ground and give a hand. Just yell out the window if you need anything."

As Aubrey turned to leave, Jim called after him. "Captain?" When Aubrey had turned around and Jim had his full attention, he pointed to the window and said, "The coward's way out is through there." For the first time ever, Jim saw Aubrey Nolan blush and it was funnier than anything he'd seen a few minutes ago on the parade ground.

A moment later Jim was considering if there was anything else he could do for Indy other than slap her awake. No sense doing that; it would scare her to death.

Tired of leaning over, Jim scooted her over a few inches and sat on the edge of the bed. She still wasn't showing any signs of coming to and he was beginning to worry. It *had* to be the heat, he told himself, going back over what he remembered happening: the heat, her high-necked, long-sleeved dress, the excitement, her delighted laughter. She probably would have been fine if she hadn't set aside her parasol.

He dipped one last cloth into the bucket and pressed it against her lips, squeezing slightly so some water would trickle into her mouth. More than likely she'd be mad as a peeled rattler when she came to and saw him, then saw herself, how she was lying there in her petticoat.

Imagining her thoughts made him aware of what he was thinking about her lying there in nothing but her petticoat. He hadn't given it much consideration while he'd been undressing her. He'd been too concerned about getting her cooled down and too annoyed that she's caused him more trouble to take close notice of what he was revealing.

The petticoat. All of a sudden the whole top of it was wet and blessedly see-through, showing the small, dark circles of her nipples, which were gently peaked and smooth-skinned in repose.

He wanted them to know his touch. He wanted to see them pucker and harden because of his touch. Without even thinking of what he was doing, he raised his left hand and felt her through the thin material, his two fingers tracing the circumference of one nipple, then only one finger rubbing its heart. The response was immediate, as he had known it would be.

And so was his. He felt that pleasurable race of heat and quickening down low and sucked in a breath. Instinctively his fingers spread out over her breast and pressed down, then gently squeezed, then massaged. Touching her, even through her petticoat, was the most exquisite torture he had ever known.

He longed to touch her all over, to rent the

damn petticoat as he had the dress and feel the satiny warmth of her bare skin beneath his palm. He hesitated, knowing to continue was wrong, but justifying it by telling himself that she had driven him to the brink, not once but several times, and the result was that he had come damn close to literally taking himself in hand and easing his own ache.

She stirred beneath his hand and made a tiny moan that awakened him to his incredible stupidity. He took his hand away, raised the other hand that still held the cloth, and began wiping her face.

He suffered the fires of hell while she hovered between sleep and wakefulness, her body tensing, relaxing, stretching. Jim stood up, looked away, not sure how much more of this be could take, but knowing he couldn't leave her until he was certain she was all right. He was about to call out her name and shake her awake when Prudence Stallard came into the bedroom.

"Captain Nolan sent me. Said you might need some help?" She moved up close and stood beside him, her astute blue gaze taking in Indy's wet bodice, then moving to him and taking in everything else. "Somehow I doubt that, but I'll relieve you just the same." She took the cloth from his hand and gave him a teasing smile. "Don't you have something to do, Major?"

"Yeah," he said, feeling like a twelve-year-old caught with his short pants down. He started for the door. "I'm pretty sure it was the heat that got to her," he said, lingering a second longer.

She tilted her head and looked him up and down. "Looks like it got to you too, Major."

Chapter 13

Dawn was still a long time yet to come when Jim finally gave up on trying to get any sleep. He sat up, ran his fingers through his hair, and leaned his back against the wall.

He hesitated lighting the lantern, then remembered that Aubrey had taken a construction detail out to work on the camp's water system, which meant he would have the next couple of hours to himself. A welcome thought. He could do with a little privacy. He had become something of a solitary man.

Without a doubt, last night ranked as one of the worst he'd ever spent. No, *the* worst! he amended. And it was his own fault. He shouldn't have touched Indy the way he had; he knew better but something had come over him, a longing so hot and thick that nothing, short of a bullet, could have stopped him.

For all the physical pain he'd suffered throughout the night, he wished somebody *had* shot him and put him out of his misery. The *fires of hell* is what it had felt like, using the expression one of his young privates had used to describe the pain of being gut shot.

If he'd had any sense, he would have found Prudence, apologized for walking out on her the other night, and taken her up on what she had so willingly offered. From the knowing, teasing looks she'd given him when she'd walked in on him and Indy, it was apparent that she knew what troubled him. Damn the woman anyway.

And damn Indy too! Damn her seductive innocence, her soft brown eyes, everything! If she didn't stay out of his way, out of his life, there was no telling what he might do. A man only had so much control.

His mood was anything but pleasant as he got himself ready for the day. At five o'clock he went down to the corrals and ordered a half-dozen horses be put in the large corral for later use.

Yesterday, Sergeant Moseley had kept the first-time riders working with the horses until every last one of them had learned the basics. By the time the training period ended, they'd know how to handle themselves on a horse as well as their cavalry counterparts, or they wouldn't go out with the Wolf Company.

After a breakfast of hard brown bread and sow belly, the men again assembled on the parade ground.

Without preamble Jim sternly ordered them to remove their hats and shirts and throw them in a pile. "From now on you're going to start looking like Apaches. As lily white as you all are now, you'd shine like a full moon on a night raid and give our position away."

There were a few laughs that were quickly stifled when Jim turned his lethal look on them. He knew his hostility was a carry-over from last night, and decided he'd better work it out if he was going to teach these men anything today. As soon as he was through giving them a few facts about the enemy they would be fighting, he'd take them into the desert and teach them some necessary survival skills.

He stood before them, hands behind his back. "Apaches usually attack in the morning from the east so the sun is in their enemies' eyes. They seldom attack unless they're sure they have all the advantages. Most times they sneak up on you quiet as a snake and strike before you even know they're there. When they do yell, it's because they're trying to scare you.

"Today, while it's still cool, we're going to start out—" He broke off—that feeling that he was being watched again. But this time, knowing who was doing the watching, he refused to acknowledge her. "—with a run," he went on. "An Apache can run all day in the sun." He turned to Sergeant Moseley. "Have all the men been issued knives as I asked?"

"Yes, sir. Nice shiny new ones."

"Very good, Sergeant. Let's go." They hadn't gone but a dozen yards when Jim realized the men were running in a column, two by two. He pulled himself to an abrupt stop and held up his hand. "What do you think this is, goddammit? Have you ever seen Apaches run in a column?" He needed say no more. An hour later he again brought them to a halt, this time to see if he had any stragglers. Surprisingly they were all together, which made him feel they might make it after all.

Out of the corner of his eye he saw the man named Ryker pull a small flask out of his trousers. Before the soldier could get the cork out, Jim had crossed the space between them and knocked the flask out of the soldier's hands. "If I had wanted you to bring water along, Ryker, I would have issued canteens. I'm teaching desert survival here. You'll find your water the same way the Apaches do."

Ryker's expression turned from surprise to undisguised hate. "I didn't ask to be in this goddamn wolf pack of yours. And I ain't gonna take no orders from a deserter." He spat on Jim's moccasin.

"You should have saved that, Ryker. You're going to wish you'd had it back."

Ryker's lips pulled back in a feral snarl. He feigned turning away, then came back throwing his right fist. Jim ducked and grabbed the man's arm, turned his back into him, and hurled him over his shoulder onto the ground. Standing back from the groaning soldier, and crouching low with his arms dangling in front of him, Jim waited for Ryker to get up. "Come on, Corporal," he said venomously. "You want to kill me so let's see you try. These men can use a good show."

Ryker struggled to his feet, then charged forward. Jim reached down, grabbed a handful of sand, and tossed it in his face, causing him to reel backward. "Had enough yet?"

Blinking the sand from his eyes, the corporal came after him again. Weary of the game, Jim decided to put an end to it and teach Ryker a lesson about fighting. "All right, you jughead, you asked for it." With that he leapt up in the air like a cat, kicked out his right leg, and hit Ryker square in the gut, doubling him over and ending the fight.

"Anybody else want to call me a deserter?" he queried the onlookers. Satisfied with the respectful looks on the men's faces he shook himself off. "When you're fighting an Apache, your life could depend on how resourceful you are. Sand thrown in his face can temporarily blind him." He picked a rock off the ground. "You can stun or kill him with a rock. You can run him down with your horse."

He walked over to Ryker and offered him a hand up. "You can never predict what an Apache will do," he added, "so don't ever assume anything." To make his point, he pulled Ryker halfway up, then backhanded him hard, forcing a loud groan from him before he went unconscious. "Ryker just made two serious mistakes. One: never cry out when you're hurt. Two: never trust the enemy."

For the next few hours the men learned various fighting techniques and practiced them on each other and on him. Looking up into the sky, Jim judged the time to be approaching noon. The men were tired and would be even more tired by the time they got back to camp, but he had no intention of letting up; they had a lesson waiting for them at the corrals.

Before starting out he told them, "Put a pebble in your mouth. It'll bring out the saliva."

*   *   *

With an escort of twenty infantrymen mounted on saddle mules, a battery of two twelve-pounder prairie howitzers, and a guide from Tucson, the new Indian commissioner, sent by President Grant himself, arrived at Camp Bowie exhausted and out of sorts.

"Riders comin' in!"

Captain Nolan had gotten back from morning fatigue an hour ago to find Jim and the troopers gone. He met the commissioner as he was getting down off his mule. "Captain Aubrey Nolan, G Troop, First Cavalry, at your service, sir," he said, saluting.

"Kindly inform your commandant that Isaiah Moorland has arrived and that I should like to see him at once."

"My apologies, sir, but Colonel Taylor is directing operations at the old Camp Bowie and won't be back until much later this afternoon. However, I am authorized to officially welcome you and to show you to your quarters."

"And my escort, Captain?"

"We have a barracks under construction, sir. The beds and bedding arrived last week. Your men should find it very comfortable."

"When the colonel returns, Captain, you will please tell him that I wish to have a word with him and you, wherever it is the most comfortable. I've been sitting this damn John Daisy for the last two days—not that I don't prefer riding mules to horses, for indeed I do, but I would welcome a well-cushioned seat, if you know what I mean."

"Yes, sir. That would be in the colonel's quarters. His daughter, Miss Independence Taylor, has made it real comfortable." With that, Captain Nolan summoned an orderly over to take the commissioner's mule. "If you'll follow me, sir."

A lone, motionless cottonwood tree stood like a tall sentry on the mountain slope south of Indy's kitchen. Indy had come to think of the tree as a quiet friend who was always there, eager to hear her thoughts and never ever critical. Yesterday morning, as she had stood within its long shadow, she had ruminated on how embarrassed she was for fainting and causing everyone so much trouble. It had been quite a scare to wake up to find Prudence beside her, wiping her face with a cool, wet cloth. Her first thought was that something terrible was wrong with her what with the way she was laid out in her petticoat like a corpse. But Pru had explained that she had fainted and that Captain Nolan and Major Garrity had brought her to her quarters and summoned help. That had apparently been the end of it.

That had also been the end of her favorite calico dress, which had been badly torn and muddied in the fall. Pru had proclaimed it beyond even her strongest lye soap and had carried it off to be burned with the other camp rubbish. Pru should know, Indy thought, lamenting the loss of the dress.

Today, she communed with the cottonwood through the open kitchen door. She had gotten a late start on her day. She had not slept well and had awakened to an all over feeling of lethargy. As yesterday, Jim was already working with the men on the parade ground when she came out into the parlor. And also as yesterday, the sight of him brought on that terrible inside-out feeling. It had been worse this morning, she thought. Much worse.

She was cleaning up the flour that she had somehow managed to get all over the place while she had been kneading the bread. The mess was a result of too much thinking and not enough paying attention. Hopefully the thinking wouldn't result in overkneaded bread that was hard as a brick.

Even now she couldn't seem to stop thinking.

Looking out at the cottonwood she asked herself if falling in love was always painful. If it was, why did people let it happen? A silly question, she thought, drawing a sustaining breath. People didn't *let* it happen. She hadn't *let* it happen. It had come about all on its own and now that it had, there was nothing she could do to ease its pain or make it go away.

She wondered if it was Fate stepping in to keep her at Bowie with Jim, that was the reason the eastbound stage operations had been suspended. And if it was, what did Fate have planned for her? She stared down at the cloth in her hand.

If Jim loved her as Pru seemed to think, he certainly had an odd way of showing it, which was not at all. Conversely, he seemed to go out of his way to ignore her, and when he was forced to confront her, as he had been in the adjutant's office, he couldn't even be civil!

It was on a sigh that she remembered what else Pru had said. That he may not yet know he

loved her. She had thought at the time Pru was
talking nonsense, but after examining her own
reluctance to admit to her feelings of love, she
knew it was possible.

But what good was admitting it? Even knowing
she loved him, she had gone to the adjutant's
office. She had still wanted to go home. And
when she had discovered him there, had she
shown him loving kindness? No. She had responded to his sarcasm with sarcasm. And yesterday, prior to the monkey drill, he had ignored her
as he came from talking to her father, and she
had pretended to ignore him.

Was that the way of love?

Sarcasm. Indifference. Ignoring the one you
loved?

It seemed a very peculiar way of behaving.
There didn't seem to be any behavioral difference
between not knowing you loved someone and
knowing you did . . .

"Ooh!" she breathed, squeezing the cloth until
her knuckles went white. "Maybe he does know,"
she whispered as if it was a secret. Her heart had
started to race. She swallowed. "Maybe he didn't
want to admit it either."

Indy hurried then to finish cleaning up. The
sooner she got done, the sooner she could get
out of the kitchen and find something to absorb
her thoughts. Maybe she could stop by Ava's and
ask to see the new baby. That would get her mind
off things . . . for a while anyway.

For fire safety, all the kitchens were detached
and set some twenty feet away from the main
quarters. Having set the bread to cool, she hur-

ried outside. She took off her apron and used it
to fan her face.

Captain Nolan came around the east side of
the building and saw her. "Do I take that as a
sign of surrender?"

She couldn't imagine what he was talking
about.

Evidently seeing her confusion he explained,
"In war, when the enemy waves a white flag it
indicates they want to surrender."

She nodded. "Oh, yes, of course." She laughed
lightly because she was too uncomfortable to
manage anything else. "I don't know what I was
thinking."

"I came by to—" He headed for the kitchen.

She held up her hand to stop him. "I know
what you came by for, Captain, and yes, I did
bake bread. As a matter of fact, I baked two
loaves, one for us and one for you." At least he
had the good manners to look suitably embarrassed, she thought. The first time she had offered him some fresh baked bread, he had eaten
more than half of her only loaf all by himself.
"It's my way of saying thank you for rescuing
me yesterday."

His brow furrowed. "It's too bad it had to happen. You seemed to be thoroughly enjoying
yourself."

"I was." She laughed in spite of herself at the
memory. "I had no idea the men would have so
much trouble just getting on their horses, let
alone staying on them. Major Garrity always
makes it look so easy, but then he seems to do
everything easily. Even the Grand March," she

blurted, unthinking, recalling Jim assuring her that she too would remember the march once they had begun. "It must have been years since he danced. And yet he didn't miss a step."

The captain gave her a long searching look, like he knew something she didn't. "At least six years. Maybe longer," he confirmed. "Back in the days when he was engaged to Tess." She felt a stab of jealousy, but her chin stayed level as he continued to talk. "It's a darn good thing he found out what kind of woman she was before he married her."

"Yes, I suppose so, but do you really think he would have actually married her?"

He nodded slowly and smiled, looking curiously pleased with himself. "Of course. He's often talked of having a home and a family—a very large family as a matter of fact."

She gave a nervous laugh. "I'm sorry I just can't imagine such a thing. He's so . . ." She waved a hand. "Well, he's so—so undomesticated. Sort of like a wild animal. Untamed, if you know what I mean."

"He wasn't always like that, you know. It's been the circumstances that have made him that way. It was the only way he could survive."

"Yes, of course, I understand."

"The right woman could tame him," the captain asserted.

She tilted her head to look at him. "The right woman? What kind of woman would be the right woman, Captain?"

He appeared to give the question serious thought. "Jim's a very irascible fellow as I'm sure you know. It would take a very special woman to handle him and to put up with him." His brow wrinkled as he looked down into her face. "Probably somebody a little like you, Indy. Somebody who's honest, loyal, very courageous. And of course, she'd have to really love him."

"Of course," she agreed on a half laugh.

"I know he's looking forward to the pardon your father promised. That will allow him to go home and live like a white man again. He's from a good family. His grandfather was a stern old man. Ruled his household with an iron fist. When he didn't approve his son's marriage, Jim's parents ran away and ended up owning a trading store just a few miles south of here. Jim was born there. That's when the Apaches and whites were on friendly terms, mind you. He practically grew up in the Apache strongholds. That's also how come he came back here. He knew he'd be welcome and that nobody would find him."

Indy was numbed by all the information. After a moment she said, "Excuse me while I go get your bread. It's been cooling while we've been talking."

She returned momentarily.

Seeing her coming, the captain stepped forward and took the still hot loaf from her hands. "Thanks, Indy. If I'm ever lucky enough to find a woman who can bake bread half as good as you, I'll marry her! Umm." He bent his head and sniffed the bread appreciatively. "I brought this along just in case," he said sheepishly, pulling a yellow kerchief out of his pocket. "I figured I'd have to hide it if I was going to get it back to my own quarters without anyone seeing it. If Jim gets wind of it, I won't even get a bite."

"He likes fresh baked bread, does he?"

The captain rolled his eyes. "He'd kill for it."

She glanced over the captain's shoulder. "Well, then, you best eat it quickly." At his questioning look she pointed behind him. "I wouldn't want to be responsible for your death, Captain."

"Jerusalem!" The captain carefully covered the loaf with his kerchief.

Indy's stomach muscles knotted as she watched Jim and his company running toward her. He was dirty, sweaty, but she thought he had never looked handsomer. He stopped a few feet from Captain Nolan and waved the troopers ahead.

"Be at the corral in one hour," he told them. They ran ahead as ordered.

"How'd they do?" the captain asked.

Indy noticed that Jim was looking at the captain in a very odd way. His eyes had darkened and narrowed. It almost looked like he was suspicious or . . . jealous!

The captain, however, seemed completely unaware of it, and Indy, wanting to see more before she drew a conclusion, kept silent and continued to watch.

"They did well." He looked like he wasn't going to elaborate, then he did. "I've got one trouble-maker so far, Corporal Ryker. I had him help me demonstrate some of the more advanced fighting techniques." His hard gaze didn't let up. He stood with his hands on his hips, legs vee'd. His chest rose and fell with exertion.

"Do I need to send a detail after him or did he come back under his own power?"

Indy recognized the jest. If Jim did, he wasn't going to let on.

"He came back with the rest of them," Jim answered in a tight voice. Covering his mouth with his hand he turned away to spit a pebble out of his mouth.

It was then that Indy noticed the bloody scratches on his back. "You have some bad scratches, Major. I'll get some water and clean them for you."

Before he could say one way or another, she was gone and through the kitchen door. She returned a minute later with a tin cup, a cloth, and a bucketful of water. She set the bucket down and dipped the cup into it. "I figured you'd probably be thirsty too." Indy's heart pounded at the nearness of him, the near nakedness of him.

"Thanks." Without another word he took the cup and drank greedily.

"You shouldn't drink that so fast when you're overheated," the captain warned. "It could make you sick. You know that."

Jim gazed at the captain over the rim of the cup, accusing him with a piercing look. "Yeah, I know," he said, his voice an ominous bass. He handed the cup back to Indy.

"By the way," the captain said conversationally. "The Indian commissioner arrived a little while ago. Unbelievably, he came in from Tucson, accompanied by a whole military escort. The colonel's over at the old camp and won't be back until later so I took him to his quarters to rest up."

Turning to Indy, he said, "He wants to meet with your father as soon as possible in someplace comfortable, with a cushioned chair. Sounds to me like that would mean here." He inclined his head toward the back door. "I thought you'd want to know."

For a moment she was too dazed to realize what he was saying. "Oh, yes," she said, nodding her head like a Chinaman. "I'll need to make preparations."

"Speaking of making preparations, I've got to get back to my quarters. More than likely I'll see you both this evening." He turned to leave, then glanced back. "Thanks for thinking of me, Indy." He gave her a wink and walked off, whistling "The Girl I Left Behind Me."

As the captain walked away, Indy stood next to Jim, holding her cloth, thinking he looked very angry indeed. The captain's wink had cinched it. Jim was jealous. And that meant he loved her. She breathed a sigh of relief and dipped her cloth into the bucket.

"Turn around and I'll clean those scratches," she ordered.

He obeyed and she was filled with an intoxicating sense of power. She started dabbing at the bloodied area. It was possible he still didn't know his feelings, she reminded herself. Prudence had said men were sometimes slow to recognize such things. Would it be too terribly bold of her to give him a little nudge in the right direction? she wondered. After all that the captain had said— about Jim wanting a home and family and such— she knew she had been wrong to think they couldn't possibly make a life together. A home and family was what she wanted too, and she wanted it with Jim Garrity. No other would do.

A furtive smile curved her mouth.

The scratches had looked worse than they really were, but she didn't need to tell him that, she realized with great satisfaction. "You might want to see Doc Valentine," she suggested, dipping the rag, swishing it around as if it had gotten very dirty, then squeezing it out and reapplying it to his back, to a much broader area than the scratches actually encompassed.

"They'll heal fine without Doc."

"All right then, but give me a minute or two to make sure I clean them out real good."

"I'm in no hurry."

She put her hand on his shoulder and froze. Her hand was so small and white next to his wide, sun-browned shoulder. His flesh was warm, firm. His shoulder muscles flexed and tensed beneath her fingers. It was easy to be brave when she didn't have to look into his eyes.

"Neither am I," she said, delighting in the feel of him. She had to at least pretend to bathe his scratches.

"About my little fainting spell yesterday," she said, speaking the first thought in her head. His whole body spasmed. "I'm sorry, I didn't mean to hurt you."

"You didn't hurt me," he said between his teeth. "What about yesterday?"

"I wanted to thank you for coming to my rescue. I'm a little embarrassed by the whole thing. If I had just kept my parasol with me I probably would have been just fine. Prudence told me the whole story."

"She did, did she?"

"I hope I didn't cause you any trouble."

"Trouble?"

"I mean. Well—I took you and the captain away from your men and all."

"Oh. No. It was no trouble."

"That's good. I wouldn't want—"

"That's enough, goddammit!" His voice crackled with savagery. He whirled around, facing her. Grasping her upper arms, he pulled her up against him with such violent force that it was like the other night when she'd had the wind knocked out of her.

"What did I do?" Her voice was high and thin.

"You really don't have any idea, do you?"

She started to shake her head but his hand lifted her chin, tilting it back so she had no choice but to meet his glittering, black eyes— *killing eyes.* It felt to Indy that he was hovering over her—like a hawk and the look on his face told her he had just found his prey.

His head swooped down and he kissed her. His lips were bruising, punishing. He captured her tongue and drew it into his mouth, tasting it, holding it prisoner as he held her body prisoner. Then he let it go and plunged his tongue into her mouth, leaving no part of it untouched.

"God, Indy. Do you know how much I've wanted to make love to you?" His lips breathed against hers. He kissed her again, wrapping his arms around her, holding her with such powerful urgency that she knew something was terribly wrong. Or was it terribly right?

Suddenly she had something she had to say. And she had to say it now. Placing her hands on either side of his face she managed to slide her mouth from his. "I love you," she whispered breathlessly. She gave meaning to her declaration then by placing fevered kisses aside his cheek, then working her way back to his mouth.

Something was wrong. He was silent. He was still.

He moved away from her so quickly that her arms were still raised and her hands still curved to the lines of his face. He stepped back from her, as if she were a rattler ready to strike.

"Don't love me, Indy. I'm not the man for you. We're worlds apart."

He turned and left.

The cottonwood stood silent, sad.

Chapter 14

"Camp Bowie is a crucial outpost, not only to the War Department but to the future of this territory." Indian Commissioner Isaiah P. Moorland had the attention of all present: Colonel Taylor, Indy, and Captain Nolan.

He was a tall man, incredibly tall, Indy thought, and narrow as a bed slat. His long, thin face was gaunt, with deep hollows beneath his prominent cheekbones. His eyes were his one saving feature, blue as a summer sky and keen with intelligence. He had been carrying the conversation, which really wasn't a conversation, but a speech, for the last quarter hour without let up.

"How Bowie is or isn't managed is of vital concern to President Grant as he intends this outpost to play a major roll in his plans to civilize the territory. Hence, it is my job to see that his concerns are dealt with.

"At this point in time the basic function of Camp Bowie, as the President sees it, Colonel Taylor, is to provide military escorts for all persons, military and civilian, through Apache Pass; to protect the neighboring ranches and towns from raids; and to keep the Apaches contained and under control. The reports I have received, sir, indicate that you have failed in every regard. Would you care to explain yourself?"

The colonel stood stiffly, clearly on his guard. "I would indeed, Mr. Moorland. I don't know whether you are aware of it or not but the War Department made a terrible mistake, which they have yet to rectify. I was given the wrong assignment. As soon as the President won the election, I applied for transfer to Washington. It was my wish to work closely with the President in whatever capacity he desired. Grant and me, we're very old friends, you know. We were boys together at the Point," he added portentously.

Indy saw the remark as an attempt to elevate his station in the commissioner's eyes. She also saw it didn't work. The commissioner remained unimpressed.

"I studied engineering," the colonel continued. "Thus, I spent my war years mapping out battle plans on paper and helping coordinate troop movements, also on paper. I *never* professed to have any kind of knowledge about the frontier or Indians."

Indy had never seen her father on the defensive before. His hands were balled into tight fists and his knuckles were white with strain.

She knew as well as he did that if the commissioner didn't like what he heard and saw during his visit, which would be through the end of the following week, his report to the President would not be a favorable one. That could lead to all sorts of ramifications. He could use his authority to relieve her father of command and send him home. In that event, the likelihood of him getting another command, with such a scar on his service record, was little to none. Or, worse yet, the commissioner could even have him discharged. Either way it would be a terrible disgrace and the end of a long, hard-won career that had not been totally without merit.

Indy had told herself she wouldn't care one way or another what the commissioner's report said or how it affected her father. He deserved what he got. But she did care. How could she not? In spite of everything, he was her father. The only father she would ever have. The only family she had left.

"On behalf of the War Department, Colonel, I extend my apologies for the error. Rest assured that I will have the matter looked into and rectified as soon as possible. However, that does not excuse you, Colonel. You, sir, are a West Point trained officer who served in the war. I've seen your service record and while it isn't outstanding by any degree, it is an adequate record and it indicated that you were qualified to command a frontier garrison.

"Most of the officers sent west for duty such as yours have far less education and experience than you do. The point being, Colonel, for all intents and purposes, it appears that you blatantly shirked your duty here, perhaps as a form of rebellion for the error?"

The colonel's face turned red with rage. "I most certainly did not, sir."

"This afternoon, Colonel, in your absence, I had Captain Nolan escort me around camp so I could personally speak to the men. What I learned, not just from one source but from many, was that you refused to take the good advice of your experienced officers, who had been in residence here during Major Clarke's command, and who were familiar with his methods and his operations—successful operations I might add—that were in effect and working at the time of his death.

"The men were extremely cooperative and made their complaints clear by way of this petition, which apparently they held back from sending at Captain Nolan's request." He unrolled the petition and turned it around for the colonel to see. "Were I to take the time to verify all these charges and discovered them to be true, Colonel, you could be subject to military court-martial."

The colonel's expression went from indignation at having been publicly rebuked to extreme alarm. "Court-martial?"

Indy gasped and put her hand over her mouth. She had thought a discharge at the worst, but a court-martial had never entered her mind. She'd had no idea that the problems were so serious. Turning to her father, she saw him go white with shock and take his seat at the end of the table, where he had sat so imperiously the day the captain brought Jim Garrity into her parlor. He rested his arms on the tabletop and clasped his hands.

Showing no trace of sympathy whatsoever, Mr. Moorland leafed through several papers in his hand. "Now then, Colonel," he said as he crossed one long leg over the other. "Now that you know where things stand, why don't you tell me what steps you've taken to remedy the situation here at Bowie."

In a voice Indy hardly recognized, her father gave a concise explanation. "I've reinstated the escorts through the pass and have patrols going out on a regular basis to check the ranches."

"Where, may I ask, were your patrols when the San Simon stage station was attacked by Cochise and his raiders?"

"We can't put patrols everywhere at once," was the colonel's explanation.

"I realize that, but the stage station, like Camp Bowie itself, is a vital point of travel and communication that should have been protected all the time. Is that the extent of it?"

"Yes—I mean no. There's the training," said the colonel, shaking his head.

To Indy, it appeared he had given up trying to help himself and had resigned himself to whatever fate the Indian commissioner decided.

She *had* to help him. "Commissioner Moorland," she ventured, not sure she was doing the right thing by coming to her father's aid, but knowing she had to try. "As you can see my father isn't quite himself. If I may speak on his behalf, sir, I'd like to tell you about the new training program."

Mr. Moorland cut a quick glance to the colonel, then came back to Indy. "This is a highly unusual request, young lady . . . but yes, I'll allow you to speak on Colonel Taylor's behalf."

Now, Indy was the one who was nervous. She wanted to do the best by her father, which would mean presenting a definition of the training in a clear, concise manner. Keeping her sentences short and choosing her words carefully, to sound very military, she explained that it was Captain Nolan's idea to train a group of soldiers to become Indian scouts, who would then be able to think and fight like Apaches, thus making them capable of accomplishing in the field what regular troopers could not.

Moorland nodded and mumbled as she spoke. Then the captain filled in where Indy was lacking information or expertise and between the two of them they gave the commissioner a complete picture of the training program and what it would accomplish once it was put into use.

"An excellent idea, Captain Nolan! Most ingenious of you. And you, Colonel, I commend you for approving Captain Nolan's idea and allowing the experiment to proceed." He bent his head and quickly scrawled some notes on the pages in his lap. "I'm sure President Grant will be most pleased with this piece of news. He was extremely worried. I will, of course, want to see this *training* for myself to judge its merit before I make my final analysis. And I want to meet this Major Garrity, whose talents have been praised so highly. He must be a most unusual man."

Captain Nolan spoke up. "You did meet him, sir, or rather you saw him. This afternoon at the corral. He was giving his men instruction in tracking and trailing skills."

The commissioner shook his head. "The only thing I saw, Captain, was a group of shirtless

FIRES OF HEAVEN   271

soldiers standing around watching an Indian poking through horse dung."

"Yes, sir," the captain chuckled. "That Indian,
sir, was Major Jim Garrity. He was showing his
men how examining horse dung could help them
estimate the numbers of Indians in a party, and
how by looking to see how dry it was toward the
center, they could determine the length of time
since the party passed by."

"Is that a fact, Captain?"

"Yes, sir. That's a fact. What Major Garrity
doesn't know about tracking and trailing isn't
worth knowing. He says he can tell if a party of
Indians includes women because of where the
urine is in relationship to the hooves. Women
apparently are the only ones in the Indian society
who ride mares."

The commissioner looked suitably impressed.
"It seems to me that the service Major Garrity is
performing is of the utmost importance and
value. If he and his men are successful at rooting
out the savages, there could be other such soldier
training programs. So, why isn't he here? I should
like to speak with him."

Captain Nolan stood up. "I'll get him if you
like, sir."

"Yes. I would indeed."

Indy left her chair. "I'll make a pot of coffee.
Would you like a slice of fresh bread, Mr. Moorland? Baked it just this morning."

"Yes. Thank you, Miss Taylor."

Indy was glad to escape the tension that filled
the room. Mr. Moorland was a stern, demanding
man, who obviously didn't concern himself with

such things as diplomacy. She hoped he was a fair man and considerate in his regard of her father, his long-standing military record, the War Department's error, and the steps he was taking to put things to right.

She delayed her return as long as she felt she could, carefully slicing the bread and putting it inside a calico cloth to keep it fresh, arranging the tin coffee cups neatly on a tray, and making sure she had a thick cloth with which to pour the coffee. God forbid that there should be a repeat of her last coffee disaster.

And God forbid that when she went back inside, and Jim Garrity was there, that she let him see how much she loved him in spite of what he had done this afternoon. After spending her afternoon in the shade of the cottonwood outside her kitchen, she thought she knew what had happened between them, though she hadn't known at the time. Her little *nudge* had turned into a big *push* and she'd pushed him too far.

He did love her. Of that she was sure in spite of what he'd said when he left. And he wanted to make love to her. He'd been almost crazy with need. His hands, his lips, his body—they'd translated his thoughts in a language even her untutored body could understand.

And she wanted him. She wasn't sure what that entailed exactly, but she knew it must be something very special and wonderful. When he had left her, she had been stunned, not hurt, for she understood completely how he felt.

But now was not the time for her to show her love or understanding. It would only confuse and befuddle him even more than he already was. He needed his wits about him to talk to the commissioner, for only Jim and what he was doing could save her father.

Jim was telling the commissioner his background when Indy came in through the back door. She adroitly avoided visual contact with him, but could feel him watching her. She could always feel him watching her. It was an odd intangible link that she had never experienced before.

He had taken her chair, which would mean if she wanted to continue to be a part of the discussion, she would have to take the only chair left, directly opposite him. And that would mean that she would *have* to look at him every once in a while.

She let out a silent sigh as she put the coffeepot and tray down on the table. With an effort, she put a smile on her face as she turned and offered each man a cup of coffee and a slice of bread.

"And you, Major Garrity," she extended her offer to him last. "I understand you would kill for fresh baked bread."

He looked up at her, his eyes unreadable. "Not unless I hadn't eaten in a week, Miss Taylor." He reached in and took a piece.

"As I was saying, Major, about your very interesting tale. I don't believe I've come across a white man who's lived with the Apaches before of his own free will. I can see why the captain thought you would be the man for the job. I expect you know the Apaches as well as any man alive, but I do have to wonder about your personal feelings in this matter. You will, after all, be training men to hunt and kill people you must have considered your friends."

"Yes, sir. I still consider them to be my friends. That's one of the reasons why I made the bargain with the colonel." Jim went on to explain his conversation with Toriano and their conclusions about the Apaches' future. "Either way, extinction or being herded together on reservations— the Apache people are doomed. The sooner they're brought to do the white man's bidding, the fewer lives will be lost. I see my role as bringing the inevitable about just that much sooner. That's how I have to look at it, Commissioner, otherwise I probably would have to consider myself a traitor even though the Apaches would never see it that way."

"How do you mean?"

In spite of herself, Indy could not keep her eyes off Jim. She loved him and admired his courage and nobility. She prayed that knowing his efforts would ultimately save lives would be enough to sustain him through the difficult times yet to come.

Jim hesitated a long time before speaking. "They have no central form of government. Each tribe is broken down into so many divisions and subdivisions that there is no unity among the people. Without that there is no reason to be loyal; there's no one to be loyal to. Captain Nolan tells me that some commanders are already employing Indians as scouts. That means that they're being paid and given *things*. Material things, Commissioner. Material wealth and status are of the utmost importance to them. To acquire these things at the expense of their own is of no consequence. Again, because they have no one to be loyal to." He sat forward, his elbow on his thighs, his hands in front of him.

"An interesting culture, Captain. I'm certainly glad we white eyes don't have the same beliefs. There would be utter chaos!" He laughed, but he was the only one, and when he realized it, he sobered immediately.

"What do you call it then, sir, when one soldier murders another soldier? Or when one neighbor steals from another? Is the murderer or thief charged with disloyalty? Is he branded as a traitor?"

The commissioner cleared his throat and nodded. "Your point is well taken, Captain."

It was late by the time the gathering broke up. The commissioner's last words had let Jim know that he would be taking a serious interest in his training methods for the next few days, and that at some time tomorrow he wanted to discuss the *bargain* Jim had mentioned.

Jim and Aubrey had stopped to talk at the far eastern side of the parade ground. They had been holding up the hitching post there for the past ten minutes.

"I'm sorry, Jim, that I made you mad this afternoon. I was just trying to make you jealous is all."

"You succeeded," Jim answered testily. His tone of voice did an about-face when he said, "And then I succeeded in making a jackass out of myself by forcing myself upon her, kissing her like some savage animal, then running away."

"You ran away? From a woman?" Captain Aubrey Nolan was incredulous.

"You could say that," Jim admitted none too happily.

"Christ, Jim. What did those Apaches teach you, anyway?"

"That's the second time you've asked me that. They taught me a lot of things, dammit. One of them being to respect women! They don't rape, you know. At least, not as a rule. If I'd have stayed one minute longer with Indy, I would have raped her."

Aubrey's brows shot up in surprise. "Ooh! Well then, I guess it is a good thing you ran away. And you had the nerve to call me a coward! At least your experiences are proving to me that it's best not to let emotion have anything to do with choosing a wife."

Jim turned to him, frowning. "What are you talking about?"

Aubrey sighed as if it was a lot of trouble to explain. "Watching you suffer convinces me that falling in love is nothing but pure hell! I don't want any part of it." He took a flask out of his pocket, uncorked it, and put it to his lips.

A moment later Jim grabbed it away from him. "Give me that thing before you drink it all."

"I thought you didn't drink."

"I don't. Except when I drink."

Aubrey simultaneously shook and nodded his head as Jim guzzled down the contents of the flask. "You know what you're going to feel like in the morning, don't you?"

"Can't be any worse than I feel now."

"Wanna bet?"

"I'm not a gambling man."

"Except when you gamble, right?"

"Right." Jim wiped his mouth dry against his sleeve. "Thought you'd want to know, we've got a problem with the colonel," he said on a more serious note as he looked up at the moon.

"We've got a lot of problems with the colonel. One of them being that he is a colonel and in charge of this garrison."

"I mean it, Aubrey. I was in his office and saw something that really bothered me. He had newspapers and Army reports all over his desk. You would have thought he was studying up on how to do his job except that all those newspapers and reports had to do with Cochise. I have a bad feeling that the colonel has acquired a big ambition."

"Of capturing Cochise?"

Jim nodded. "It would make him famous to be the man responsible for Cochise's capture. It would give his career a big boost."

"I see what you mean." Aubrey stared off into the night, obviously contemplating the significance of what he had just learned. "He may not have a career in the next few days. I don't think I would worry about it too much. The commissioner doesn't appear to have taken to Colonel Taylor." Aubrey took his empty flask back. "I'm going to turn in."

"I'll be along after a bit. I just want to think a few things out."

"Might as well while you still can," Aubrey said over his shoulder.

The moonlight softened Bowie. The adobe buildings almost looked pretty beneath the white light. The responsibility of training the men lay heavy upon him now, more now than before and he wasn't sure exactly why.

Jim found himself staring at the light in Indy's bedroom window. He wished he'd exercised more control with her this afternoon. But, damn! She had nearly driven him crazy with her soft hands touching him like that. He hadn't meant to hurt or scare her. He loved her, for God's sake! But he just couldn't see himself making her a good husband, not after everything he'd been through these past six years. Not even if he got his pardon. What he had told Prudence was true, that he had lived with the Apaches so long he had forgotten what it was to be a civilized man.

A civilized man would not have forced himself on her the way he had.

She had looked so stunned when he'd backed away from her. Stunned, he thought, but not frightened!

He was about to turn in when he heard the colonel's wrathful voice, loud as a pistol shot.

"How dare you presume to do such a thing! Don't you *ever* talk for me again as long as you live!"

Jim took off, running toward the officers' quarters.

"I won't. I'm sorry. I only wanted to help you."

"Can't you understand? I don't want your help? I don't want anything from you. Not now. Not ever!"

Jim heard a door slam. From a hundred feet away he saw Indy coming into her bedroom and felt an incredible sense of relief. He kept going until he was at approximately the same spot he had been the other night, and, like the other night, told himself he was watching her to make certain she was all right.

She was rubbing her upper arms and he realized she was in pain; her father must have grabbed her and hurt her. Then she bent her head and put her hands in front of her face and began to sob.

"Jesus." His throat suddenly ached. He wanted to go to her, to comfort her, but he held himself back. That would only make matters worse. He couldn't touch her, let alone hold her and comfort her, without making love to her. He didn't have the moral or physical strength to resist her another time.

"*I love you,*" she had whispered to him this afternoon as if she could hardly wait to tell him the joy that was in her heart. He was sure she had expected him to return the words.

A deep, unaccustomed pain exploded in his chest as he thought of the cruel way he had left her standing there with her arms raised, and her hands holding nothing but empty air.

After a moment she stopped crying and looked to be recovering herself. She picked up the water pitcher and filled the basin, then folded a cloth, dipped it into the water, and applied it to her arm, wincing as she did so.

Jim moved up a few feet closer. Now, he could see where the colonel had hurt her; the imprint of his fingers stood out on her white skin like a fiery red brand. He wanted to kill the bastard for hurting her. He *would* kill him if he ever hurt her again, he vowed.

Jim averted his gaze, anger and torment eating at his insides, but still he couldn't justify going to her knowing what would be at risk. And besides, there was nothing he could do to help her physical hurt that she wasn't already doing herself.

A soft sigh brought his gaze back to her.

She was leaning over the basin splashing her face and neck with water. By the time she had finished, the entire front of her nightdress was soaking wet and clinging to her body, but she didn't seem to be concerned. In fact, she seemed oblivious to it.

Jim was anything but oblivious to the way the nightdress molded itself to her gentle curves or the way it allowed him to see her dark nipples through the material. He cursed himself over and over for not leaving as soon as he had satisfied himself that she wasn't seriously hurt.

He heard a movement somewhere behind him and turned to see what it was. One of the camp dogs, he realized, breathing a sigh of relief when he heard it bark. It would be just his luck to be caught by Sergeant Moseley or her father. Fully intending to leave now, he glanced back at her one last time and saw her untie the ribbons that held the front of her nightdress closed and push the garment off her shoulder, baring her breast.

He stood transfixed.

"God, Indy," he whispered involuntarily, his body suddenly aching with desire. For a second he thought she might have heard him but when she didn't look up from what she was doing he knew she hadn't.

It was in his thoughts for her to pick up the cloth and touch herself with it, so that when she did he wasn't surprised. She drenched it in the basin first, removed it dripping, and placed it against her collarbone. Water trickled down over her breast and off her nipple.

Jim's mouth went dry. The throbbing pain of his erection was such that he was ready to do anything he had to do to relieve himself. Anything! He didn't care anymore how he got relief just so he got it. It wasn't as if it was a sin. A wound to his oversized male ego maybe, but not a sin. He started to reach his hand down then abruptly stopped; he couldn't do it. She pulled on the other side of her nightdress and slipped the whole thing down her body with excruciating slowness until she stood naked before his hungry gaze.

She was beautiful. Exquisite.

He felt the blood flow into him. *Move the cloth*, he thought. *Lower*. And she did. Just as he had wanted her to. He felt the tension build within him.

On a sudden, startling thought he narrowed his eyes, hardly able to believe that what he was thinking could be true, and yet he knew it was. How many times had he sensed her watching him, felt her eyes on him in silent communication? If he could feel her gaze wasn't it just as possible that she could feel his?

He watched her closely. She was performing the act of bathing herself just the way it had been in his mind, moving the cloth from one breast to the other, then across her ribs, down the center of her stomach, to the dark V between her legs.

Damned if she didn't know he was there watching her!

And damned if she wasn't deliberately trying to seduce him!

He practically ran up to her window. If he was wrong, he was a dead man. She would scream, and even if her father didn't save her somebody would hear her and come running. It was a chance he was going to take.

He vaulted over the window ledge into her bedroom.

Indy gave a start of surprise. Then her chin lifted and she boldly met his gaze, and his thoughts were confirmed.

Neither of them moved. It seemed an interminable time that they did nothing but gaze at each other. He would have to have been made of stone not to feel the silent message her eyes communicated to him now. *Come to me. Make love to me.*

Jim wanted nothing more than to come to her and make love to her. His body was weak and in agony from abstinence, but he was not a savage. He would not take her to slake his own needs. He was a civilized man, and when he made love to her it would be after he was sure she had felt everything she had a right to feel, everything he wanted her to feel.

His gaze moved over each inch of her wet shiny body. Her breasts were neither large nor small. They were perfect. Beautiful and perfect. Round, high, gently peaked. Her nipples were puckered and tight, begging him to touch her.

An almost imperceptible smile curved her lips as she turned her attention back to herself and again moved the cloth over her body, this time with a slow circular motion over her stomach, her hips, her thighs. He walked across the room, his footsteps silent as a stalking Indian on the plank floor until he stood before her. She reached out her hand, inviting him to take the cloth from her, thus giving him permission to touch her. His hand shook as he dipped it into the basin. When he pulled it out and lifted his arm, water slid backward and dripped off his elbow.

He placed the cloth against the side of her neck and slowly, only an inch at a time, moved it down her body, squeezing it as he went. He followed his hand with his eyes and when he got to her breast, he let the cloth slide away so there was nothing between them but flesh.

The feel of his hard, rough hand against her breast turned the spark into flame. She dared a glimpse downward to see his hand upon her breast. The contrasting skin tones, his so dark and hers so very white, was startling. She looked up at him then and was even more startled to see the pained look on his face, as if it actually hurt him to touch her.

"Jim?"

He met her gaze and saw her look of concern. He would have laughed except it wasn't funny. She was reading him too well and it made him feel oddly vulnerable. "How long have you known I was out there?"

"Just after the dog barked," she said guilelessly.

His gaze searched her eyes, then moved down the length of her body taking in the fact that she was breathing erratically and that her fists were clenched at her sides. Her boldness was only a pretense.

"I hope you know what you're doing," he said, thinking he needed to warn her.

She took a deep breath and nodded.

He saw her eyes widen when she happened to glance down. The urge to know her and touch her intimately was blatantly apparent beneath his clothes.

"I want you, Indy," he said on a ragged breath, "but I have to warn you, I can't go slow with you. I can't be as gentle with you as I'd like to be. Not this time. It's been too long for me. Do you understand?"

She sensed he was on a tight rein, holding himself back even as he spoke. She raised her arms and touched his face as she had done that afternoon and repeated the words that had driven him away from her. "I love you." And when he didn't move, she said, "I trust you. I know you won't hurt me."

He bent his head forward and stared down at her. Then with a moan of long-suffering desire, he reached around her and caught her up against him. He felt her arms twine around his neck and cling. His mouth took hers. Her lips parted beneath his allowing him the access he would have demanded from her had she kept her mouth closed to him. Groaning, he thrust his tongue inside the soft opening and tasted her, then pulled back and thrust forward again, making love to her mouth as he would soon make love to her body.

Her response surprised him. Delighted him. Fired him. She held his thrusts and followed his retreats. After a moment he tore his mouth away from hers and kissed her face, her eyes, her ears. "God, Indy. You feel so good," he murmured into her hair.

Somewhere outside the dog barked, reminding Jim of the open window. Cursing, he pulled away and walked over to the window and drew the makeshift curtains together. As he started back, he saw her lean over and turn the lamp down until it sputtered and went out.

Before his eyes could adjust to the darkness, he heard the bed creak and stopped dead in his tracks, afraid he would explode just thinking about her lying there on her bed waiting for him. With an effort he would have thought beyond him, he regained control, and by the time he had recovered sufficiently to make it across to her, he could see her and she was in exactly the position he had imagined her to be in.

He swallowed, suddenly nervous and unsure of himself. Six years of celibacy was a long time. What if after all these years he wasn't physically able to make love? Christ! He hadn't thought of that before. He *wouldn't* think of that! He stripped off his clothes and tossed them in a pile by the window.

And he prayed like he had never prayed before.

Indy gasped as he discarded the last of his clothes and lifted his head to look at her with his dark, fathomless eyes. She had never seen a naked man before. She wasn't sure what she had expected, but it certainly wasn't this. She swallowed, suddenly uneasy. "Jim—maybe we shouldn't—" When he took a step toward her, she halfheartedly turned away, but before she could get up off the bed, he caught her from behind and stayed her.

"Indy! Listen to me." He knelt down on the bed behind her, his strong arms encircling her, trapping her hands against her stomach. She was trembling like a leaf in the wind. "You said you trusted me. So trust me now."

"But that was before I saw—"

He bent his head beside hers and whispered close to her ear. "I'm no different than any other man," he assured her, then turned her around on the bed to face him. "I want you, Indy. I want you so much I hurt." He took her hand and moved it down between them, loosened her tightly clenched fingers and wrapped them around his engorged flesh.

She heard him suck in his breath.

"Only you can stop the hurt," he said, his hand firm over hers, holding her, squeezing her fingers to conform to his rigid length. "Only you, Indy." Then he began to slip back and forth within her hand and something twisted and coiled deep down inside her and she hurt too. A small cry of bewilderment escaped her. She had never imagined anything as intimate as this. His flesh was hot and hard—so impossibly hard. Little wonder he hurt.

She looked up at him. "I don't know how to stop the hurt," she told him, not even realizing that he had taken his hand away.

"Yes, you do. You are. You will." He knew he wasn't making sense, but it was impossible to think rationally when she was touching him like that. He felt her hold loosen and was about to protest when she began to explore him with her fingers. Her hand was trembling, yet she seemed determined to know the texture and shape of him, and he sure as hell wasn't going to deny her.

But he could stand it only a moment before he had to make her stop. Abruptly he pulled back and laid her on the bed. She opened her arms and invited him to lie beside her, which he did without hesitation.

"Jim." She paused breathlessly. "I've never—" She broke off, biting her lower lip.

He pushed a wisp of soft hair back from her face and gazed into her eyes. "I know, Indy." She reached her hand up to touch his cheek. He could see that she was frightened but it was a natural fear—a virgin's fear of the unknown. He would only see it this once, and then she would never be afraid again.

Her voice was shaky. "You'll have to teach me."

He nodded and prayed to God he could hold out long enough to teach her, to give her the pleasure she deserved. Every second he waited was pure unadulterated torment.

She twisted and squirmed as his hand roamed over her body. Her skin was like white silk. He caressed and fondled her, massaging, rubbing her breasts, tracing her nipples with his fingers, then with his tongue. He drew her nipple into his mouth and suckled her until she clung to him, saying his name over and over. Then he went to the other and repeated the action and when he was through there, he tasted her all the way down her body to her navel.

He considered going farther, then thought better of it. He wouldn't be able to last but a second if he did that. Instead, he reached down to see if she was ready for him. It was the first time he had touched her there and it was nearly his ruin when he felt a shudder ripple through her small delicate body. He fought for control, wanting to delve deeper into her moist heat but he couldn't, not unless he was willing to sacrifice everything else.

With an urgency that threatened to destroy him if he didn't get immediate satisfaction, Jim rose up and moved between her thighs. Taking hold of himself, he stared down at her as he guided himself into her enveloping softness.

"Indy . . . Now, Indy," he rasped out as he drove himself into her at last. He felt the barrier of her virginity give way to his hard, powerful thrust. He had wanted to be gentle with her but he couldn't. His body wasn't his anymore to control. It belonged to the need—the hot pulsing need that she had unleashed.

Indy cried out as he plunged his hard, urgent masculinity deep inside her, but he took the sound into his mouth and muffled it. The pain was intense but short-lived, and now she felt as if she was filled to bursting. She hadn't even recuperated from his entry when he pulled out of her and thrust into her again, going as far as her body would allow him to go.

"Wait. Please," she said, pleading for a moment to recover herself.

"I can't," he said repeatedly. "I can't."

In a frenzy of passion, he kissed and fondled her even as he pulled back and thrust forward again and again, deeper, faster, deeper still, until she thought she would go out of her mind with a need still unfulfilled. She quivered and tensed, arched and strained. Her fingers clutched and dug into his muscled shoulders. Her legs lifted, wrapped him, locked around him with the intention of holding him still but he was too strong to be stayed.

He rose up, grasping her buttocks, and found a new depth that took him to the edge of insanity. He gave a final, fierce thrust and poured his seed into her fiery heaven.

Never in her life had Indy felt anything like what she was feeling now. The steady heat that had been building inside her burst with an explosion of firebrands and left her quivering as sensation upon sensation assaulted her body. She turned her face into her pillow and wept softly.

Jim didn't move. He couldn't. He was mindless and numb. The years of stored-up need drained from his body into hers. He heard her soft sobs and was overcome with tenderness and love.

Toriano was right, he thought, bending down to kiss her soft, tear-wet cheek. She was such-a-woman. His woman. "I love you, Indy," he whispered.

Chapter 15

Jim had gone straight from Indy's bed to meet with Toriano whose smoke signal he had seen yesterday but had kept to himself for fear it would bring suspicion about his loyalty.

It had not been an easy meeting for Jim despite his resolves about what he was doing and Toriano's approval.

At first they talked of small things, insignificant things. Of Toriano's family. Of Jim's life at the soldier fort.

"They say you have the power of the wolf," Toriano commented solemnly.

"Who says this?"

"Diablo. The son of Chie. He has much hate in his heart. He has promised the mountain spirits he will kill the wolf, take his pelt, and hang it from his war lance to show his enemies."

"Chie came to steal the woman and I killed him. I told Diablo to go back to his camp and tell his father's braves that Shatto had taken Chie's power and that they should return to Cochise."

"Such-a-woman?"

Jim laughed. "Yes. Such-a-woman."

Toriano nodded his head and gave Jim a knowing look. "She will make a good wife, I think."

"I think so too."

"You must watch her with eyes of the hawk. She is in great danger. Diablo will try to honor his father and take her as his father would have taken her."

Mr. Moorland had been up since before daybreak to see his escort off to Tucson. Afterward, he inquired about where Major Garrity was and found Jim as he was coming back from the desert.

"Yesterday, you mentioned something about a bargain you made with the colonel. I want you to explain exactly what you meant."

Jim was leading his horse to the hitching post by the corral. "To train the men in Apache warfare in exchange for a full pardon and reinstatement of my rank and benefits," Jim told him offhandedly.

"A pardon? For what?"

Jim had assumed either the colonel or Aubrey would have told the commissioner about his court-martial, but obviously not. "Six years ago I was court-martialed and sentenced to hang for a crime I didn't commit," he began, even as he wiped down the big paint. He hoped the commissioner wasn't going to stand around and make a pest of himself. He had supplies to get ready for today's training. He had planned to take the men out into the desert where he could teach them to read various signs, some of which he had made himself earlier this morning.

He finished his story at the same time he finished getting everything together. "The fact is, I probably would have done it regardless of the bargain because of what I said last night. Toriano and I figure that if something doesn't happen soon, there won't be any Apaches left to tell about the great spirits who look out over these mountains. Then too, I figured if there was a chance the colonel could get me a pardon, I'd take it. The way it was, I could never go home."

The commissioner leaned his head to the side inquiringly. "What Captain Nolan did then was to bribe Colonel Taylor. In other words, the captain promised to hold off sending the men's petition if the colonel allowed you to train the men. Do I have that right, Major?"

"I think that's how it was. You'd better ask Captain Nolan to make sure. All I know is that the men—most of them anyway—weren't satisfied with things the way they were. Every time a patrol would go out under the colonel's orders, some of them would get killed."

Jim told him about the day Indy had arrived and how there had been too few men sent out on the patrol. "It was just luck that we came along when we did. We were hunting when we saw them being chased by Chie and his braves so we ran them off."

More questions about who "we" were and Chie kept Jim talking another fifteen minutes, at the end of which the commissioner crossed his arms and stood back looking into the mountains.

"I have to tell you, Major, Colonel Taylor does not have the authority to grant you a pardon."

Jim drew a deep, steadying breath. "I wasn't

sure, but I went along with it anyway. I figured if it was to be, it would be. But now at least I've got the incentive to go back and find the proof that will exonerate me. It's there. I know it is. If anybody had looked before as I had asked them to, they would have found it."

"Which is, Major?"

"That those men I killed were Reb spies. I heard them call each other by name. I remember their names and their faces. But because they were wearing Yankee blues, carrying Yankee papers, it was assumed they were Yanks. Nobody even checked to see."

"They were troubled times, Major. A lot of confusion and such."

"Yeah, I know. But you know what, Commissioner? People will call these troubled times too. And the next generation will call theirs a troubled time, and the one after that and so on. It'll go on forever, Commissioner. Every time will be a troubled time to the people who live in it."

"Of course, you're right, Major." He took a broken-off pencil out of his pocket and a square of paper and began jotting down notes.

"What are you doing?"

"Your case is somewhat familiar to me. I'm a lawyer, you see, and sometimes, just to satisfy my curiosity you might say, I look into unusual cases that I find particularly interesting. Yours was one of those cases. However, I didn't begin looking into it until after you escaped. It was quite a story as I recall. I was in Washington when it came out in the newspaper. I was particularly impressed by your testimony and particularly unimpressed with the idiot who was supposed to be representing you, for to my way of thinking, he seemed to be doing everything but representing you."

"He was a lazy bastard," Jim agreed resentfully. "I promised myself if I ever got a hold of him, I'd wring his neck."

The commissioner cleared his throat. "Yes, well, be that as it may, I wanted to see for myself if those names you gave in your testimony coincided with the muster rolls."

Jim braced himself. "And did they?" he asked tentatively.

"Yes, Major. They did. All four of them. The problem was, as I recall, that you had two of the names spelled incorrectly, which could account for your lawyer not being able to find them, if indeed he actually looked. Actually I doubt that he did, because they were easy enough to find."

Jim leaned back against the corral railing. "They were Dardis, Sinnett, Dillehay, and Corwin—Will Corwin. Corwin was the one in charge.

"If you knew I was innocent, Commissioner, why didn't you tell someone?"

"You had disappeared, Major. No one knew where you were."

"But you could have contacted my family. They would have notified me through Captain Nolan."

The commissioner hung his head. "Yes, Major, there are indeed steps I could have taken to help you, but sometimes we don't always do the right thing by our fellow man. Because we're human we are often unforgiving."

"When did you lose your Southern accent, Commissioner?"

"When I lost my home and my family, Major, to a Yankee patrol heading to Atlanta."

There was a long pregnant silence.

Jim breathed a deep sigh. "I can't say that I blame you, sir. Like you said, that was a bad time, for all of us."

"Consider yourself exonerated, Major. As soon as I get back to Tucson, I'll make a full report, which I will submit to the President. I have no doubt that he will grant you a full military pardon, reinstate your rank, and return your benefits."

"Thank you, sir."

A week later, on the parade ground, the commissioner stood before the whole garrison, with the exception of the sentries who had been placed around the entire perimeter of the camp.

"Congress has been deluged with complaints and investigations about crooked Indian agents, Army officers, and civilian contractors. Not to mention the government scandals. This June, President Grant appointed a board of Indian commissioners, of which I am a part. We are authorized to do many things as we see fit on behalf of the Indians, which includes negotiating treaties and establishing reservations."

The commissioner had made it clear that this was to be an informal gathering and that everyone was free to speak his mind.

Corporal Ryker pushed through to the front of the assembly. "Why not authorize four or five thousand troops to come in with cannons, and a freight wagon full of dynamite and blow them red devils clear to hell!" His words drew a weak cheer from several others.

"Even as I speak, Corporal, there are powerful organizations working to stop all fighting against the Indians. Because of newspapers and churchmen, the Apaches have the sympathy of the entire nation, with, of course, the exception of the people of New Mexico and Arizona. The nation wants President Grant to send good Christian men into the territory as Indian agents to establish reservations, and they want missionaries to educate the savages in Christianity and agriculture. They do not want extinction."

"One dollar. Do I hear one dollar for this fine chair, shipped all the way around the Horn from Boston?"

Indy raised her bruised arm as high as she could to signal the auctioneer. "One dollar," she shouted, though she hardly needed to. There weren't more than two dozen people in the audience, and all of them were soldiers and all of them were in a terrible hurry to get to breakfast.

"Miss Independence Taylor bids one dollar. Do I hear more? One dollar going once." The auctioneer pounded his gavel on the table in front of him. "One dollar going twice. One dollar going three times. Sold to Miss Indy!"

Indy was pleased with her purchase but felt badly for Prudence. The chair should have gone for at least two dollars and would have if any of the women had been in attendance. But because the items being auctioned off were Prudence Stallard's, the only buyers were men.

Indy placed a comforting hand on Prudence's arm and looked at her with sympathy. "I'm so sorry, Pru. You should have gotten twice as much as you did for everything. You had such beautiful things. I don't know what's the matter with the women around here. They don't have anything in their quarters that can compare with what you had here."

"It's all right, Indy. The soldiers always get everybody else's castoffs. I'm glad some of them finally got some nice things. I'll get pleasure out of knowing my things are making a few of them more comfortable."

Indy brightened. "Jim says that Captain Nolan's quarters are practically bare. I'm glad I got the captain over here and talked him into buying your table and chairs. At least he and Jim will have a place to sit down and eat at now." She shook her head impatiently. "I probably could have gotten him to buy some more things if he hadn't had to leave so fast. I guess Jim was taking the Wolf Company out around the boulders this morning to teach them to hide their tracks."

Prudence studied Indy for a moment and smiled. "So it's Jim now, not Major Garrity," she teased.

"Well—I—" Indy sputtered like a burned-down candle.

"You don't have to explain, Indy."

Indy grabbed Prudence's hand. "Yes, I do. You have to believe me when I tell you that I had no idea Jim cared for me. I know he didn't mean to hurt you and neither did I."

"Independence Taylor! Nobody ever knows

when they're going to fall in love. It's just a thing that happens. Don't you think I know that? And you didn't hurt me. The night I ran into Jim, I was just feeling a little lonely is all and looking for a good man to share my bed."

"Shhhh!" Indy put her fingers to her lips and looked all around to make sure no one had heard Prudence. "You shouldn't say things like that. Somebody might have heard you!"

"Oh, pish posh. What do I care who hears me?" She deliberately raised her voice and then grabbed Indy by the arms and squeezed her excitedly.

"Ouch!" Indy pulled back and rubbed her arms where her father had hurt her.

"What's the matter?"

The bruising inflicted by her father was still tender. "It's nothing. I just strained my muscles."

"Doing what?"

Indy thought a moment. "Lifting an old box." She dropped her arms back down to her side and tried to make light of it. "I should have called someone to help me, but you know how it is? You don't want to trouble people."

"Indy," Prudence said gravely. "Jim Garrity, he is a *good* man, isn't he?"

What an odd question. She seemed so serious. "Yes, Pru. He seems to me to be a very good man. I've come to greatly respect him . . . and love him."

"That's not exactly what I meant." Seeing Indy's confusion, she explained. "When he made love to you, he was gentle and kind, wasn't he?"

Indy gave a start. She couldn't believe anyone

would ask such a bold and intimate question. Yet, when she met Prudence's gaze, she realized that it wasn't curiosity that had prompted it, but concern.

"I—I don't quite know what to say."

Prudence waved her hand dismissingly. "You don't have to say anything. It's none of my business. It's just that . . . well . . . he did live with those savages for all those years. There's no telling the kinds of bad habits he picked up from them. I was a little worried he might have forced you to do something you didn't want to do."

In spite of her best efforts, Indy felt her cheeks burn with remembrance.

"I can see I need not have concerned myself," Prudence said, the teasing back in her voice.

It occurred to Indy then that it was her own lie about lifting a box and straining her arm muscles that had prompted Pru to ask such a question in the first place. A thoughtful smile came to her lips. "I truly do appreciate your concern, Pru," she said in earnest. "Please believe me when I tell you that Jim didn't force me to do anything I didn't want him to do." Indy decided a change of subject was badly needed. "When do you leave?"

"Day after tomorrow." Prudence drew herself up proudly and gave herself a look of importance. "Commissioner Moorland will be accompanying me. We're going to Tucson together."

Indy played along, glad for a lighter mood and a safer subject. "Oh, well! La-dee-da! Aren't you the one?"

"I certainly am. But believe it or not, I'm going

to miss Bowie, not this Bowie but the old one, across the way. That's where the major and I came after we were married. We went through a terrible rainy season there together."

Tears smarted at the backs of Indy's eyes. "I'm really going to miss you, you know. Once you leave, I won't have anybody at all to talk to."

"You'll have Jim. I used to talk to Major Stallard for hours and hours at a time. He said the most interesting things." With a faraway look in her eyes she continued, "He used to tell me about all the places he had visited and the amazing things he had seen. He made everything so exciting and he described everything so clearly. Why I could see those places in my mind, just as though I had been there myself." Her head bent. She looked up at Indy through her lashes. "That's what I miss most, him taking me to all those distant places."

Indy solicited the help of two young enlisted men on their way to the mess hall to take her new chair back to her quarters and then spent the next ten minutes trying to decide where to put it. She wished now she had thought to purchase it from Prudence privately rather than at the auction. That way she could have offered her more money for it. Prudence would need all she could get to start her new life in Tucson.

Before beginning the morning dusting, she stepped outside a moment to shake out her dust cloth, when she saw Jim at the far end of the officers' quarters talking with Doc Valentine. She had thought Jim was with his men this morning outside the camp, but apparently she had misunderstood.

Whatever Doc was saying, he was certainly adamant about it. He showed Jim the palm of his hand as if it represented whatever point he was trying to make.

"You've seen smallpox enough, Jim, to know what it can do," Doc was saying. "A few days after the fever comes the rash, most times on the face but just as prevalent on the extremities," he explained. "As to scarring—depends on the individual. Some people are lucky and don't scar at all. Others, the rash leaves terrible scars on the face. Or like me"—he turned his hand over, palm up, for Jim to see—"this is my little reminder." Jim looked closely at the deep scars crisscrossing Doc's palm. "There's more on the soles of my feet, but ain't nobody gonna see them 'cept an undertaker."

Fury flashed white and hot within Jim. He looked toward the adjutant's office where he had seen the colonel go a few minutes ago. *You son of a bitch. You blamed her, but it was you!* Jim turned his gaze to Indy, knowing she had been watching him. It was everything he could do to keep his anger under control so that she couldn't see it, feel it.

How was he going to tell her that her father had lied to her—that all these years he had been hiding his smallpox scars from her so she wouldn't know he'd had it too? On second thought, maybe he shouldn't tell her; she'd already mentally distanced herself from him. Knowing about the scars would only hurt her more, but knowing about them would also free her from her guilt—a guilt that would haunt her for the rest of her life.

She smiled at him when he glanced her way and he took it as a sign that telling her would be the right thing to do.

He smiled back and Indy felt herself go weak with wanting him. Ever since that night he'd made love to her, she couldn't look at him or think about him without becoming all warm and tingly inside, the way she'd felt when she had realized he was outside her window watching her. Even now, she couldn't imagine what had possessed her to act so boldly wanton. Just the thought of what she had done made her blush.

She thought it uncanny that she could *feel* his eyes upon her and understand what it was that he was thinking. She wondered if this sort of thing happened to other people, or did she and Jim have something rare between them? It would be nice to think it was indeed an uncommon ability that only they shared.

Jim turned back to Doc who was still talking about the effects of smallpox, when he caught sight of a cloud of dust rising out of the mountains to the east. His first thought was that it was a stampeding herd of wild horses. He had seen them many times. They numbered more than a hundred, but he had never seen them this far west.

Putting a silencing hand on Doc's shoulder, Jim lifted his head to listen. He could hear them now—hear the rumbling of horses' hooves. At least a hundred, he thought. Riding fast. Riding hard. Too hard!

Not wild horses! Apaches!

He grabbed Doc's shoulder. "Get to cover. It's a raid!" Bolting away from Doc, Jim raised his carbine and shot into the air. "Apaches!" he called out. "Sound the alarm!"

He ran toward Indy, who was standing out in the open. He had to get her to safety.

Indy heard the shot and saw Jim running toward her, but before she could fathom what had happened, the camp erupted into chaos and everything seemed to happen at once. She whirled around at the sound of rumbling hooves.

From out of the blaze of the morning sun, dozens of warriors spewed forth from between buildings at a thundering gallop to pound down on the parade ground.

Nearly deafened by their savage war cries, the rumble of hooves, and the shouts and cries of Bowie's men, women, and children, Indy couldn't think what to do. Fear held her captive. She couldn't move.

"Indy! Get inside!" Jim called to her as he ran.

The bugle blared, drowning out the warning.

Indy watched in horror as a group of soldiers, armed only with knives and forks, ran out of the mess hall, squinting and shading their eyes. They barely had time to digest that they were under attack when the Apaches wheeled their ponies into their midst and cut them down where they stood with bullets and lances.

Over and over the trumpet sounded the alarm, then ended on a sour note and didn't blow again.

Indy saw Prudence running just a few yards in front of a warrior on a galloping horse. Fear for Prudence mobilized her and she picked up her skirts and ran to save her friend. She saw Prudence stumble and prayed she wouldn't be trampled beneath the Indian's horse.

The warrior was nearly upon Prudence now, leaning off the side of his horse, ready to sweep her up and carry her off.

"Pru!"

There was only one thing Indy could think to do. She positioned herself directly in the path of the galloping horse and jumped up and down, frantically waving her arms and screaming.

As she had hoped the horse shied. While the warrior attempted to regain control, Indy grabbed Prudence and pulled her to her feet.

"Come on. Let's get out of here!"

"I can't," Pru cried. "I've twisted my ankle."

"I don't care if you broke it. Hop if you have to, but come on!" Indy put her arm under Prudence's and half carried, half dragged her toward the closest row of buildings. She glanced over her shoulder and saw that the Apache was heading toward them. "Hurry, Pru, hurry!" They had made only a few steps when Prudence's ankle gave out, and despite Indy's efforts to keep her moving, she fell.

Jim stopped, knowing he couldn't reach them in time. "Get out of my way," he yelled at a young private who had bumped into him. He ripped his knife from its scabbard and put it between his teeth. Then he raised his carbine, aimed, and fired.

Concurrently, Indy heard the report of the carbine and saw the Apache fly backward off his horse. She silently thanked whoever had saved her and Pru. Again, she bent and struggled to pull Prudence to her feet but she was a dead weight. "Help me, Pru."

"Leave me, Indy," Prudence begged.

Indy caught a glimpse of her father running out of the adjutant's office. He was only thirty feet away. "Father! Help us!" She saw him turn to look at her. Relief washed through her. Then he looked away and took cover behind a buckboard next to his office.

It was then that Indy saw the two warriors bearing down upon them, leaning low over the sides of their ponies. One of them was Chie's son.

"Oh, God." Indy wheeled around. "Father! Please, we need you. Help us for God's sake!" But she knew it was useless. He wouldn't help her. Jim! she thought. Where was Jim? She had seen him only a moment ago. "Jim!" she called, turning toward the direction she had last seen him.

It was bedlam. People, horses, mules, everywhere! Fire licked at wagons. Desert dust whirled and lifted. Arrows fell from the sky like rain. Black smoke coughed from revolvers and carbines.

Jim cursed himself for not recognizing the sounds of attack sooner. An arrow whizzed by his head. He ran headlong into a civilian, using up precious seconds to untangle himself from panicked, grasping arms. Finally, he made the center of the parade ground where he had last seen Indy, but now she wasn't there.

A horse went down in front of him, flinging its rider clear. He leapt over the animal even as it struggled to gain its feet. All around him, sabers rasped from scabbards, rifle fire crackled, revolvers echoed.

When he broke from the melee, he saw Indy. Diablo was reining up next to her. He scooped her off the ground, set her in front of him, and raced off. Jim raised the carbine, then tossed it aside and grabbed his knife, afraid the bullet that would kill Diablo would kill Indy too. He drew back his arm, and took aim.

Too late he heard the warrior's conquering cry. His horse ran past Jim, knocking him off his feet a second before he could release the knife. He felt a white-hot pain rip across his forehead and through his hair.

Then nothing.

Chapter 16

Jim reared and bucked like a stallion when he came to, thinking he was still in the middle of the fight.

"Easy now, Jim." Aubrey Nolan pressed him to the cot to hold him still until he was fully awake and rational.

"Let me go, goddammit!" Jim raged. Everything was blurry and he had black spots in front of his eyes.

"Simmer down, will you? Doc's going to stitch you up, put a bandage on you, and get you out of here."

"Where's Indy?"

"They took her, Jim. They got Prudence and the commissioner too."

Jim ran his hand through his hair and felt blood. His memory started coming back in fragments. "I should have killed him that night. I never should have let him go," he said in a low, tormented voice.

"Killed who?" Aubrey took his hand away and let Jim up.

"Diablo! Chie's son. Toriano warned me that he would try to get revenge, but it never even occurred to me he'd attack Bowie." He slammed his fist into his hand. Between his teeth he said, "I just got through preaching how unpredictable Apaches are, and told the men never to assume anything where they're concerned. You'd think I'd listen to my own advice!"

"You can't know everything, Jim."

He was too distraught to see the logic of Aubrey's words. "How long have I been out?"

"Twenty minutes is all."

"That's twenty minutes too long. We've got to go after them right now."

"If you don't let Doc sew you up first, you won't make the first mile. Now be sensible and sit back and shut up. I've sent Moseley to round up the men. By the time Doc's finished with you, they'll be outside, mounted and waiting ready to go." As Jim started to speak, Aubrey cut him off. "I've taken care of everything. I told them to pack light, except for weapons and ammunition, and I told them to dress for the occasion—moccasins instead of boots and such."

Jim passed a hand over his face and looked up at Aubrey. "There's just one thing I want to know. Why didn't the sentries alert the camp of the attack?"

"I don't know yet, but I mean to find out. My guess is that there weren't any, that they were doing something else."

Doc was quick with his needle and thread and had Jim sewn up and ready to go in five minutes. Aubrey handed him a red kerchief to use as a bandage. Jim tied it around his head Indian fashion and strode out the door.

As Aubrey had promised, the men were mounted and waiting when he exited the hospital. They looked mean, tough, and anxious, just the way Jim wanted them to look. Aubrey handed Jim his knife and his carbine and while Jim was checking his cartridge belt, the colonel came stomping across the parade ground.

"What the hell is going on here?" When Jim ignored him, wouldn't even acknowledge his presence, he became enraged. "I asked you a question, Major Garrity, and as your commanding officer, I demand an answer!"

It was Captain Nolan who stepped forward to answer the colonel's question. "With your permission, sir, we're going after the captives."

"Permission denied, Captain," he answered sharply, emotionlessly.

Jim glanced up from loading his carbine.

"Begging your pardon, Colonel," said Nolan, "but I don't think you understand. One of those captives is your daughter."

"You think I am not aware of that, Captain? I saw them take her."

"Well then, if you saw them take her, how can you deny us going after her?"

"I am deeply saddened that those savages captured my daughter, Captain. However, I cannot allow my personal feelings to interfere with my duty as commander of this garrison. Nor can I allow a whole company to go chasing around the territory for God only knows how long on an off chance that you'll find them. The welfare of Camp Bowie is at stake! That may have been the first of many raids. Taking a company of troopers out now, when the camp is in such a state of turmoil, would leave Bowie severely undermanned."

Without warning, Jim grabbed the colonel by the neck of his uniform, drew him up close, and laid the sharp edge of his blade across his throat. "I saw what you did, you miserable bastard," he hissed into the colonel's face. "Indy called to you, begged you to help her, and you turned your back on her and hid behind the buckboard."

The color drained from the colonel's face and he started to shake. "No. No, I didn't. I—I wanted to help her but—" he whined plaintively, his eyes bulging with fear.

Jim shook his head. "You're a liar. I saw you! You turned your back on her. You could have saved her."

"That's not true! There was nothing I could do."

"It is true," Jim answered in a low, savage voice. "But you didn't make an effort to save her because you hate her. You hate her so much you made her believe she killed her mother and brother. There wasn't a day that went by that you didn't blame her for their deaths. But she had nothing to do with it." Slowly, purposefully, he slid the knife blade an inch to the left, cutting a shallow crease in the colonel's throat. "It was you. You're the one who carried smallpox into your house."

"You're crazy. You don't know what you're saying! I never had smallpox."

Jim's mouth twisted with anger. "Then you won't mind showing the Doc here the palms of your hands, will you?"

The colonel struggled against the blade, then seemed to realize it was useless and stopped fighting.

"You won't mind, will you, you son of a bitch?" Jim persisted, letting his blade do the coaxing.

The colonel held out his hands, palms up. Doc stepped forward and looked down at them.

"Yep. Those are smallpox scars all right," Doc vouched.

To no one in particular Jim explained, "All these years he's hidden those scars from Indy, from everyone." To the colonel he said, "You're the one who's crazy—crazy with hate. You probably figured the Apaches were doing you a real favor by capturing her. That way you'd never have to see her again. That goes for the commissioner too." Jim charged, "With him gone, you don't have to worry if his report to the President is a good one or not, do you?"

"No. No. You can't believe that," the colonel protested vehemently.

Jim exhaled loudly. "You're right. I can't believe that. I can't believe anyone would do such a thing, but you did."

"Leave him alone, Jim," Aubrey cautioned.

"If anything happens to Indy," Jim said slowly, threateningly. "I'm going to come back here and show you the Apaches' favorite method of torturing their captives," he stated, forcefully shoving the colonel away from him.

Colonel Taylor staggered backward and came up hard against a support post. "I'll see to it that you never get that pardon," he spat. "I'll see you hang!"

Captain Aubrey Nolan pushed Jim aside and addressed the colonel. "Begging your pardon, Colonel, sir. But with all due respect, I'd like to state my objection," he said.

The colonel wiped his hand across his throat and stared at the blood. "Objection to what, Captain?"

"To you, sir. To your position as commander of Camp Bowie." He drew back his arm, made a fist, and slammed it into the colonel's face. "I've wanted to do that a long time," he said, smiling with satisfaction as he brushed his hands against each other.

The sun was high in the sky and the temperature still rising when the company rode out. They totaled only twenty-five now. Three had been wounded and two killed in the raid.

Twenty-five against a hundred or more. Yet, Jim refused to let the odds depress him. He glanced back at his hard-eyed wolves and an unexpected surge of pride lifted his spirits. They were good. Damn good. They were as skilled as any Apache warrior who had been prepared from infancy to fight and kill. In an incredibly short time they had become superlative horsemen, skilled trackers, and masters of warfare and survival. Those skills combined with good horses beneath them, the latest weaponry, and the white man's innate sense of logic would make the Apaches think twice before raiding another military outpost.

Twenty-five against a hundred or more. The odds were in the wolves' favor.

The ground around Bowie was charred and still smoking where the Apache raiders had fired it on their way out of camp, no doubt hoping the flames would spread to Bowie itself. But with no breeze to stir the embers, the flames had quickly consumed their sparse meal of dry chaparral and died out.

The smell of smoke was thick in Jim's nostrils and his eyes watered and stung. Just beyond the blackened area, he picked up the tracks of the band's unshod ponies and determined that they had headed east into Apache Pass.

A mile into the pass, Jim scanned the sheer mountain walls, the enormous rocks that looked ready to fall, and the blue-shadowed crevices. Until now, this moment, he had always found beauty and peace here in the pass, the kind of peace that comes with long familiarity. Now, the mountains, with their myriad of secret hiding places where Indy might be right at this moment fighting for her life, with the giant boulders that needed only a strong nudge to send them tumbling into the long, narrow channel below, seemed ugly and forbidding, and he cursed himself for having ever thought otherwise.

They rode slowly, steadily, deeper and deeper into the pass. Jim kept close watch on the ground for a sign that the band had dispersed, but so far nothing, which testified to Diablo's lack of leadership and skill. A wizened leader would have broken the band up by now, agreeing to rendezvous at another place and time.

When Jim wasn't looking down at the ground, he was watching the mountains for the glint of a mirror or a white plume of signal smoke. The Apaches had many ways of communicating with each other and most of them were silent.

Near the eastern end of the pass, before it sloped into Siphon Canyon, he saw evidence that the band had finally separated, half of them heading north, the other half south. Jim got down off his horse and followed the tracks to the north several dozen yards. He took his two best trackers with him and explained that he was looking for three sets of deeper hoofprints; those being the horses carrying two riders. When they didn't find them, they examined the tracks to the south and there they found what they were looking for.

The trail through the Chiricahua Mountains was windy, steep, and treacherous. They were forced to ride single file at a slow walking pace. The silence of the desert, which was like no other silence, surrounded them, broken only by the occasional ring of an iron-clad hoof striking a rock. At last, they descended into a wide-mouthed canyon surrounded by towering rock formations. Vegetation was sparse with only an occasional cedar or scrub oak precariously rooted into the side of the mountain.

Jim raised his hand to halt his men, then signaled them to circle him. "We'll pull up here. There's a stream two miles ahead of us. If Diablo listens to the older braves, he'll have them make camp there for the night. It's the only water in any direction for fifty miles."

Aubrey, like the others, appeared to accept Jim's knowledge of what was up ahead without question. "And if he doesn't listen to the elders?" Aubrey asked.

"Let's just pray that he does. Picket the horses. No fires. No smoking. We don't want to give our position away."

As soon as Aubrey had picketed his horse, he walked over to Jim, who was staring into nothing. "What do you figure to have us do?"

Jim met Aubrey's gaze. "I'm going to take Ryker and Moseley and scout ahead. Once I locate the band's exact position, I'll be able to determine their strengths and weaknesses. Then I'll come back and we'll lay out the plan of attack."

"We'll get her back, Jim." There was deep compassion in Aubrey's tone. "We'll get the three of them back alive and unhurt."

"Yeah, we'll get them back," Jim echoed Aubrey's words. Moseley and Ryker signaled their readiness. "We'll be back in an hour. Be ready to move out on foot."

True to his promise, Jim, Ryker, and Moseley returned an hour later, just as night was stealing over the mountains. Jim gathered the men around him and hunkered down and told them what he had observed. "They're camped about two miles up ahead." Using the dull side of his knife, he smoothed the ground in front of him, then cut out a large circle to represent the Apaches' encampment. "They've made camp in a sort of horseshoe canyon," he explained. "The walls around the canyon are almost perpendicular. The stream runs along the east side of the camp," he said, making a squiggle in the dirt. "The horses are picketed here, just up from the stream. There's only one way in and out, in front of the stream. Ryker will take six men up into the rocks to take out the guards. The rest of us will stay on the ground. We'll come in by the horses. Once we see Ryker's signal, we'll strike." He spent a half hour going over each aspect of his plan, then he stood up. "I don't know how this is going to turn out, but no matter what happens, I want all of you to know that I'm proud of what you've accomplished." Turning slowly, he looked at each of them. Then he said, "Let's go."

They had ridden for hours beneath a blazing sun. Indy could tell by the way her skin had begun to tighten that her face and neck were badly burned. She was stiff and sore, aching in every bone of her body, but no part of her hurt as much as the insides of her thighs where they had rubbed raw from straddling the horse with nothing between her skin and the horse's hair-rough hide to stop the chafing.

She had fought Diablo at first, struggling, scratching, biting, kicking him and kicking his horse, until he had pulled out his knife and slashed the back of her hand as a small example of what he would do to her if she didn't cease her struggles.

After that, she had calmed down, realizing the futility of it all. Even if she did manage to get away from Diablo, there were still the other braves to contend with.

Now, in the inky darkness of the night, slumped against a large boulder, Indy sat cross-legged in miserable silence with her hands tied behind her back. She was so weary she felt sick to her stomach and she was half-crazed with thirst.

Not a drop of water had passed her lips since early this morning. Her lips were swollen and her tongue was thick and dry inside her mouth. She remembered the trick Jim had used to draw the saliva into his mouth and searched the ground around her for a small pebble. Seeing one, she struggled to uncross her legs and sobbed with anticipated relief as she slowly rolled onto her hip, then to her arm and shoulder.

Bending her head to the ground, she picked up a pebble between her lips and drew it into her mouth. It tasted of grit and dirt but none of that mattered if it worked.

"What are you doing?" Pru choked out, obviously as thirsty and dry as Indy.

Rising slowly back to her sitting position, Indy closed her eyes and concentrated on working the pebble around the inside of her mouth. Without realizing it, she began to make little whimpering sounds when she felt it begin to work. After a long moment, she answered Pru's question. "It helps relieve the thirst," she whispered, her voice still raspy.

Prudence did try it and was soon enjoying the same relief that Indy had felt. "Do you think they'll torture the commissioner?"

"I don't know. I hope to God they don't."

"Indy, do you think Jim will come after us?"

"Unless something happened to him during the raid, he'll come for us," she answered with confidence.

"But there must be fifty or more Apaches and there's only thirty scouts," Pru lamented.

Indy refused to abandon her faith. "I know, Pru. But you mustn't think about that. If Jim can, he'll find a way to rescue us. I know he will."

"You're very sure of him, aren't you?"

Indy's eyes smarted with tears. "Yes, he loves me and he knows I love him."

"Then he'll come," Prudence whispered. "He'll come."

Fully armed and stripped down to nothing but breechclouts and moccasins, the scouts advanced slowly and cautiously. A portion of the trail they were obliged to follow had once been a stream. Dried up long ago, the streambed was littered by round, smoothly washed stones and boulders. A whispered word of caution passed from man to man to tread lightly so as not to disturb the stones, which if knocked against each other would send a echo through the canyon and give away their approach.

Jim held up his hand for the men to halt when they reached the mouth of the canyon that led to the encampment. He gave Ryker last-minute instructions, then sent him and his men on their way. The others he told to remain where they were until he came back.

Asking Aubrey to accompany him, Jim ran into an outcropping of boulders, and climbed the stone fortress until he found a fissure through which he could view the Apache camp.

Aubrey followed close behind and climbed up near to Jim.

"There's the guards," Jim told Aubrey in a low whisper, pointing out each one. Holding on to their rifles, the guards stood on rock ledges high above the camp, casually watching the activity below.

A large crackling fire lit the center of the camp. The Apache raiders sat back in small groups from the leaping flames, laughing and talking among themselves.

"There's the commissioner," Aubrey observed. "He's alive but it looks like they've carved him up some."

"If they had wanted to kill him, they would have already," Jim offered, his knowledge of Apache traditions giving him an advantage. "More than likely they're planning on saving him for their victory dance once they return to their stronghold."

"To do what with him?"

"Give him to Chie's relatives. The women are the experts when it comes to getting revenge. They take a lot of pride in the way they torture a man. And with Chie having been such an influential member of the band, they'll take their own sweet time."

"But the commissioner didn't kill Chie. You did."

"Doesn't matter. One white eyes is as good as another."

The captain looked away and searched the camp. "I don't see Indy or Prudence anywhere."

"They're back there in the shadows." Jim pointed to the far end of the camp. When he had seen them earlier, they had appeared unharmed. He prayed that was still the case.

The Apaches were settling down for the night. Jim thought it best to wait until everything was quiet and most of the braves were asleep before he signaled an attack. He told Aubrey his plan and had started to climb down when he heard a woman's scream.

Indy!

He turned back and peered through the fissure, his face pressed against the rock.

Diablo had Indy by the arm and was dragging her to the center of the camp near the fire. Her arms were tied behind her back and she looked exhausted and terrified, but much to his relief, she still appeared unhurt. His heart wrenched at the sight of her and he wished he could tell her help was coming.

Aubrey was beside him, anxious and worried. "What do you think he's going to do with her?"

Jim held his hand up to silence him. Diablo had started speaking. His voice was loud, carrying. It echoed against the canyon walls. Every warrior had turned to look and listen.

Jim listened and translated at each pause. "He says that the success of the raid on Bowie proves he is no longer a boy but a great warrior. He says he's even more clever than his father because he succeeded in capturing the *nantan's* daughter where his father could not."

One of the older braves stepped forward and spoke with fierce determination. He waved his arms, pointed his finger, and scolded.

"What did he say?" Aubrey asked.

"He's challenging Diablo, claiming Indy for his own." Jim turned to Aubrey. "I've changed my mind. This could get out of hand. We can't wait."

Aubrey breathed in sharply. "You're afraid one of them will rape her, aren't you?"

Jim nodded. "It could get to that."

"You told me Apaches don't rape."

"It's not their custom. They think it puts them at risk of losing their luck, but this was a revenge raid. That changes things."

Jim and Aubrey left the boulders, returned to the men, and outlined what had been seen and overheard. Everyone overwhelmingly agreed it would be better to strike now, not wait.

Jim stood alone before them and looked at each now familiar face. He would have liked to have spent more time working with them, developing and fine-tuning their skills before he had to put them to the test. But time had run out and now they were here, and all he could do was hope and pray that they, his wolf scouts, would bring about a miracle.

"Let's go," Jim said.

Slowly, steadily, their footsteps hushed by moccasins, the scouts made their way to where the Apache's horses were picketed. One, two at a time they slipped into the herd, taking care not to disturb them, patting them soothingly as they crouched and moved around the horses' legs.

Hiding himself behind a small shrub, Jim looked up into the rocks, impatiently waiting to see the glowing red tip of Ryker's cigar—the signal that the videttes were dead and that Ryker

and his men were in place and ready to provide
cover for the ground troops.

Seeing the signal at last, Jim waved his scouts
forward. On hands and knees, they moved out of
the herd and threaded through the brush border-
ing the camp.

Closer. Ever closer. On all fours like wolves.
Stalking.

Now, he thought. "Now!" He jumped up, his
hand slashing the air. The wolves sprang from the
shrubs, howling, yelping, and ran into the camp.

The surprise lasted only seconds. Then the
Apaches scurried for their weapons. From above,
Ryker and his men kept up a steady stream of
carbine and revolver fire, giving cover to their
comrades below.

Sergeant Moseley made for the commissioner,
cut his wrist bindings, and helped him back to
the safety of the boulders.

Captain Nolan ran for Prudence, swooped her
up in his arms, and carried her into the shadows
behind an outcropping of rocks.

Jim headed straight to the center of camp, his
carbine belching fiery streaks of lead. When he
had fired the last shot, he wielded the carbine
like a broadsword, striking out at each new chal-
lenger, causing as much injury with the wooden
butt as with a bullet. One by one he cleared
the way.

And then he was where Diablo was, where
Indy was.

Diablo held her before him like a shield.

Jim stopped, lowering his carbine to his side.
"Let her go, Diablo," he warned, his gaze never

wavering from Diablo's. He didn't dare look at Indy. Not now. One look would give away his emotions and give Diablo the advantage. "You have nothing to gain by killing her."

"She *nantan's* daughter," Diablo spat venomously. "Much good to kill." He wrenched Indy's arms up behind her until she cried out in pain.

Jim swallowed. His mind was going crazy with fear, but he refused to let it show. "Only a coward would kill a woman! Kill me instead and your people will call you a great and fearless warrior." He tossed his carbine aside.

Diablo laughed. "Why will they do this, white eyes?"

With all the bravado of a shaman, Jim played on Apache superstition. "Because I have much power," he said in an imposing tone. "You kill me, you take my power." Behind him the sounds of the battle raged on, but he couldn't allow himself to think of anything but Diablo and Indy.

Indy was making small whimpering noises, like a wounded animal, and looked to be near collapse. Pulling his knife from its scabbard, Jim turned it in his hand, taunting Diablo. "Fight me. Prove you are a brave warrior, not a coward!"

"I will kill you both!" Diablo shouted and at the same time thrust his knife into Indy's side. Then he flung her away from him and ran toward Jim, screaming like a giant eagle.

Jim twisted out of Diablo's path, then jumped on him as he ran past. Diablo fell hard, Jim on top of him. Grunting and struggling, they rolled out of the firelight into the shadowy void beneath the rocks. Seconds later they came up, crouched and spitting like two cats.

Diablo moved to the left. Jim watched, waited. Having fought Diablo before, he knew his strengths, his weaknesses. He had only to step back when Diablo lunged for him.

"You want to try that again?" Jim taunted. His silvery blade caught the reflection of the fire.

"You will die, white eyes!" Diablo vowed, swiveling to lunge again.

And again Jim adroitly dodged his attack.

In spite of the awful, burning pain in her side, Indy managed to stay conscious. She had told Prudence that Jim would come and he had. Because he loved her.

She would have been afraid for Jim had she not seen him fight Diablo before and knew that he was the more experienced and capable. She had no doubt how it would all end. It was only a matter of time. She watched Jim closely, his face that never gave away his intent. He easily feinted Diablo's knife thrusts and dodged his lunges, and it occurred to her that he was merely playing with him, teasing him until the time was right to kill him.

Then, for no reason Indy could think of, Jim turned his back on Diablo and walked away.

A scream of warning tore from Indy's throat when she saw Diablo go after him, his knife held high, ready to plunge it into Jim's back.

Jim had deliberately turned away from Diablo, remembering the last time Indy had watched him kill a man, remembering the look of fear he had seen on her face afterward. He was determined that she would never again witness him killing a man with such ruthlessness and savagery.

He heard Indy's scream, but continued walking away. With not a second left to spare, he ducked and whirled around, ramming himself and his blade deep into the Apache's gut.

They were face-to-face, eye to eye. Diablo opened his mouth to speak, but no words came out. A muscle twitched alongside Jim's mouth. "You were a fool, Diablo. You should have known you couldn't win. I have the power of many men."

A look of fear contorted Diablo's face and then his mouth opened and his jaw fell slack. Even before he hit the ground, Jim was heading for Indy, shouting her name.

But she didn't answer.

Jim knelt down and gathered her to him. She was still conscious, but barely.

The fighting was over. The stillness of death was everywhere. The Wolf Company had won and proved themselves to be the superior warriors.

With stricken looks on the men's faces, they watched helplessly as Jim lifted Indy in his arms and carried her across the encampment toward the stream.

Prudence ran ahead of them, limping badly, struggling to rip her skirt off. "Aubrey, help me," she pleaded when her own attempts failed.

"What do you want me to do?"

"Use your knife. Quick!"

Aubrey made fast work of slicing through Prudence's skirt, then helped her spread it out on the ground.

"Jim, lay her here."

Dropping slowly to his knees, Jim carefully set Indy down. In spite of his gentleness, she groaned in pain, the sound tearing through him like a lance. He had never been afraid of anything in his life, but seeing the blood gushing from Indy's body, knowing that she could die, a cold knot of fear clenched and twisted his stomach.

She looked up at him through pain-glazed eyes. "Jim," she breathed his name raggedly.

He unsheathed his knife and slit her dress to get to the wound. "Shhh. Don't try to talk."

Weakly, she raised her hand and touched his arm. "I have to tell you . . ." she whispered insistently.

Jim probed the wound with knowledgeable fingers. It was deep, but clean. If he could stop the bleeding . . . "What, Indy? What do you have to tell me?" he asked as he placed his hand firmly against the wound and applied a hard, steady pressure.

A loving smile touched her lips. "I wasn't afraid because I knew you'd come. I told Pru—" she broke off to catch her breath.

Jim felt his throat constrict. "I'll always come for you, Indy," he told her in a husky voice. "No matter where you are. I love you. I love you more than you can possibly know." His eyes blurred. He had never felt for a woman what he felt for her. And he had never wept for a woman before. Her hand fell away and he saw her eyes start to close. "No, Indy! Come back to me," he shouted, fearing the worst had come. "Dammit, Independence Taylor. I love you, woman. I need you!"

Aubrey pushed Jim back, bent over Indy's

breast, and put his ear against her heart. "She's not dead, Jim. Her heartbeat is slow and shallow, but she's alive."

Jim averted his gaze and thanked God for not taking her. When he turned back, he was full of renewed purpose. "Prudence, take my knife and cut her petticoat away. Then tear it up for bandages. If we can get the bleeding stopped, she might have a chance."

Chapter 17

With Indy cradled in his arms, Jim led the company and the Apaches' horses out of the canyon.

Indy had not regained consciousness but her heartbeat was stronger than it had been before, which gave him hope.

With no time to waste stopping, Jim sent several of the men to ride ahead and build a travois that they could put the commissioner on when they got out of the canyon. Meanwhile, the commissioner rode behind Ryker, securely tied to him so he wouldn't fall. His entire upper body was scored with knife slashes, some of which would require stitching. Aubrey had used what was left of Indy's petticoat to wrap him in bandages.

Jim rode in silence, thinking about the many dead they had left behind—Apaches and soldiers.

In the seclusion of his thoughts, Jim recalled a recent conversation he'd had with Indy. They had talked for hours. Indy had wondered if the conflict between the Apache and the white man would ever end, and he had explained that the root of all the hatred was the land.

"But there's so much of it," Indy had said. "Why can't we share it?"

"Because they each want to use it differently," he had told her.

"That's the only reason?"

"To the Apache, the land is power, harmony, and beauty. They believe it belongs to everyone, yet to no one in particular, where the white man wants to claim the land as his own."

She was so eager to understand, he thought, glancing down at her. She was also eager to love and be loved. He prayed she wouldn't be denied that opportunity.

It was midmorning when they came within sight of Bowie. Jim again sent riders ahead and told them to warn Doc to get ready for patients.

A half hour later, the remainder of the company rode in. The entire population of Camp Bowie had come outside and were standing, quiet as statues, in the blazing sun, to watch the scout company return.

Jim heard the officers' wives' gasps of alarm as he passed by, but ignored their frightened exclamations and concerned questions over Indy's condition and well-being. Indy had either been blind to their ostracism or had chosen to ignore it. On several occasions he had seen her go out of her way to befriend them and receive nothing in return but scornful looks.

It wasn't Indy they actually resented, Jim was sure of that. It was her father, and how his unscrupulous methods affected their husbands. Excluding Indy from their social circle was their way of getting revenge. He understood, but he couldn't forgive them. She could have used their friendship had they offered it.

Jim looked straight ahead, seeing the camp as it had been before he'd been knocked out—the people running this way and that, the carnage in front of the mess hall when the troopers had come outside to see what all the noise was about. All traces of what had happened a little over twenty-four hours ago were gone, vanished. Bowie looked just as it had before the attack.

Two stewards were waiting to take Indy out of his arms when he reined up in front of the hospital. They came back momentarily to get the commissioner.

Aubrey and Prudence reined up and dismounted. "She'll be all right, Jim," Aubrey said with a confidence he couldn't possibly feel. "She's a survivor."

Prudence pushed past them. "I'll see what I can do to help."

Jim stood in the open doorway and watched Doc examining Indy's wound. He'd seen Doc at work before and knew he was better than most army surgeons, but was better than most good enough to save Indy? He had no way of knowing that and even if he did, and Doc wasn't good enough, he was still all there was. Indy was too weak to take all the way to Tucson. His inability to control the situation frustrated Jim, making him want to punish something—someone—for allowing this to happen. The muscles of his forearms tightened and bunched. With a vicious oath, he pulled the hitching post out of the ground and threw it as far as he could.

"Come on, Jim," Aubrey coaxed. "Let's go get washed up and put some grub in our bellies. By the time we get back, Doc will probably be able to tell you how she's doing. Hell, she might even be conscious by then."

"No. You go ahead," Jim said, pushing Aubrey's hand away. "I can't leave her. Not until I know."

"All right, but—" Nolan hesitated when he spotted the colonel coming across the parade ground, flanked by four burly troopers.

"My daughter—is she all right?"

Jim glowered at him. "She's alive . . . but I don't know for how long," he retorted icily. He hated the colonel as much as he loved Indy.

The colonel turned his gaze, ordered the troopers to wait for him outside, and went into the hospital. Jim had considered barring his way but thought better of it at the last second. If Indy was dying, the colonel had a right to spend those last moments with her whether she was conscious or not. She was his daughter; it was his right.

Under a broiling Arizona sun, Jim paced back and forth in front of the hospital building. Waiting for news had never been such agony. When Aubrey came up behind him, he nearly swung on him, his nerves were so tightly strung.

"Whoa! Jim," Aubrey shouted, raising his arm in defense. "For God's sake, you're not doing anyone any good acting like this. It isn't going to help Indy and it won't help make you feel any better."

"Shut up, Aubrey," Jim snapped, hating himself even as he spoke. "Let me be the judge of what will or won't make me feel better. And don't you dare say that you know how I feel, because you don't and you never will because you won't let loose of your emotions. You're going to find yourself a woman who's *suitable*. A woman who will make a proper officer's wife. Whether you love her or not has nothing to do with anything. You think love is nothing but a big nuisance—a bother!"

Aubrey gave Jim a look that said, "Are you finished yet?" and abruptly turned when Doc came out and called Jim over.

"She's conscious, but right now that's about all I can say. There's nothing more I can tell you. Her father's with her."

"When will you know if—"

Doc put his hand on Jim's shoulder. "You can't rush these things. It's a serious wound. The big worry is infection and fever. Prudence and me, we're going to keep a close watch on her."

"We're all three going to keep a close watch on her, Doc. I'm not leaving here. Understand? I'll sleep in a chair if I have to, but I'm not leaving."

"How's the commissioner?" Aubrey inquired.

"He's in a real bad way. He's not as young as Indy. Doesn't have the strength of youth. I already told the colonel that I don't think he's going to make it, but he could surprise me."

"I hope he does, Doc," Aubrey said slowly. "He's a good man. The territory needs him."

Moments later, Colonel Charles Taylor stepped outside, squinting at the bright sunlight. With four troopers at his side, he approached Jim and Aubrey.

"As commander of Camp Bowie it's my duty to inform you, both of you as a matter of fact, that I am placing you under arrest."

Flourishing their Navy Colts, the four troopers stepped forward and surrounded Jim and Aubrey.

"What's the charge, Colonel?" Aubrey flared.

"Charges, Captain Nolan. Insubordination. Disrespect to your commanding officer. Striking or threatening a superior. All of them punishable by a garrison court-martial. However, the latter, Article of War number twenty-one, is punishable by death, or as decreed by a court-martial." The colonel crossed his arms in front of him. "Of course you, Major Garrity, already have a punishment pending, so I doubt that any additional punishment will be required. After all, you can only hang a man once."

Something had awakened her. A light. A noise. She wasn't sure what. She only knew that she resented the disturbance—resented being torn from her dreams.

"Doc," Prudence called over her shoulder, "I think she's coming around."

Indy groaned and turned her head away from the noise, trying desperately to recapture those fading dream images.

"Come on now, Indy. Wake up," Doc said, patting her cheek.

They didn't understand. She didn't want to wake up. She wanted to stay where she was— where the people were warm and friendly, the scenery was beautiful—where it was safe.

Reluctantly she opened her eyes.

"Good morning," Doc greeted her. He was grinning from ear to ear. She felt the hospital bed sink beneath his weight, heard the crunch of straw. "It's good to have you back with us."

Everything was blurry, but she knew instantly where she was and what she was doing there. She opened her mouth to speak but nothing came out. Determined, she tried again. "H-how long have I been—"

"Two days," he told her. "We were real worried about you there for a while, but now it looks like you're going to be just fine."

Her eyelids felt so heavy she could hardly keep them open. "Two days," she repeated. "Where's Jim?"

Prudence was leaning over her, wiping her face and neck with a cool, damp cloth. "He left just a few minutes ago, honey. Your father had something he wanted him to do, but he said he'd be back. I know he'll be upset when he finds out he wasn't here when you woke up. He's been awfully worried. I never saw a man fret so."

A small smile curved her lips. "He loves me," she whispered. Against her will, her eyes closed and she found herself slipping back into the dream.

After that, Indy awakened every few hours, always with the same question. "Where's Jim?" The answer was always the same too. "He just left, but he'll be back." Three days later she was beginning to get frustrated with herself for sleeping so much, and with Jim for not waiting for her to wake up.

"Sleep is the best medicine," Doc told her when she grumbled a complaint.

"No," she contradicted him. "Jim is the best medicine."

On the sixth day, Indy asked Pru to raise her up in bed, thinking it would help keep her awake. "Tell Jim I want to see him."

"I'll do it, but you may have a long wait. The colonel sent him and Captain Nolan out on patrol bright and early this morning."

"Has he been here? My father, I mean. Has he come to visit me too?"

Prudence hesitated. "He came when Jim brought you in, but not since."

"Has he even asked how I'm progressing?"

Prudence swallowed and shook her head. "No. The only one he's asked about is Mr. Moorland. He seems particularly concerned about whether or not the commissioner is going to recover."

Indy dropped her gaze and chastised herself for thinking that just because she had nearly died, her father would realize the error of his ways and their relationship would change—that overnight it would become the father-daughter relationship of her dreams.

"*Will* the commissioner recover?"

"Doc didn't think so at first. He was running a high fever and his wounds weren't healing the way they should, but he started showing signs of improvement yesterday."

Indy managed to stay awake for more than four hours on that occasion, during which Prudence fed and bathed her.

"You sure do look funny with your face peeling like that," Prudence said as she dried Indy's face.

Indy grabbed Prudence's hand. "How many were hurt and killed in the raid?"

"Seven killed," Prudence answered, her voice solemn. "Six wounded, but with all the noise they make in here, I'm sure you probably thought there were twenty or more."

"I want you to know how very grateful I am to you, Pru. I'll never forget everything you've done for me. You've been a true friend. When you leave—"

"Oh, I forgot to tell you," Prudence interrupted. "I've decided not to leave after all."

"But—but you sold all your things. What happened to make you change your mind?" When bright red splashes of color appeared on Prudence's cheeks, Indy opened her mouth in astonishment. "Pru! Why . . . I do believe you're blushing."

"Oh, pish posh. I am not." She tried to back away but Indy kept hold of her hand. "It's just hot in here is all. Now, why don't you lie down . . ."

Indy thought a moment. "It's Captain Nolan, isn't it?"

Prudence's hand squeezed Indy's lightly. "He's part of the reason," she admitted in a stern voice. "I've only really just gotten to know him, but he seems very kind, a lot like Major Stallard. But the other reason, the main reason," she emphasized, "is that I discovered something about myself that I didn't know until I started helping Doc. I like nursing folks. It gives me a real good feeling inside, being needed and all, and Doc says I have a natural talent for knowing what makes sick folks feel better."

It had been a full week since the raid. Following reveille, Indy raised up into a sitting position. She was through with sleeping and through believing Doc's and Prudence's lies that Jim had been coming to visit her. Something was wrong and she was determined to discover what it was. The moment Prudence came in carrying her breakfast tray, Indy confronted her.

"All right." Prudence set the tray down. "I guess the time's come for you to know." The foreboding in Prudence's voice, her somber expression, caused Indy to conclude something terrible had happened to Jim. Maybe he was one of those badly wounded men on the other side of the hospital. He could have been lying there all this time without her knowing it. She hadn't even thought to ask if he had been injured during the rescue. Or, God forbid, maybe he was dead! "Doc and me," Prudence proceeded, "we've been trying to keep it from you until you felt better, because we were afraid it would upset you and slow your recovery, but—"

"Prudence! For God's sake tell me where Jim is!"

"Your father put him and Captain Nolan in the guardhouse."

Indy was outraged. "Why? What did they do?"

Prudence sat down on the edge of the bed. "Doc says that right after the raid, Jim wanted to take the scouts out to find us, but your father ordered them to stay, claiming it would leave

Bowie dangerously unmanned. Jim got mad and accused him of all sorts of things, including lying to you about never having had smallpox. Then he threatened him with his knife and warned him that if anything happened to you, he'd show him how the Apaches torture their captives. Aubrey finished it off by knocking your father out, after which they disobeyed your father's order and left, taking the Wolf Company with them."

Indy felt the blood drain from her face. Her hand flew up to her throat.

"Your father pressed charges—"

"What kind of charges?" she asked, barely able to choke out the question.

Prudence sighed deeply. "Insubordination. Disrespect to the commanding officer. Striking or threatening a superior."

"Oh, God," Indy breathed. She knew the Articles of War as well as any army regular and knew the prescribed punishments that accompanied them. Captain Nolan might get off with minimal punishment, but Jim—for Jim there was no hope. Indy didn't doubt for one second that her father would relish the opportunity of telling the court about Jim's previous crime and the punishment he had escaped.

"I'm really worried, Indy. Your father's arranging a court-martial, but the way things are, with the Apaches at war on the whole territory, and travel being what it is, it's going to be hard to get a whole board of officers to come here. It could take months!"

"You sound anxious for the trial," Indy exclaimed, horrified.

Tears filled Prudence's eyes and rolled down her cheeks. "I am," she acknowledged. "Anything would be better than—"

Indy's eyes widened in alarm. "Than what?" When Pru averted her gaze, Indy shook her by the shoulders. "Better than what, Pru?"

"As of yesterday, your father decided to make an example out of them and punish them. They spent the whole day spread-eagled in the middle of the parade ground for the entire garrison to view. It was terrible, Indy. It was so hot! The sun was beating down on them. They were refused water. The flies were—Oh, God. I can't talk about it."

Indy passed a shaking hand over her forehead. She knew she was on the verge of becoming hysterical and fought hard to ward it off. Hysteria would serve no purpose and neither would self-indulgence. This was the time to be strong, stronger than she had ever been. She couldn't sit back and allow her father's tyranny to continue. She had to find a way to stop him.

It could mean Jim's life. Captain Nolan's too.

This was the time to be clever and calculating.

With purpose taking hold of her, Indy insisted that Prudence help her get out of bed. She needed to get her physical strength back as soon as possible, and the longer she stayed in bed, the longer it would take.

Surprisingly she wasn't in all that much pain and by afternoon was getting back and forth across the room without help. Seeing that the commissioner was awake and cognizant, she sat down beside him and told him what her father had done.

"That's outrageous! He knows better than that. The rules of discipline are clear. That kind of punishment was outlawed in '61 along with flogging. He's acting illegally."

"Can you stop him?"

"I can threaten him, but no, I don't actually have the power to stop him. My powers are limited to negotiating treaties, auditing the books of the Office of Indian Affairs, recommending changes and improvements and such."

Indy sighed. She had hoped he would be able to do more.

Seeing her disappointment, he offered, "Tell him I want to speak to him. I'll do what I can to convince him that what he's doing will assure a court-martial."

Doc came up beside them. "I wouldn't do that if I were you, Mr. Moorland. It's my professional opinion that Colonel Taylor is not acting rationally. I'm of the opinion that he would not have ordered the arrests in the first place if he had thought you were going to live. He fears you greatly."

"That's true," Indy agreed. "He was terribly upset at that word of your coming. It was only then that he made the bargain with Major Garrity to train the men, thinking you would see it as an indication of his making an effort to improve things at Bowie."

Understanding dawned on Commissioner Moorland's face. "I see."

"My father has had his eye on Washington for

as long as I can remember. A bad report from you to the President would have jeopardized, if not ended, his career."

"Indeed, that's exactly what it will do. I only wish I had the authority to do it here and now!" He paused in thought and a moment later his mood became suddenly buoyant. "What's the date?"

"October the eighteenth," Doc supplied, looking curious.

"General George Stoneman was scheduled to visit Fort Lowell around this time. As the commander of the District of Arizona, *he* would be able to stop the colonel. If you could send someone to Lowell to fetch him—I'll write him a letter explaining everything that's going on here."

"But what if he's already left or doesn't come for several days?" Indy shook her head, regretfully rejecting the commissioner's plan. "We have to do something now or Jim and Aubrey may not survive my father's punishment."

"We could arrange for an escape," Prudence suggested from behind. Each turned to look at her at the same time. "I think I might know a way to get the guards' attention," she said, tilting her head suggestively. "It wouldn't hurt to try."

Indy rose to her feet. "Oh, Pru! Do you think you could get their attention long enough so that someone could sneak in and unlock their cells?"

"I haven't met a man yet that I can't seduce if I really want to—with one exception," she said, clearing her throat.

The longer the foursome discussed the idea, the more they knew it was the only answer. Later, after General Stoneman was brought back to Bowie, the situation could be resolved legally.

It was decided to enlist the aid of Sergeant Moseley, who could ride to Tucson carrying the commissioner's letter and bring back General Stoneman as soon as possible. For all intents and purposes his unauthorized departure would look like a desertion, which was nothing out of the ordinary, and wasn't likely to arouse the colonel's suspicions.

Doc Valentine suggested that the commissioner's recovery be kept a secret. "The colonel's already broken military law. There's no turning back for him now. No absolution for his crimes. If he were to learn of your recuperation, he might decide to—"

The commissioner held up his hand. "I get your meaning, Doc. As far as the colonel is concerned, let's continue to let him think I'm dying."

"So who's going to let them out of the guardhouse?" Prudence inquired, looking at each of them.

"I am," Indy replied.

Doc shook his head. "Oh, no, you aren't, young lady. You aren't strong enough to be out of my care yet."

"I'm sorry, Doc, but nothing is going to stop me from helping Jim. Nothing."

As soon as the bugler blew taps, Sergeant Moseley headed for the horse he'd hidden behind the storehouse and rode out for Tucson. Doc, in spite of a chorus of grumbles and complaints from his patients, turned down the lanterns and declared an early bedtime in the hopes it would discourage a visit from the colonel if he decided to inquire about the commissioner's condition. Prudence rummaged through an old trunk and dragged out a scarlet satin dress—a remnant from her saloon days. She combed her hair and doused herself with enough lilac water to make a skunk turn tail and run the other way.

And Indy waited.

She had returned to her quarters that afternoon and was appalled to see that it looked much the same as the first time she'd seen it. Only now the table in front of the window, instead of being covered with dirty dishes, was strewn with papers containing myriad notes and hand-drawn maps— all of them focusing on the Apache chief Cochise.

Toward evening, she heard her father come into the parlor and sit down at the table. She wondered if he even knew if she had returned. She wanted nothing more than to confront him with all her grievances, but realized it would serve no purpose and could end up with him hurting her the way he had after the last confrontation.

Indy waited patiently, and near midnight he retired to his room. She waited an hour before turning off her light—the signal she and Pru had agreed upon. Then, bracing herself, she carefully lifted one leg over the window ledge, then the other, and lowered herself to the ground. She took a moment to steady herself and regain the strength she had used getting herself out the window before going on. The guardhouse was across the parade ground, on the opposite side of Bowie.

The only way to get there from where she was without being seen, was to take the long way around, walking behind the buildings.

Because of her injury, which was beginning to cause her some pain, she had to stop often to catch her breath. Nearly fifteen minutes later, she peeked around the corner of the quartermaster's store and saw Prudence dressed in her ruby-red satin gown, drunkenly angling her way across to the two guards. She had a bottle and a tin cup in her hand.

One of the guards stepped forward as she approached. "Sorry, ma'am, but I'll have to ask you to stay away. Our orders are not to let anyone near the prisoners."

"I don't want near your prisoners, Private. I was just passing by, on my way home from visiting a sick friend."

The young private glanced down at the bottle in her hand. "He must not have been too sick because he didn't take all his medicine."

Indy made a face at Prudence's tinkling laughter.

"Well, I'll be. He sure didn't, did he? What a pity. This San Francisco blend is the best medicine I know. Pure and smooth. Aged to perfection."

"San Francisco blend?"

Prudence uncorked the bottle and put it up to the private's nose for him to smell. He inhaled deeply and sighed.

"That sure do smell good. Bet that would fix my gout up real good."

"Oh, yes. It would," Prudence assured him. "Would you like to try just a little bit? I bet it would take the pain away just like that," she said, snapping her fingers.

"Riley!" the other guard warned. "If the colonel catches you, he'll have you hung up by your thumbs."

"He ain't gonna catch me. Besides I'm jes' gonna have me a little sip or two. To relieve the pain, you understand."

Prudence poured in two finger's worth and handed it to him. "Slow down, honey. That's expensive stuff. Not so much at one time."

"That sure is a pretty dress you're wearing," said the private, boldly looking Prudence over.

"Why, that's real nice of you to mention it. I thought it was kinda pretty myself."

Indy was just wondering how Pru was going to entice the other guard when he stepped forward and asked for a drink, claiming he'd been suffering from a stomach ailment. Half the bottle later, Pru sat down on a long bench in front of the guardhouse. Her two companions joined her momentarily and a short while later were slumped down and fast asleep.

Indy left her hiding place and headed toward Pru, who was obviously very pleased with herself.

"How did I do?"

"You should be on the stage," Indy whispered.

Pru took Indy's hand and halted her before she could enter the guardhouse. "Maybe you should let me go in. I'm not sure what condition they're in."

"No. You stand guard at the door as we agreed," Indy insisted, her determined expression brooking no argument.

The instant Indy stepped inside, Jim called to her in a low whisper.

"Indy! My God. What are you doing here?"

A low-burning lantern revealed that both Jim and Aubrey looked haggard, but she couldn't stop and worry about that now. They were strong. They would recuperate.

"Breaking the two of you out of here, that's what."

She spied the keys lying on the table beside the lantern and went for them, then hurried over to the cells, ignoring the burning pain in her side.

"Doc saddled your horses and packed your saddlebags with ammunition and a week's supply of rations. They're behind the hospital. We've sent Sergeant Moseley to Tucson to fetch General Stoneman. The commissioner says the general will make everything right."

She opened Aubrey's cell door first because it was the closest, then Jim's. As soon as he was free, he took her into his arms and held her tight.

"I've been so worried about you," he whispered, nuzzling his lips into her hair. "The men were ordered not to speak to us, so I didn't know if you were dead or alive. It was hell."

"For me too," she murmured, savoring the sweet seconds in his arms. "Jim," she said, sudden intense emotion bringing tears to her eyes. "I love you. If anything happens . . . to either of us, I want you to remember that."

"I love you too, Indy. But nothing is going to happen to us. We've both been through enough. Everything is going to be all right now. I'm sure of it. It will just take a little time."

Captain Aubrey Nolan walked over to the door and asked Prudence to step inside a moment. "When I get back," he told her, "We're going to get to know each other a little better."

Prudence looked up at him and smiled. "I'd like that, Captain."

"Good," he said, smiling down at her. "But just so you don't forget me . . ." He pulled her into his arms and kissed her long and hard. When he was through, Indy thought Prudence looked positively stunned and delighted.

Reluctantly, Indy pushed herself out of Jim's arms and hurried the men on their way. "Go on now, both of you. We don't have any more time to waste."

Jim made for the door, Aubrey in front of him. He stopped and looked back, his gaze full of emotion. Then he was gone.

The two women hurried out after them. Prudence insisted she help Indy to her quarters and Indy let her, knowing she was fading fast and might have trouble getting back into her room. They made it, however, without incident but Indy was in so much pain, she could hardly breathe.

Prudence searched Indy's face. "I should get Doc. You look terrible."

"No," Indy protested vehemently. "I'll be all right. You can do as much as he can. Besides, we don't want to cause any kind of disturbance. They need time to get away. How long do you think the guards will sleep?"

"A long time. Doc put an awful lot of laudanum in that bottle."

Chapter 18

From her bedroom window, Indy watched her father march determinedly across the parade ground toward the guardhouse. Clearly, he had been informed of the prisoners' escape and was going to investigate.

She wondered what action he would take, and worried that the two guards would be severely punished for their drunkenness.

In all her life Indy had never seen her father appear in public or private looking anything but immaculately groomed and clothed. This morning, however, his uniform was rumpled and dirty, obviously slept in. His boots were dull and dusty, and his hat askew on top of his head. There was nothing about him that in any way resembled the Colonel Charles Taylor she had known in St. Louis. There was nothing about him that resembled the father she had once loved.

He was a stranger to her now, a cold, hard, stranger.

She had meant to question Doc about why Jim had accused her father of having had smallpox, but had forgotten. How could Jim have discovered such a thing? she wondered. If there were

scars, yes, but there were no scars. Had her father said something to Jim, or had he just guessed
it? Something must have happened; Jim wasn't
the kind of man to make unwarranted accusa-
tions. If he had accused her father of having
smallpox, then he had.

In which case, that meant . . .

She gasped. Shock grabbed her and held her
rigid. No! No! He wouldn't, couldn't, she
thought, vehemently denying the most probable
explanation. He was her father! Surely to God he
wouldn't have blamed her for something *he* had
done. Would he?

He would.

He had.

She could see that now. All these years he had
let her believe she had been the one to bring the
smallpox home. And maybe she had, but he had
brought it home first. She remembered now that
he had been away for several days. Army business. On his way home, he had stopped by the
orphanage to ask her to be sure to come home
for supper. He had good news.

She had been late. Supper was over and her
father had already retired to his room, complaining of fatigue. It was her mother who told her
Justice was coming home the next day for a short
leave from West Point.

Indy closed her eyes, trying to remember. So
many orphans. So few women to tend them. There
weren't enough hours in the day. She doubted
she saw her brother more than a few hours, and
then several of the orphans took ill and she spent

all her time with them, not knowing what ailed them.

One of the servants brought word that her mother and brother were ill and she went home.

She recalled her father coming out of Justice's room, looking ravaged, utterly destroyed.

"Smallpox," he had said, looking down at his hands, as if he couldn't believe it. "I had no idea. . . ."

She remembered feeling faint with shock. Smallpox. *That* was what ailed the orphans. And she told her father so, but he had said nothing.

It wasn't until after the funeral that he accused her of being the one to bring the dreaded disease upon them. And every day after that—in one way or another—he accused, blamed, condemned.

Indy bowed her head and prayed. "Dear Lord. Forgive him."

General George Stoneman arrived at Camp Bowie three days after the escape. He found the colonel absent, on patrol somewhere in the mountains. With Sergeant Moseley assisting him he was quickly introduced to Commissioner Moorland, Doc Valentine, Indy, and Prudence, who filled him in on why he had been summoned.

Indy found it painful to hear her father maligned in front of the general, but it was all too true. He was all the things they said about him and more. She had talked to Doc and learned about the scars on the palms of his hands— testimony to him having had smallpox.

After that first interview, the general approached her and offered her compassion.

"Miss Taylor," he said, his expression compassionate, "I first met your father many years ago and I remember him as a fine, upstanding officer. I remember your brother, Justice, as well. He was a cadet at the Point—a very promising young man. As I recall, your father had great ambitions for him, but he and your mother were lost in a smallpox epidemic. A terrible tragedy," he said, sighing. "We met again about five years ago when I was visiting St. Louis. My impression was that your father had not yet adjusted to his loss and had, if I may be so bold to say, become somewhat embittered. I heard the rumors, of course, that he blamed you for their deaths, though I was loath to give the rumors credence. One cannot really be *blamed* for contracting and passing smallpox. And now, with what Doc Valentine has told me, I think I have a better understanding. Perhaps even an explanation. I would venture to guess that your father couldn't bring himself to think he had given his family smallpox. Because he desperately needed to place the blame elsewhere, he blamed you. He was weak. He wronged you terribly. I hope you can forgive him."

"I'm trying, General. But I only just learned of his deception." It had been easy to ask God to forgive her father and she knew that He had. And she would too—someday—when it didn't hurt as much. With Prudence by her side, Indy returned to her quarters where they awaited the patrol's return.

The patrol, or what was left of them, returned at dusk. At the head of the column, was Major Jim Garrity. Beside him rode Captain Aubrey

Nolan. Of the forty men the colonel had taken out, twenty-two, not including Jim and Aubrey, were returning alive.

With her hand covering her mouth, Indy slowly walked to the center of the parade ground. She scanned the faces of the returning men but didn't see her father among them. Wearily, Jim dismounted and came over to her, and put a comforting arm around her shoulders.

"You don't need to see this, Indy."

"See what? Where's Father? Tell me what's going on here!"

"Aubrey and I found the patrol after Cochise attacked them in the pass. Your father is dead, Indy. We brought his body back for burial. We brought all of them back."

"Take me to him."

"No, Indy. Trust me. You don't want to see him."

She twisted against him. "I have to see him, Jim. I have to. I need to tell him I forgive him!" She looked up at him, beseeching him to let her go.

"We'll tell him together."

General George Stoneman listened attentively to Captain Nolan, several of the enlisted men and officers, and finally to Major Garrity. He asked detailed questions and occasionally instructed the thin-faced, bespectacled man beside him to make a note.

When he had heard all there was to hear, he officially addressed the group. "As far as the charges the colonel imposed on Major Garrity and Captain Nolan . . . they no longer exist. I find you both innocent on all counts." He paused. "But as to your past charges, Major Garrity, I'm a little at a loss as to what to do in spite of Commissioner Moorland's testimony that he knows you to be innocent. Though I have no reason to doubt him, I can't simply take his word for it and acquit you. He claims there's proof of your innocence and says he knows exactly where it's located. So, what would you say to surrendering yourself to my custody, coming back with me to Tucson, and waiting until the proof is located and brought forward? Then I will personally present you with your pardon."

Jim looked across the room at Indy. They could never have any kind of life together unless he was granted that pardon. But what if the commissioner was wrong or the records had been lost? It had been six years after all. If the records couldn't be found, he'd find himself dangling at the end of a rope. It was a risk, he decided. Indy smiled at him and he knew it was a risk he was willing to take.

"I say yes, General. On two conditions."

Stoneman frowned. "You're hardly in the position to be making conditions, Major. What are they?"

"One: that Indy and I be allowed to see each other in Tucson while we're waiting. Two: that you send Captain Nolan back East to find and bring back the proof. He's the only one I would trust."

"But he's needed here at Bowie, Major." He stared at Jim, then shook his head. "I suppose

Sergeant Moseley could handle things for a short while, though it's highly irregular. All right, I'll accept those conditions after you accept one of mine."

"Which is, General?"

"While you're in my custody, I want you to teach me and some of my officers all you know about the Apaches and train us in Apache warfare. This is going to be a long and bloody war, and I want to be as prepared as possible."

"Sounds like a bargain to me, General."

"Shall we shake on it?"

"I'd like that, sir. Just as soon as you put the terms of our bargain in writing."

The general laughed and nodded. "Of course, Major."

The white light of a three-quarter moon shone into Indy's bedroom window. A soft breeze, redolent with the smell of rain, billowed the curtains. Indy held her breath as Jim quickly removed first her clothing and then his own. She couldn't help trembling with anticipation.

I love him, she thought, reaching her arms out to him and pulling him near. She kissed his mouth, his chin, his implacable jaw. *And he loves me.* It was the strength of their love for each other that had given her courage during those frightening hours of her capture, sustained her through her recuperation, and helped her through the emotional upheaval following her father's death.

"I love you," he whispered as he drew her into his embrace. She didn't need to hear him speak the words aloud; he spoke them in silence every time he looked at her and touched her. He loved her in a way no one had ever loved her.

"I hope you know what you're getting into," he told her. "I'm not your St. Louis gentleman. You know that, don't you, Indy? There's so much I've forgotten about being a white man, I'm not sure I know how to act civilized anymore. I don't know that I'd ever be able to fit in again. And frankly I don't know that I want to. Those mountains out there—they're my home now. Do you understand?"

She raised up on one elbow. "Are you trying to frighten me away, Jim Garrity? Because if you are—it won't work. I'll love you whether you're wearing a uniform or a breechclout, whether you're Major Jim Garrity or Shatto, whether we live in a wickiup or in officer's quarters. Do you understand?"

"Toriano was right about you."

"And who may I ask is Toriano?"

"An Apache friend of mine who lives on the other side of that mountain." He turned toward the window. "The Valley of Thunder."

"How does he know me?"

"He was with me that first day I saw you."

"So what did he say about me?"

"He said you were such-a-woman. And he was right."

Epilogue

It had seemed to Indy that this day would never come. The wait had been interminable, but winter and new Apache uprisings had made travel hard. Outside her quarters, Fort Lowell's infantry company was shining up, preparing themselves for the ceremony and the festivities afterward.

Jim had been gone nearly a month, helping to build a road through the White Mountains that culminated at the new post, Fort Apache. It was there that the army was planning to set up a reservation.

Captain Nolan had left for the East within a few days after the general had dropped the charges against him. Throughout the winter there had been only one message from him—an affirmation that he had found the needed proof and would be presenting it to the necessary officials at the War Department.

He had returned a week ago with not only the pardon signed by the President himself, but with Jim's parents, who had insisted upon coming so that they could be present when their son received his pardon. Upon the captain's return, a detail had been sent to bring Jim back, using the pretense that General Stoneman had returned to Arizona and needed to speak with him about a new and desperate situation arising in Tucson.

Indeed, General Stoneman had returned, leaving his new San Francisco headquarters as soon as he had received the news that Captain Nolan was on his way to Fort Lowell.

"If you don't stop pacing, you'll wear holes in your shoes," Prudence Stallard told Indy.

"I can't help it. I can't just sit and wait. I have to do *something*. What time is it?"

"Patience, Indy. Jim just rode in. He'll have to clean up. You don't want him appearing before all those people covered with trail dust, do you?"

"No, of course not." She shook her head.

Prudence consulted her new timepiece, a gift from Captain Nolan upon his return. The way the two had greeted each other, there was no doubt that they had missed each other and would waste no time in renewing their relationship. Indy could not have been more pleased. Prudence had become a dear and special friend.

"I suppose we could walk over there now," Prudence announced.

Indy stopped in midstride, looked at Prudence, and took a deep breath. "Let's go."

The room was crowded with spectators. Commissioner Moorland sat in the front row beside Sergeant Moseley and Doc Valentine. Captain Aubrey Nolan stood at the front door.

"Are you all right, Indy? You look a little white."

She touched the sleeve of his dress uniform. "I'm just nervous. This means so much to Jim, but I have to wonder if surprising him was such a good idea."

Nolan smiled. "Everything will be fine, Indy. A little surprise never hurt anyone."

"I hope you're right." She squeezed his arm, then walked away and took her seat. Prudence was beside her and Indy had never been more glad for her company.

Jim's parents turned around and smiled at Indy. In just the few days she had known them, she had come to care for them as if she had known them all her life. It had been nearly seven years since they had seen their only son and she knew they were as anxious as she. They were also proud.

From the side door General George Stoneman entered the room and took his seat behind a large, imposing desk. He squared his broad shoulders and gazed out over the assemblage, his expression void of emotion of any kind.

He lifted his head and looked straight at Captain Nolan. "Bring in Major Garrity, please."

"Yes, sir."

Moments later the door was opened and Jim Garrity stepped inside. He stopped abruptly and surveyed the scene before him. Indy bit down on her lip and turned her head ever so slowly.

"Good evening, Major," said Stoneman. "Won't you come forward? I have some news that I think you'll find to your liking."

With a nonchalance that made Indy smile, Jim walked past the assembly to the front of the room. "And what might that be, General?"

"I'm a man who keeps his promises, Major. I

have here, from President Grant himself, a paper that gives me the authority to grant you a full pardon—to reinstate your rank and your privileges." He held out the paper. "On behalf of the army, Major, I would like to extend an apology for all that you have suffered."

"I didn't suffer, sir, except maybe for this last month." He turned around then, faced the assembly. Indy was halfway to him, smiling and crying at the same time.